A Stone's Throw

Louise Maclennan

First published in Great Britain in 2025 by
Louise Maclennan.

ISBN: 978-1-9193628-3-0 (paperback)

To those

who

allow

us to

be

ourselves

PROLOGUE

NOW

A brimstone butterfly flew down and landed on the windscreen wiper of the parked car, her pale, yellow-green leaf-shaped wings fold together as she rests, waiting. She is vulnerable here, yet she remains, deciding her next move. Her adult life expectancy is a year, if she survives the threat of predators. She must learn to avoid and outwit those who seek to destroy her, adapting her behaviour and developing strategies to survive her tortuous encounters.

TWENTY YEARS BEFORE

He'd been a familiar face in the regular early morning tube crowd that trickled onto the platform and habitually gathered in unvarying spaces. Same time, same place, same people, waiting, yet never so much trading a nod in acknowledgment. It was a normal Tuesday, to begin with. The distant rumble from the tunnel prompted the collective folding of newspapers, shuffling of feet moving forward and polite positioning of bodies as the crowd readied to board the 6.32am. The train arrived, collectively they swarmed into the carriages to occupy their usual seats. Newspapers were unfolded and reading reconvened. Clara reached into her bag, feeling for the familiar touch and comfort of her favourite book. The train moved forward, then stopped with a jolt. Her life took a turn she would live to regret.

'Good mornin' all. I'm afraid we're gonna sit here for a while 'cos there's an incident ahead.' The driver's weary voice broke the familiar silence that inhabited the carriage. The announcement made little impact. Clara glanced at her watch – 6.34am. At 6.39am she sensed some of her fellow commuters beginning to look up from their papers and books – still no eye contact. It took a further three minutes for them to acknowledge each other's existence as an exchange of half-smiles and rolling eyes were shared through the carriage. At 6.51am conversations began to spread around her, just like the cold virus they'd circulated between them last winter, as her fellow passengers broke their silence to communicate with the people they'd purposely ignored for years. Unwelcome chatter seeped into the pages of her book, splintering her concentration. She closed it and sighed.

'Jane Austen can have that effect on you.'

She would have happily ignored the comment if she hadn't been reading Pride and Prejudice, but now common decency required her to acknowledge the unwelcome interruption. She guessed he was around 5 or 6 years older than her. He'd folded his paper onto his lap and was looking directly at her. He was the guy who always read The Financial Times, whose shoes were always highly polished, whose hair was always immaculate, who had never even glanced in her direction these past two years. And that was the moment, right there. Without asking permission, he stepped into her life and began to slowly tear it apart.

Clara would soon begin to regret her choice of book that day. His familiarity with the writings of Jane Austen led them into easy conversation and her into believing they were kindred spirits. Had he set out to capture her? She'd been easily duped, like a moth to a flame.

'See you tomorrow?' he'd asked. She'd hardly noticed the train had begun to move again, yet here they were at her stop.

'Yeah sure.'

For those first few months Dan was funny, charming, caring, generous, thoughtful and loving. Until he wasn't.

1

NOW

Clara painstakingly paired together the opposite corners of the cream serviette that lay on her lap, ensuring each point met the other perfectly. Satisfied she had captured each crumb within the bundle, she twisted the corners into a spiral to make a neat parcel. Congratulating herself on a job well done, with not a single flake of evidence remaining of her drive-time snack, she opened the car door and stepped out onto the driveway. Noticing a butterfly resting on her windscreen wiper, she wafted the parcel in its direction until it flitted away.

Clara headed towards the black dustbin standing at the side gate, lifted the lid at arm's length, quickly threw the parcel in, then stepped back as the lid crashed back down. She returned to her car, took a bottle of hand sanitiser from the glove compartment and squirted a large amount of the cold liquid into her palm. She hated the stickiness of it, but this was just one of her little foibles she felt compelled to do, even though they often irritated her, she felt more at ease after she'd performed them, a couple of times. Still, little things make tidy minds. If she chose to, she might be able to remember a time when she was less pernickety.

The small, compact garden to the front of the little bungalow was beginning to welcome spring. Tiny green shoots poked their noses above the ground, the advance party sent to investigate to see if it was safe to sprout. Clara didn't share her mother's horticultural inclination for complete lack of symmetry, with her bold displays of unruly sprawling shrubs and free-spirited weeds.

If Clara had a garden of her own its manicured inhabitants would mirror her lifestyle; ordered, uncluttered and uncomplicated. Only carefully picked accessories made their way into her life these days. The result was a clean, tidy, minimalist lifestyle in which she spent evenings and weekends alone in her apartment as often as she could.

She pushed the car door closed, enjoying the rather satisfying solid 'clunk' sound it made. A company car was an extravagant treat, although she daren't look at the tax she paid on her monthly salary slip, but as the dark blue Porsche 911 gleamed in the evening sunshine she was satisfied it was worth every penny. However much that was. She would take it to be cleaned this weekend as usual. Looking at her mother's dusty Ford Fiesta, she guessed *it* hadn't been cleaned this side of Christmas, and most probably much longer.

The same brass key she'd been awarded on the day she started high school turned easily in the lock, and as she pushed the front door of the bungalow open the familiar smell of freshly baked ginger cake filled her nostrils.

'I'm home,' she called out as she hung her jacket and bag on the old coat stand and placed her shoes neatly in the hall cupboard. Clara closed the front door, blissfully unaware that her perfect life was about to unravel at the edges.

'A letter came for you. It's on your bed,' her mother's voice called out as Clara carried her weekend bag through the living room. She caught a glimpse of her mother in the kitchen.

'I'll just get changed mum,' she called as she walked past and into the small hallway leading to the rear of the bungalow.

They had moved here when she was born, just the two of them, and since leaving home she had visited the first weekend of the month almost without fail, these past twenty-three years. To the left was her mother's bedroom. A faded silk pomander nine-year-old Clara had proudly presented to her mother one Christmas morning still hung on the door handle. It's sweet smell of oranges a distant memory but her mother kept it regardless, its aroma now reminiscent of 'eau de dust', but to her it was a priceless heirloom. Straight ahead the bathroom door was slightly ajar, as usual, '*to let the air blow through'* as her mum used to tell her. Turning right, Clara opened the door to her childhood bedroom and saw her reflection staring back at her in the long mirror hanging on the opposite wall. She was sure it had hung there forever. Over the years it had watched the baby girl grow into a woman; quietly studying her many hair styles, decorated with varying shades of pink, red, blue, and even green when the process had gone horribly wrong the day before Clara's 17th birthday. It observed her changing fashions as it stared back unflinching all through those colourful teenage years and hung to attention, steadfast, always ready to listen and never pass judgement. Her adult reflection stared back at her in her old friend. Her chic, dark brown, shoulder length hair and swept fringe nowadays were maintained exclusively by a highly skilled hair stylist. No longer did she lop lumps off with the kitchen scissors and stain the bathroom sink with hair dye.

Clara opened the door of the single wooden wardrobe, carefully hung up her suit then folded her blouse, putting it into her bag to be washed when she got back to London. She swapped her work suit for a pair of faded jeans, an oversized pink denim shirt and a pair of crimson woolly socks, morphing into being back at 'home' in the process, to a time before any of *that* had happened.

An envelope lay on the folded blanket at the end of the single bed. Clara sat on the edge of the mattress to open it.

'Dear Miss Richmond...'

'Mum!' she called out, walking back through the living room to the kitchen. 'Who was David Reid? And why has he left me half a house?' With the letter still in her hand she entered the kitchen and kissed her mother on the cheek. Two cups of freshly poured tea stood on the table, Clara looked at her mother quizzically, holding up the letter as evidence. Linda slowly removed her flour-covered apron and hung it on the back of the kitchen door before turning to look at her daughter.

'I can give you a proper hug now,' she held out her arms and Clara folded herself into them. 'I've made some ginger cake 'specially for you. Here, let's have a sit down.'

Linda produced two plates, each bearing a large slice of her 'magic ginger cake', placed them on the table and sat at her usual chair. Over the years her magic ginger cake had come to the rescue on countless occasions, helping to dissolve a myriad of young Clara's distresses and traumas. How she hoped it would work its magic now.

Clara sat at the remaining chair, eagerly awaiting a response. 'Has there been a mistake? We don't know anyone called David Reid, do we?'

Their gaze met momentarily. A tear glistened in the corner of her mother's eye. Clara watched it slowly trickle down her face then drop onto the table. She began to dread the answer to her question.

Still wide awake in the early hours, Clara was sure every spring from the single mattress was sticking into her. Linda had bought it when Clara was eleven from a neighbour whose adult daughter had left home. *She probably left so she could get a good night's sleep,* Clara concluded, turning onto her side in the hope that less springs sticking into her would allow her to finally drift off.

'Nope!' She threw the cover to one side, got up and quietly

made her way to the kitchen.

Her mother's bedroom door was slightly open, and a faint glow shone from a plug-in light. Clara always believed her mum was secretly afraid of the dark, even though Linda insisted it was so Clara could find her in the night if she needed her. She smiled to think her mum still left the light on for her. The contrasting brightness of the kitchen light made her eyes squint. She closed the door and pressed the switch on the kettle.

Too often Clara experienced a night where she couldn't sleep, where tiredness hid just around the corner out of grasp, usually until around 4am when she could finally drift off, only to be woken an hour and a half later by her alarm. The doctor had put it down to her age. *Bloomin' cheek,* she muttered under her breath as the barely thirty-something, most probably newly qualified GP, spouted his sparse amount of knowledge on pre-menopausal women. *He's probably been reading his mother's weekly women's magazine, she decided.* But tonight Linda's revelation ensured sleep was a bit like Christmas – you're really looking forward to it, but it's still only October. Clara sat at the table, re-read the letter and recalled her mother's confession.

* * *

'I've been waiting for this day to come, dreading it in so many ways. I've gone over it in my mind many, many times working out the best way to say it all.

A large envelope arrived two weeks ago addressed to me. Your envelope was inside.' Linda asked her to listen until she had finished speaking.

David Reid, Clara discovered, was her uncle, her mother's much older brother. Linda was twelve years younger and her conception had come as an unwelcome surprise to her older parents. They had been blessed with a boy the first time around, ensuring the family farm would be safely passed down to him and keeping it in the family name. So another child hadn't been necessary. With such a large age gap between them she rarely had anything to do with David, and as granny lived with them, Linda grew up being cared for by her. Her parents worked long hours with David alongside them as he grew older; upon reaching sixteen he worked on the farm full time. Linda had been good company for granny.

'Now the next part...'.

Linda explained how she had been sworn to secrecy until such a time as she was given permission to tell Clara, or anyone at all. If she did, there would be desperate consequences.

Linda had been allowed to join the local Young Farmers group at age sixteen. Granny had sadly passed away three years earlier, and with the family busy on the farm, the concession was in exchange for Linda agreeing to take care of the home and family instead of finding a job. They accepted she would benefit from spending time with people her own age in the farming community. At her first social event, and her first taste of alcohol, she 'became friendly' with a lad from Kent who was visiting his cousin in Norfolk. He was 18, tall, quite handsome, and had given her a lift home in his car.

'I rather liked him. He was funny and sweet. It was the first time I'd felt in control of my life, and so... I thought I would. It was a one-off,' Linda said, blushing. 'I knew what I was doing,' she assured Clara. 'I suppose I thought it couldn't happen the first time. Anyway...'

Clara listened as her mother told her how her parents had been horrified when they discovered she was pregnant, and to avoid bringing shame on the family Linda's father announced she and the boy must marry.

'My father kept several shot guns and he would have blasted Gavin if he'd clapped eyes on him.' Linda paused, as if to imagine the scene. 'Arrangements were made for me to move immediately to Kent,' she continued '...but when I got here, I was told I'd be living with Gavin's grandma and caring for her in exchange for a roof over our heads. His parents didn't want a scandal for their only son who was destined to become a solicitor, and they were determined his future wouldn't be jeopardised by the distraction of a young wife and baby.'

Linda remained living in Tonbridge caring for Gavin's grandmother while his parents took him to live in Southampton for a fresh start.

While growing up Clara knew that Linda and Gavin had been separated before she was born, and Linda had told her that she didn't have any family. Even a young Clara had sensed it was a fragile subject, and over the years it hadn't mattered. With only seventeen years between them Clara and her mother had always enjoyed a close relationship. Forty-four years later, people often assumed Linda was her older sister.

Pausing, Linda boiled the kettle, refilled the teapot, and returned to the table to tell the rest of her story. Ordinarily, Clara would have filled such a gap with a torrent of questions, but today she did as her mother had asked and sat in silence.

'I never saw my parents again. They told their friends I was working abroad as an au pair. When I was seven months pregnant Gavin's grandmother died very suddenly. This was her home. My parents bought it from Gavin's parents and allowed us to live here on the understanding that I didn't return home to reveal the truth and bring a torrent of shame on them. They vowed to make us homeless if I did. I wasn't allowed to tell anyone about them, not even you, for as long as a member of the family was alive. Now, with David gone… well here we are. I never even expected to hear from any of them again.'

Across the table Linda took her daughter's hand in hers. Clara saw the fear and pain of a young girl staring back at her.

'I was so scared they would be true to their word, and they told me I didn't exist to them anymore. I changed my surname by deed poll so your parents would have the same last name on your birth certificate. I wanted to save you from any scandal too. That's how it was back then.'

Linda steeled herself for the cross examination she'd always anticipated; but Clara found herself lost for words. She knelt beside her mother and put her arms around her.

'So, what happens now?' Clara asked. 'And why would 'Uncle David' leave me half a house if he was ashamed of me?'

'He was ashamed of me, not you,' her mother reassured her.

Clara had enjoyed a happy childhood; money had been scarce, but she knew her mother loved her unconditionally, despite her own parents' inability to love her. Clara finally declared that David must have had a guilty conscience in his old age.

* * *

Linda found her daughter asleep on the sofa the next morning, the solicitor's letter lay on the floor beside her. The property, 'A Stone's Throw,' was being sold at auction and Clara would receive half the proceeds. The envelope had contained a smudged photocopy of the sales particulars from the auction house, with a few pictures and a brief description:

'This charming brick and flint cottage has remained in the same

*family for many generations and stands in a large plot measuring approximately two acres sts. The property comprises of 3 double bedrooms, living room, study, kitchen and downstairs bathroom. The property is situated close to the North Norfolk coast. *See special conditions of sale.'*

The main photograph was blurred, but Clara could just make out an old cottage standing behind a hedge, with a wide driveway to the right-hand side. An enormous Christmas tree that must have been planted many years ago stood proudly at the front of the property. Linda remembered the cottage as it was her grandmother's home until she was unable to live independently. It was rented out to a farm labourer for a number of years, then her brother David and his wife made it their home when they married. They had a son, Michael, who was the other beneficiary of 'A Stone's Throw'. It was Michael who sent the envelope to Linda. It arrived by registered post, with no accompanying letter from him, no acknowledgement of her brother's passing, no introduction, nothing other than the information from the solicitor. Inside were the deeds to the bungalow in Tonbridge that had been transferred into her name over 40 years ago by her parents. David had uncovered them shortly before he died, the solicitor had been instructed to pass on his apologies. It was a bittersweet parting gesture, and Linda seemed genuinely moved by it.

On the drive home Clara recalled how over the years she'd sensed a deep sadness in Linda that she tried to mask, but their close bond meant that neither of them could disguise their true emotions. Linda hadn't shown the slightest surprise when Clara announced that she and Joe were getting divorced scarcely six months after their quiet registry office wedding.

'I guessed as much,' she replied, hugging her daughter tightly. Clara had since reverted to her maiden name, preferring to put her failed marriage behind her.

'What a weekend!' Clara exclaimed to herself out loud arriving back home in London and opening the door to her 5th floor apartment. Closing it behind her she put her overnight bag in the closet and flopped onto the sofa where she awoke an hour later.

Pouring herself a large glass of red wine her thoughts returned to her mother. Abandoned by her own family and Gavin's, Linda was just seventeen when she gave birth to her, alone and without support. Social services had questioned how she could cope with a baby on her own, but she'd proved them all wrong. The government provided some financial assistance for food and bills which they somehow managed to survive on, but food wasn't their only sustenance as Linda's love and positivity kept them in good spirits and health.

Clara wondered what the cottage was like inside. *Probably old, smelly, dilapidated and covered in cobwebs like Miss Havisham,* she imagined. Looking around her own home she remembered why she had bought it so many years ago. It was affordable, functional and convenient. Clara was thankful she'd had the foresight to buy off plan as the subsequent rise in property prices had made it a solid financial investment. If anyone had visited, they'd have mistaken it for the show home; spotless, sparse and soul-less.

Contemplating the prospect of an impending windfall, Clara felt butterflies dance in her stomach. She wondered whether she would move to a larger apartment, or maybe just add the funds to her pension pot and top up her investments, which she acknowledged was boring but less messy. The prospect of moving seemed overwhelming, and she wasn't sure the upheaval and stress would be worth it. Besides, gazumping was commonplace among young professionals vying to get on the property ladder, and she hated the thought of getting into a bidding war. Perhaps she'd go to the auction to find out how much she was going to get so she could let her financial advisor know. She wondered if Michael would be there too. Would he speak to her?

Inheriting half a house from a family she knew nothing about was the sort of thing that happened in films, not to ordinary people like her. The more she thought about it, the greater her curiosity got the better of her, and the more she was determined to see the cottage before it was sold. Clara called the auction house and was surprised to learn there was an open day planned for potential buyers which coincided with the last day of her trip away with the girls from work, also in Norfolk. Deciding it was best not to reveal her true identity, as she only wanted to be nosey, she gave her married name.

2

It was strangely out of character for Clara, but somehow she'd found herself agreeing to a *Jolly Girls'* weekend away with the marketing department. Ordinarily, she would never have said yes. Ordinarily, they would never have invited her. 'Stuffy Clara,' who rarely stepped outside her office, had scored 1/10 in the marketing department's annual Christmas 'Who, What, When, Where' quiz for 'Who would you most like to get stuck in a lift with?' Daisy was the sole person who had voted for Clara as she thought she had sad eyes and needed a hug! Ironically, Teagan and Daisy were in the lift with Clara when it got stuck between floors.

She had thought twice before getting in with them as she detested the kind of small talk that made lift journeys seem endless, but she was late for a meeting. During the 27 minutes it took for the engineer to arrive and release them, Clara and Daisy quietly endured Teagan's relentless monologue, expressing her penchant for all things related to gin, including an atomiser that infused her home with the aroma of her favourite rhubarb flavour. Clara wasn't sure that was all Teagan sniffed when she was at home! Thankfully Daisy came to her rescue just as Teagan took a breath and prepared to reveal yet another fascinating aspect of her life, and quickly interjected.

'I'm hoping to get a new cat at the weekend. I'm just waiting for some paperwork then I can pick him up. His name is Bing.

Apparently, he was named after some singer from years ago. His owner passed away recently and the family need to rehome him.'

'Bing Crosby. He's famous for singing 'White Christmas', Clara informed them.

'Never heard of it, or him.' Teagan jumped at the chance of taking back control of the conversation. 'Anyway, haven't you already got like five cats? I don't know how you fit them all into your flat, I'm surprised your George puts up with them.'

'He loves them too,' Daisy protested. 'Bing's the third cat we've rescued,' she explained to Clara. 'I volunteer at a cat rescue charity at weekends. We're really short of helpers, do you like cats Clara?'

Before Clara had the chance to respond that she wasn't keen Teagan looked up from filing her nails and announced, 'They'll be even more short-handed when you go away for the Jolly Girls weekend, perhaps you should stay at home. Kate's pulled out, so you'll have to pay more for a single supplement. I can easily find two new people to fill your room.'

Clara observed Daisy's head drop as Teagan's cruel quip stung her like a slap in the face. Clara was amazed how calm Daisy remained.

'I'll find someone, and George is going to help out with the cats instead of me.'

Incensed by Teagan's flagrant cruelty to poor, kind-hearted Daisy, who didn't appear to possess the ability to offend anyone, Clara quickly stepped in.

'When are you going Daisy?' She wasn't quite sure why she was asking but felt a need to protect her, she'd heard that Teagan could be a bully. Daisy looked up, her eyes searching Clara's.

'Would you like to come?'

Daisy was overjoyed to have found a new roommate and grateful that Clara had come to her rescue. Teagan on the other hand wasn't impressed and let Daisy know it on their way back to the office.

'Daisy! Are you freakin' mad? She's the last person I want to spend a weekend with. What will the others say? I hope she's not going to spoil it for everyone. Well, I'm glad you're sharing a room with her.'

Daisy ignored Teagan's objections; she was extremely happy with the arrangement. Last year she'd shared a room with Kate who'd thrown up over Daisy's bed then collapsed on her own, snoring as her head hit the pillow. Daisy had spent the night on a sofa in reception.

The girls in the marketing department had a reputation for their often outrageous behaviour, but Daisy didn't fit the mould. When Teagan broadcast the news to the others there was a collective 'No!' aimed at Daisy. They were looking forward to their drunken weekend away but 'stick-in-the-mud, divorced-no-boyfriend Clara' was going to spoil it all.

That was a few weeks' ago and now Clara was running late. Teagan had given her strict instructions to leave work on Friday by 3.00pm which she guesstimated would give her an arrival time at the East Coast Holiday Village in Norfolk of 5.30pm with enough time to 'glam up' before dinner.

The exodus from London on a Friday afternoon was predictably hectic. Although Clara hated being late she had chosen not to leave earlier to take account of it. She grew frustrated as she found herself hemmed in at all angles, cursing the motionless queue of traffic. *Damn, why am I going on this stupid weekend anyway? I'm going to hate every minute of it.* She'd managed to feign illness for last year's company away-day. *Why didn't I think to do that? Oh….. crap. It's going to be crap.*

Clara rarely swore apart from in exceptional circumstances, and this was definitely one of them. She knew she was old-fashioned in that way. No-one seemed to bat an eyelid at work as her younger colleagues littered their sentences with expletives. Her self-approved 'exclamations' consisted mainly of 'flippin', bloomin', blinkin', blimey, bloody, bum, poo, crap, damn and shit. The latter only used in serious situations.

Slowly, the swarm of traffic ahead of her evaporated as the offending vehicles migrated off in varying directions like bees returning to their hives for the weekend. The last part of the A11 allowed her to indulge her love of speed; a tinge of excitement rippled through her body as her Porsche 911 responded immediately to the gentle but determined pressure she applied to the accelerator. It was her one guilty pleasure, apart from her Monday night Mars Bar. She wished she'd brought one with her as she wasn't sure this weekend away would be much of a treat.

Clara had developed a favourite way of slowly and satisfyingly devouring a Mars Bar. Firstly, she would bite off the chocolate around the sides, then slowly peel back the top layer of chocolate-coated caramel with her fingers, place it on her tongue, close her mouth, and wait for the sweetness to explode on each and every taste bud. Leaving the best bit 'til last, she would relax back on the sofa with her eyes closed as each bite of the sticky nougat melted in her mouth and slid down her throat. Heaven!

Arriving two hours later than instructed, Clara drove through the entrance to the East Coast Holiday Village. She lowered her car window as the security guard approached and asked for her name.

'Clara Richmond, I'm with Teagan Sanders' party.'

He checked his list, nodded, uttered 'nice car,' and raised the automatic barrier before retreating back to his wooden gatehouse. Winding her way around the car park looking for a suitable space she chose a spot at the end of a row, away from trees where birds like to perch, and next to a shiny black Range Rover Eclipse. Clara judged that the owner would be sufficiently careful of their own car as to not open their car door onto hers. Stepping out she felt a keen breeze coming off the sea.

'Wow, that'll blow the cobwebs away,' she announced to a passing seagull.

Clara loved the month of May with its promise of summer and the heat of the sun that would at last warm her bones through to her core. She hated being cold with a passion. In an attempt to eliminate any thoughts of winter and cold weather-related seasons from her mind she had devised her own system. 'Summer' was followed by 'late summer', November through to February became 'après summer', moving into 'pre-summer', and before she knew it 'summer' arrived again round about the beginning of May. It was a most satisfactory alternative. Clara's least favourite day of the year was 21st June, the longest day, when so many people around her liked to announce, 'The nights will be drawing in soon.' Aaaaargh, she wouldn't listen to them, the very thought of cold weather and shorter, darker days made her grumpy. Whenever possible she would walk on the sunny side of the street, and on gloomy days she'd stand next to windows to feel the light, as long as there wasn't a draft, and preferably if there was a warm radiator. Some people may have considered her 'odd.' Clara preferred to say she was 'particular.'

Clara had been oblivious to the annual 'Jolly Girls' Weekend' that had been a ritual for the girls in the marketing department for the past eight years, and now she was about to become part of its apparently rich history.

Manoeuvring her heavy suitcase across the bumpy carpark, its small wheels clearly unsuitable for any kind of off-road excursion, she doubted if she would need all the things she had been instructed to pack. "It's important to be prepared for all weathers," Teagan had informed her. Clara had also added her hairdryer, straighteners, various hairbrushes, makeup, toiletries, bottles of sanitiser, two packets of antibacterial wipes, her own towels, laptop and charger, iPad and charger, phone charger, power bank and favourite book, Pride and Prejudice, in case she became bored. She left her pillow in the car; she'd collect it later. She didn't want them thinking she was strange.

The automatic doors to the holiday village reception had barely slid open when she saw and heard her rowdy crowd in the bar.

'Here she is.' Teagan's voice was unmistakable and much louder than usual.

'You've missed dinner and you're way behind us with drinks, so you'll have to be on doubles the rest of the night,' she laughed.

Pulling her overloaded case towards them Clara noticed the table was littered with empty glasses and wine bottles. It seemed they'd started several hours earlier and laughingly boasted they'd had shots for starters. Seven 'girls', five of whom she didn't recognise, all lifted their glasses towards her.

'Cheers! Here's to another great Jolly Girls' Weekend.' Clara managed a weak smile in return.

The seasoned 'Jolly Girls' had booked a half-day holiday from work. They'd lounged in the sauna, lazed in the jacuzzi and now sported fresh manicures. They'd already eaten their evening meal and were taking full advantage of the all-inclusive drinks package. Daisy had arrived half an hour before Clara and was still on her first glass of wine. Clara made up the eighth 'Jolly Girl' but definitely didn't feel worthy of the title.

Happily accepting a large glass of red wine Clara sat in the one available chair listening to the noise and shrill laughter as they discussed their weekend itinerary. What *had* she let herself in for?

Clara followed Daisy to their room to prepare for the evening ahead. Clara suggested Daisy shower first, then when it was her turn, cleaned the entire bathroom with the antibacterial wipes before taking a shower. She hadn't shared a room with anyone since Joe, but Daisy didn't seem to notice her surreptitiously cleaning the light switches and door handles. *I can do this!* Clara quietly told herself.

Having both missed the evening meal in the restaurant they were accompanied by a few other late arrivals and invited to eat in a small bar area where a cold buffet had been supplied. The rest of the girls joined the masses for bingo. Daisy sipped her glass of wine while Clara ordered herself another.

'Don't you like wine?' Clara asked, and offered to order her something else.

'I'm driving tomorrow so I'll be up early; I'll try not to wake you.' Her response took Clara completely by surprise. She'd assumed they would stay at the resort all weekend. Was leaving even an option? Daisy explained that the rescue shelter where she volunteered had a sister centre in Norfolk, which is mainly why she came away for the weekend. None of the others seemed to notice that she slipped away during the day as she'd done so these past 3 years. It was a much larger rescue centre with horses, cows and sheep. Daisy liked to walk the dogs who were waiting to be rehomed and that's where she was going tomorrow.

'Can I come with you?' Clara heard herself ask, surprised and slightly embarrassed by her outburst, but thankful for an opportunity to escape the drinking games and line dancing the others had planned for the next day. To her surprise Daisy didn't object,

'We can walk twice as many dogs,' she replied.

Clara's thoughts turned to Minty, but she quickly brushed them aside, took another large mouthful of wine and changed the subject.

* * *

Minty had been Clara's beloved childhood dog. He was a yellow Labrador who adored her as much as she adored him, and very probably more. He arrived on her 8th birthday, and she'd been told he was hers to care for; feed, water, walk, train, love and, of course, clear up after. She hurried home from school each day to find him waiting at the front door, his tail wagging so much his rear end swayed from side to side, his mouth smiling and eyes shining at the sight of her. He was her constant companion. He cheered her on from the side-lines while she played hockey on Saturdays, lay under her desk while she agonised over her homework, stayed on guard in his basket beside her bed each night, sat through all the soaps on TV, and gave unwavering moral support during her exams by bringing her his ball to throw, giving her a well-earned break from revision. He stayed up with her all night while she cried over Mark Stevens who had told her he loved her then was seen kissing Sally Jacobs outside the cinema. Mark had bravely owned up before he could be 'squealed on'. Minty was there to hear his confession, and licked Clara's hand while she was dumped as delicately as any 15-year-old boy can manage. Clara said nothing in response, she and Minty simply turned on their heels and walked away. If Minty had been able to cry there would have been two floods of tears that night.

The morning after her 20th birthday Clara woke early, the sun was already streaming through the curtains on that June day. She rolled onto her side as she did every morning to say hello to

Minty, but on this day, he didn't look back up at her or wag his tail. He didn't stir. On this day, he lay still, silent and seemingly asleep. On this day, he reluctantly relinquished his post, and quietly crossed over the rainbow bridge.

Clara had been completely distraught and taken a week off work, giving the loss of a close family member as the reason to the personnel department. She'd not made a fuss of another dog since.

* * *

After their meal Clara and Daisy joined the others in the theatre where they were over-excitedly informed that Tanya had almost won £190 at bingo, as she'd only needed one number and they were all sure the next one to be called would have been hers if only the woman in the short pink dress hadn't beaten her to it. Their disappointment was soon forgotten by the announcement that it was time for the evening performance and would they all please take their seats. Clara watched the others as they drunkenly sang along with the singers and clapped the dancers as they performed their energetic and dynamic routines in perfect synchronisation. She secretly admired their lack of inhibitions and couldn't remember the last time she'd let her hair down.

Clara and Daisy trailed behind the others as they staggered to the late-night bar, then slipped away unnoticed for a reasonably early night ahead of their secret day out tomorrow. Clara knew she wouldn't have trouble sleeping tonight, she'd never been one to hang out with large groups of people, she'd found the evening's noise and chatter quite overwhelming and exhausting. She and Linda had led a quiet life at home, so she was looking forward to her outing with Daisy tomorrow. Perhaps deep down she felt some affiliation with the deserted animals, hadn't she and her mother been abandoned by her family?

In the morning, following a hearty breakfast, the two fugitives left the holiday village and set out early for Heathfield Animal Sanctuary. Clara found herself beginning to relax in the passenger seat, a position she rarely found herself in. Perhaps it was the hypnotic rhythm of classical music that filled the car, or the mesmerising view of the Norfolk countryside slipping by the window, or the four large glasses of wine she'd consumed the previous evening, or even the full English breakfast she'd polished off before they left, that lured her into a gentle slumber and an all too familiar dream.

* * *

Clara found herself walking a familiar path, barefoot at the water's edge, feeling a gentle tickle as the water lapped around her ankles and toes. Her heels slowly sank a little into the soft warm sand, her jeans were rolled up to just below her knees and the water splashed at her calves as she walked a little further into its waves. Goose bumps prickled the skin on her arms and legs as the water became cooler. She stood, looking out to sea, the large breakers just a little further out, displayed their plumes as if enticing her like male birds to a mate, their ritualistic dance inviting her closer. She felt the temptation to walk towards them, drawn forwards, their energy pulling her nearer. As she took a half-step further, she felt the current strengthen, almost pull her feet from under her and she quickly stood firmly again to regain her balance. The wind began to whip the breakers into a frenzy, the rollers preceding them becoming taller and fiercer. The water was pulling at her hips, trying to drag her deeper in.

Looking around, clasping desperately at the water, she realised something was missing. Something, or someone? Momentarily she wasn't sure who or what had been here. But now she was. Yes, it was someone. They had been there, for a long time, forever since she could remember, and now they were gone. Her heart pounding in her chest, she could barely breathe, a huge wave swept over her, then just as quickly, she was on a beach laying on a towel, sunbathing, the brightness of the sun visible through her closed eyes...

* * *

Just at that point, as usual, Clara awoke. She wiped away the beads of sweat on her forehead with the back of her hand and quickly looked across at Daisy who was quietly humming to herself, oblivious of the distress her sleeping passenger was suffering. Clara had dreamt this same dream at least once a month for too many years than she could remember. She'd even visited a Dream Interpreter who concluded she was searching for her father; Clara hadn't been entirely convinced.

'Is it much further?' Clara asked, glad to be awake and eager to forget her dream.

'It's this next turning on the right, then about quarter of a mile down on the left.'

They pulled into the entrance barely two minutes later and were greeted by an assortment of odours and noises.

'Welcome to the countryside,' Daisy exclaimed, the excitement in her voice noticeable in its stark contrast to her usual quietness. She parked her car haphazardly in a muddy spot and jumped out, her walking boots squelching as they sank into the sludge. Clara opened the car door and was relieved to see a sparse square of clean grass within her reach, if she stretched far enough. She hop-scotched her way across to a path, stepping over the muddy puddles in a pointless attempt to keep her boots clean. She followed Daisy as she strode off towards a dark green converted shipping container that served as an office. Her boots caked in mud, Daisy stepped straight into the office. Horrified, Clara stopped outside, fully aware of the devastation the mud on her boots would inflict on the office floor, but Daisy and the staff seemed oblivious of this fact, to Clara's utter astonishment. While she stood in the doorway deliberating on how to join them without making a mess Daisy was greeted like an old friend, hugging each one, telling them how great it was to be back. There were some 'in' jokes aimed at Daisy, who helped at the cat rescue, accusing her of slumming it in the country and being a far cry from "sitting pretty in the city cuddling kitties!" to which they all laughed, and someone meowed.

'Come in,' a tall lady with greying hair past her waistline beckoned to Clara, 'we don't bite!' 'No, but Blue will!' a voice replied, and they all laughed at another 'in' joke. Blue, it transpired, was a black pony who liked to bite and kick.

'You *will* be black and blue if you don't move out of his way in time,' Tina, the lady with long grey hair explained. He'd been mistreated and subsequently surrendered by his owner having been reported to the RSPCA. He's a 'work in progress' they all declared. Clara watched their easy banter and relaxed camaraderie, surprised at how these scruffy, muddy, fur-covered colleagues all seemed at ease with each other. It was the polar opposite of her own work environment where she shut herself away in her office.

'I suppose we'd better be useful as we're here.'

The sound of Daisy's voice snapped Clara out of her thoughts and back into the present. They followed Tina to the kennels and heard the volume of barking increase as they drew closer. Tina opened the tall metal entrance gate housing a small community of homeless dogs of varying shapes and sizes. Clara was filled with mixed emotions as she passed the cages. The occupants pressed their noses to the wire mesh, eager to discover if she was that special person, the one who would choose them and invite them into a loving home in return for their unconditional devotion. Tina explained that Saturdays were usually busy with volunteer dog walkers but as the weather was so good after a whole week of rain many of them had gone away for the weekend.

'So, you can both walk your boots off today,' she laughed. They stopped in front of a cage where a smallish black dog with long ears resided.

'Smudge here is 7, he's an American Cocker Spaniel and is waiting for a home check to be completed. He walks well on the lead but isn't keen on dogs bigger than him. His owner had to go into a home and was heartbroken to let him go. He was very well looked after and is soon to be re-homed with a mature lady who has recently retired. She lives alone and enjoys walking. They are the perfect match,' Tina informed them.

Clara wondered if Tina had such an encyclopaedic knowledge of all the residents in her care. Tina put a collar and lead on Smudge, handed him to Daisy and looked at Clara.

'Do you have any experience with dogs?'

Clara felt the full force of the question hit her in the chest with the might of a hammer as she remembered Minty.

'Erm, yes,' was all she could manage as a lump formed in her throat. She followed Tina in a slight daze, shocked by how her raw emotions gripped her so tightly. She fought to keep her composure, resisting the urge to run. Tina was talking to her, yet she was oblivious to her words as she was handed a lead. Clara unconsciously took it. With the familiar touch of a handle in her grasp, she slowly looked down at the end of the lead where she saw a small black and tan face gazing back at her. She quietly thanked God that it wasn't a yellow Labrador. She could breathe again. It had been twenty-four years since she'd lost Minty, how were her emotions so strong even after all this time? Hadn't she buried them deep enough?

Clara and her four-legged companion followed Daisy and Smudge out of the kennel and up a grassy track to a large field. The dogs were not to be let off the lead, they could be given treats, and all 'mess' was to be cleared up and put into poo bags which had been supplied. There were water bowls along the route and poo bins where they could deposit the used bags. Clara was grateful for the keen early morning breeze that gusted towards them as they fought against it up the hill to the field.

'This wind makes your eyes smart,' Clara called out to Daisy, grateful for an excuse to finally let the tears roll down her cheeks. She must pull herself together, she told herself, taking a deep breath and wiping them away on her sleeve.

They stopped at regular intervals whenever Smudge or Treacle found something of great importance to investigate. Clara hadn't heard Tina tell her the dog's name and looked confused when Daisy said, 'isn't Treacle sweet?' then laughed out loud saying how funny that was. Seeing Clara's blank expression Daisy felt the need to explain.

'Treacle, the dog... she's sweet, and so's... oh never mind, I thought it was funny.'

Clara suddenly caught on and laughed politely, 'Yes, good one.'

The woodland at the far end of the field belonged to the centre and soon Clara found herself enjoying the sound of twigs breaking beneath their boots, the smell of damp composting leaves littering the ground and the quiet whistling of the breeze as it swished through the trees. Looking down at Treacle, who had found herself a sizeable stick to carry, her head raised in an attempt to keep it from dragging on the floor, Clara smiled at the little dog's determination as she refused to give up. Fifty minutes later they returned to the kennels fresh-faced, with wind-blown hair and red cheeks. Clara and Daisy made a fuss of Smudge and Treacle as they handed them grudgingly back to Tina.

'Cup of something hot?' she offered.

Warmed by a large mug of tea they returned to the kennel to find their next walking partners. Tina handed Daisy a friendly husky-cross called Charles, who, she warned, 'could pull a bit' and then admitted he was actually like a coiled spring! He'd recently arrived at the centre and was 'undergoing training'. She needed a calm dog to walk with her who wouldn't be disturbed by his antics and had 'just the one'. Elsa was a cross between a Saluki and a Lurcher. She was placid but timid with strangers, a trait which meant she had been overlooked many times. Having been a stray, and with no known history, prospective adopters had been cautious, and she'd spent the past year at Heathfields. Tina told them the vet had estimated she was around 5 years old when she arrived. Clara stroked Elsa's soft creamy fur from her head to her tail, but she didn't respond. She stood completely still as her collar and lead were attached, and obediently walked slowly alongside Clara as they followed Daisy who was way ahead of them, trying to dig her heels in the mud to stop Charles pulling her along. Clara laughed at them both as Elsa wandered along beside her, the epitome of good manners.

Daisy and Charles were half-way around the field when Clara and Elsa reached the top of the track. Clara stopped to stroke her, but Elsa had long since stopped reacting to the many kind strangers who would all eventually return her back to her cage. Clara headed towards the woods to see if anything would spark her interest there. Daisy and Charles had already completed a quick lap of the field before Clara reached the woods. Daisy gesticulated from afar that she was taking Charles back to the kennel; arm and lead outstretched ahead of her as he hauled her along in whichever direction he chose.

Unlike Treacle, Elsa found nothing of interest to sniff, nor could she be enticed with a rather attractive stick. She simply stood patiently, waiting until she was encouraged to move on again. Clara allowed herself to remember Minty and how he loved chasing balls, sticks, slippers, birds and cats. With Elsa ambling along beside her Clara wondered about her past. Had she been loved once? Alone in the woods Clara confided in Elsa all about Minty. They reached a fallen tree which served as a convenient resting place. Clara sat while Elsa lay among the leaves at her feet. Clara stroked her head and ears as she allowed her tears to flow at the memory of her beloved childhood companion, but also for the young Linda who had been so cruelly abandoned. If Elsa was confused by the grieving lady quietly weeping and sharing her sad story then she didn't show it, she was happy to listen. There was something quite soothing about the sound of her soft voice that lulled Elsa into a light sleep as she lay on the woodland floor.

They returned to the kennel to find Daisy eating bacon sandwiches with the staff.

'We were wondering where you'd got to,' she mumbled with her mouth full. Clara bent to stroke Elsa one last time as she handed her lead back to Tina. Clara watched as she made her way quietly back into her cage, lay down in her bed and closed her eyes.

With a bacon sandwich and bottle of ketchup thrust into her hands Clara quickly balanced them on her lap whilst fumbling in her bag for a small bottle of sanitiser. She looked around for a sink where she could wash her hands with soap and hot water, but as a hot mug of tea appeared from somewhere she was forced to take it politely, silently dreading how many germs she was about to ingest.

They filled the journey back to the East Norfolk Holiday Village with chat about the dogs they had walked, a further two each that day, and the staff who looked after them. Daisy had to borrow a spare uniform as Charles had pulled her over in the mud on their way back to the kennel. Clara laughed, saying she'd wished she'd have seen it and could she do it again tomorrow when they went back?

They repeated their now familiar bathroom routine, dressed for the evening ahead and made it to dinner in time to hear everyone's news. Teagan noisily reported the day's events with tales of their activities and shenanigans. Although they were both tired and would have preferred an early night, Clara and Daisy managed to stay up to watch the show but snuck back to their room while the others were en-route to the late-night bar again.

Clara volunteered to drive the next day. She borrowed the bathroom towels to keep the car seats and floor clean on the way back.

'We can sit on them and put them in the footwell,' she told Daisy who was suitably impressed with her car, but not sure why they needed quite so many towels.

Pulling into the entrance to Heathfields Clara spotted a grassy area in the car park, away from the mud. This time she stepped straight into the office to join them all, no longer feeling like a stranger, but experiencing of a sense of belonging that she hadn't known in years.

Daisy was asked if she could help muck out the horses as Sarah had a plumbing emergency at home and they were a pair of hands short. If Clara was happy to walk the dogs she might like to visit the stables later, as long as it wasn't with Charles! She followed Tina to the kennels where she met Ralph, a 10-year-old beagle, and they spent a pleasant hour following a scent he picked up. He trailed Clara through the woods, around the field then back into the woods, several times. The source of the smell eluded them both but Ralph's enthusiasm never waned. She eventually coaxed him back to the kennel with treats then had a quick cup of tea with Tina. Clara spent the next twenty minutes trying to convince a very nervous Corgi-cross called Bertie to go for a walk. He could only be persuaded to take a few steps forward before sitting down. It was a painful experience for them both so Clara gave in before they even reached the field and turned back towards the kennel. He pulled her all the way back and wagged his tail when he was returned to his cage and snuggled into his bed, turning his back on Clara. Feeling slightly dejected she asked Tina to point her in the direction of the stables.

'Why don't you take Elsa with you? She's not been out today, and it'll give her a change of scenery.'

Elsa sauntered alongside Clara, instinctively turning left towards the field when they reached the well-trodden track. Confused by the slight tug on her collar she stopped momentarily, unsure what it meant.

'Come on Elsa, this way today,' Clara reassured her, and she obediently followed without objection. Long before Clara could see, hear or smell the stables Elsa was sniffing the air, her head and ears raised, her delicate senses alert to the potent aromas and sounds emanating from the stables.

Daisy had a shovel full of something smelly and steaming when Clara and Elsa found her. Her cheeks were glowing pink and her dishevelled hair was randomly accessorised with fragments of straw. Beads of sweat on her forehead and neck glistened in the sun as she greeted them with a beaming smile.

'Come to help?' she asked Clara.

'Not bloomin' likely. Elsa and I are far too delicate,' she replied holding her nose and stroking Elsa's head and silky ears as if to reassure her they definitely wouldn't be participating.

'But it's so exhilarating.' Daisy laughed.

Lizzie was in charge of the stables and invited Clara to meet the residents. Elsa followed, waiting patiently as Clara stroked the horse's noses, except for Blue, she remembered his reputation.

As the kettle was boiled for yet another tea break Clara washed her hands under the large outside tap, spraying her trousers in the process, then took the bottle of sanitiser out of her bag. Lizzie laughed.

'You've only stroked a horse's nose Clara, it's not like you've been picking up their shit like Daisy!' Clara felt her face flush red. No-one had commented on her 'funny ways' since Joe, but then she'd not let anyone else close.

* * *

Joe had been patient at first, not seeming to mind her need for cleanliness, as she had been able to keep much of it at bay to begin with, but it soon crept back in. He even began to carry his own bottle of sanitiser for emergencies, not that Clara forgot hers. When they moved in together he'd loved living in a clean and tidy home, especially as Clara insisted on doing it all as she liked it done 'just so.' Over time her obsessions spread from cleaning to checking; checking she'd locked the car, checking she'd locked the back and front doors and turned off the lights downstairs each night-time, with several trips back downstairs just to make sure. She wasn't sure exactly when Joe had started to mock her, pretending to be joking at first, then the anger came.

'Can't you just get the fuck into bed without jumping up and down like a friggin' Jack in the Box? Christ Clara! Why don't you just stay the hell downstairs and save us both the trouble?'

She learnt to hide her obsessive behaviour to avoid the confrontation it caused, and they slipped into an easy compromise of her waiting until he had fallen asleep before going back downstairs to check what she feared she had forgotten. Eventually, Clara would finally allow herself to climb into bed exhausted.

Six months after they were married Clara emptied all the cupboards in the spare bedroom to wash and clean the inside of the drawers. As she pulled out a bedside cabinet to hoover behind, she found an earring that wasn't hers. 'How cliché,' she scolded the offending object as it lay in the palm of her hand. Joe owned up to his infidelity, and with the same amount of delicacy as Mark Stevens, announced he was leaving. Initially, Clara was surprised at how easily she settled into life without him but soon began to spiral even deeper as the obsessional behaviour began to consume her. The day she was too exhausted to get out of bed and go to work Clara contacted a Counsellor, 'I need someone to help me.' In time she learnt how to control her impulses and urges, using strategies to settle her mind and help choose to change her behaviour. She had it all under control now, didn't she?

* * *

Clara bit her lip, steeling herself for Lizzie's next cutting comment she took a deep breath, ready to endure the disapproval, the criticism, the scolding that was so familiar to her. She had never been able to confide in Joe where it all came from, how it all started. After he left, she was glad she hadn't given him her secret to take with him.

But Daisy was beckoning to her, smiling. Clara stood, unsure of what to do next. 'Come and have a cuppa and a biscuit, I've got some news to tell you.' Clara took the offered mug of tea. The sun streaked through the clouds as the three women relaxed on bales of hay among the smells and sounds of the horses. Elsa, waiting patiently, had intuitively observed the pain Clara had quietly endured and began to uncharacteristically sniff at her hand.

Clara found herself stroking Elsa's soft ears and back, with each stroke she relaxed more, as if she was absorbing a magic potion. She held a biscuit out to Elsa who took it gently.

Daisy broke the spell as she announced in an excited voice that she had something to tell them. She was leaving Coopers & Leigh and moving to Norfolk with her boyfriend George, hopefully next year. They could afford a bigger property here than in London and George had enquired about a transfer from the Metropolitan Police. Clara stared at Daisy, admiring her new friend's bravery. She'd never considered leaving London herself, at least until she retired, when she presumed she'd move close to her mother. She felt privileged to have been trusted with Daisy's secret and promised to keep quiet. Lizzie suggested she apply to the centre, if they had any vacancies, she was sure they'd employ her.

No-one seemed to mind that tea break ran well into an hour as they deliberated over where Daisy and George would live, how much they could sell their two-bedroomed flat in Wanstead for and how many acres they would need for the five children Daisy wanted, plus the numerous stray cats she was likely to adopt. Clara was surprised at the house prices in comparison to London. While Daisy's future was being meticulously planned, Elsa quietly demolished the rest of the biscuits that had been carelessly but conveniently left on the floor, then softly lay her chin on Clara's boot and closed her eyes.

Clara and Daisy agreed they ought to return to camp sooner rather than later as it was their last night. Clara and Elsa wandered slowly back towards the kennel.

'Well, what do you think of that Elsa, Daisy moving to Norfolk? That's a big step.'

As the kennel came into view Clara stopped. She looked down at Elsa, standing, waiting patiently. What would her future be? Would anyone give her a new home?

Why was she feeling like this? When did she become so attached to her? Clara knelt in front of Elsa and for the first time they made eye contact. Stroking Elsa's velvety head and ears, Clara felt a tear trickle down her cheek.

'I'm sorry I have to take you back. I wish I could take you home with me.'

Clara felt a warm wet tongue brush her face as it washed the tear away. She put her arms around Elsa's neck and knew that somehow, although she had no idea how or what made her think it, they would be together again.

Reluctantly saying their goodbyes to everyone Daisy promised she'd be back again next year, hopefully when she moved up. As they returned to the car Clara half-jokingly scolded Daisy.

'You're lucky to get a lift back in my car smelling like that,' and threw a pile of towels at her to sit on. Clara couldn't remember laughing and being silly in so long, she desperately didn't want it to end. The complete strangers she'd met only yesterday seemed more familiar now than any of her colleagues whom she'd worked alongside for so many years. The journey back passed quietly, both lost in their own thoughts, both sad to be leaving Heathfield.

During dinner that evening Teagan proposed a toast to The Jolly Girls. 'Cheers to you all, thanks for yet another fantastic weekend away, it's been great. Let's enjoy ourselves one last time before we get back to reality.' Clara raised her glass along with the others, those last words echoing in her head. '...back to reality.' They winded her like a belly flop when you're learning to dive and momentarily stunned by the pain as you land squarely on the top of the water. She could only mouth the word 'cheers' in unison with the others.

Reality? Back to what? What was her life? What was the plan? Hadn't she felt more alive these past two days than any she could remember? Where did she belong? A stream of questions scrambled around in her brain, stuck on repeat. Returning from previous holidays abroad, after she'd spent two glorious weeks lounging around in the sun and overindulging in far too much food and wine, she knew that wasn't real life. But this weekend visiting Heathfield and the staff that worked there, this *was* their life. She wasn't ready to go home. Thankfully, the detour to inspect her inheritance at the open day would prolong the inevitability of it. She wondered if there would be many people there.

After breakfast they all said their goodbyes and wished each other a safe journey on their way back to London, each claiming they would arrive first. Clara waited until they had all left and then turned out of the car park in the opposite direction.

3

Driving slowly along the narrow lane searching for the property, Clara carefully negotiated potholes, and a pheasant that ran back and forth in front of her car until finally disappeared into a hedgerow. She was surprised by the flatness of the Norfolk landscape in comparison to Kent's rippling hillsides, which although beautiful to look at, but crippling if you ventured out for a Sunday afternoon bike ride. Clara was sure she could cycle for miles in Norfolk.

Despite the calm of the lazy countryside she was hot and bothered, having left the East Norfolk Holiday Village later than planned as Daisy had lost her keys. They'd hunted high and low for them in their room several times, each emptying their bags twice and checking under the beds. Clara eventually found them wrapped in a towel Daisy had been sitting on after mucking out the horses. Now she was running late.

Finally, she spotted a wooden weather-worn sign propped against a large stone, with the words 'A Stone's Throw' barely visible as they'd been etched into the wood many years ago. As Clara carefully manoeuvred the car through the entrance, ensuring the hedge didn't scratch the sides of her car, the cottage stood before her. The sight of it made her stop.

'Wow!' The rustic charm of the brick and flint cottage caught Clara's breath, she was sure she'd never seen such a beautiful setting. *Yes, I agree. It all looks a bit tired and it probably needs a lot of work,* was her assessment. She was intrigued to see inside. That's when she realised there ought to be more cars for the open day, she looked at her watch.

'Damn, I've missed it!' Clara exclaimed out loud in disbelief, hitting the steering wheel in frustration and momentarily sounding the horn, startling herself. 'Bloody Hell!'

As she'd come all this way it made sense to at least take a look around the outside and peer through the windows. The driveway was empty except for an abandoned, dusty old car parked in front of a dilapidated greenhouse, whose roof and sides had long since shattered and now lay lost among the long grass. She parked neatly next to it, smiling to herself as she pictured the car park of her apartment block and its occupants standing in line. *I guess old habits die hard.* As she stepped out of the car the stiletto heels of her shoes disappeared among the stones, and she realised she'd dressed more appropriately for a business meeting than an open house in the countryside. Who was she trying to impress?

Looking through the overgrown shrubs, Clara spotted a small wooden shed further into the garden, it was lop-sided and partially hidden by the vegetation. It's crude repairs over the years were obvious and made her curious as to why someone would go to so much trouble to maintain it. Intrigued, Clara ducked under the branches of the trees to take a closer look. The well-worn metal latch opened easily at her touch and the door quickly swung open, taking her by surprise. Clara caught it just before it hit her and took a sharp intake of breath. Far too late she realised her mistake, unable to breathe out quickly enough to stop the assault on her nasal passages from the stench of what she now realised was an outside toilet. The sickening smell engulfed her and triggered her gagging reflex. She took a step back as far as she could and declared out loud 'Oh my God. That stinks!'

This wasn't her first encounter with an outside toilet, she had once been incredibly brave and used one during a trip to the Blue Mountains in Australia many years ago. The presence of several spiders in the outback dunny had required all her courage to enter and she'd made her exit as quickly as possible. The alternative she had been told was to squat behind a bush where there may or may not be a snake or two. Clara chose the lesser of two evils. She was sure this one smelt far worse.

Stepping back and breathing in the fresh air, not wishing to get close again, Clara left the door open and turned back towards the cottage to see a man locking the front door. Horrified he would leave without seeing her, as she was partially hidden by the shed, she began running towards him, waving over-enthusiastically and calling out.

'Hello!' As she ran the heels of her shoes sank into the ground again, and her oversized shoulder bag swung around her neck. Clara momentarily wondered what on earth she must look like as she gambolled towards him. *Like a startled gazelle,* she guessed, but didn't have time to worry about that, this was her only chance to look inside. Thank goodness he hadn't seen her reaction to the outside lavvy! Desperate to gain his attention, the thought of a wasted journey propelled her forward. Stopping a few feet before him, relieved he was still there, she stood momentarily to gather her composure. The man smiled at her as she straightened her hair and took several deep breaths in an effort to calm her breathing. Clara's gaze met his blue eyes, then slowly moved down to his well-worn jacket and trousers, then finally his very dusty shoes. In that moment she realised the abandoned car must belong to him, and her ungainly jaunt across the stoney drive had been an embarrassing and unnecessary spectacle!

Gaining some of her composure Clara introduced herself,

apologising for her late arrival and hoping she would still be able to view the property. Breathing heavily from her short sprint she made a mental note to cancel her gym membership because paying a monthly fee clearly did not guarantee fitness, actually attending the gym was a requirement for that. The agent smiled again and informed her that he'd heard her arrive from the other side of the garden and was unlocking the door to let her in!

Trying to conceal her own embarrassment, Clara didn't notice the agent surreptitiously rubbing the top of each shoe on the back of his trouser leg in a futile attempt to remove some of the dust. Uncomfortable about his own shabby appearance in front of this clearly sophisticated, attractive woman, who didn't appear to be wearing a wedding ring, he wasn't quite sure why it bothered him so much.

'I see you've found the facilities,' he laughed looking over her shoulder at the open shed, hoping to distract her and lighten the moment. Clara's face reddened as she realised he had clearly witnessed her reaction to it.

'Yes, a lovely water feature in the garden,' she replied, pleased that she could retort with a witty reply and hoping it would make up for her entrance.

'Oh! there's no water. It's a compost toilet,' he informed her, reddening with embarrassment and a sinking feeling that he'd blown any chance of appearing cool, calm and collected.

He introduced himself as William. He was happy to stay for longer as it was his day off and he was standing in last minute for a colleague. He turned the tarnished handle of the front door and opened it for her to enter.

'Take your time, I'll be outside if you have any questions.' William turned and walked away, cursing his disastrous attempt at a joke and wondering why he should care.

As the door swung open the stale smell of 'musty old house' wafted into Clara's nostrils, but to her its scent was comparable to an elegant perfume in contrast to the stench of the shed.

Structurally the cottage seemed in a reasonable condition, although it appeared no one had lived there for some time. Many of its original features remained and Clara was impressed by the light and spacious rooms with views overlooking the overgrown gardens. Somehow it felt strangely homely, despite the eclectic mix of varying decades of furniture, curiously patterned carpets and curtainless windows. It was a stark contrast to her London apartment. The kitchen was sparse and dated, *…but you could live with the units for a while*, she considered. *It has enough space for a big table and leads out to the garden. Actually, if you knocked that wall out, put bi-fold doors in and combined the kitchen and study that would be a fantastic space.* Clara unconsciously began planning how the property could be improved. *What am I doing? It's not like I'm going to live here,* she silently reprimanded herself.

Upstairs the three bedrooms were all of a good size, each one had a built-in cupboard which functioned as a wardrobe, complete with ill-fitting wooden door, a single hanging rail and a few cobwebs. In one corner of the second bedroom a pale pink pedestal washbasin stood proud. *It's a shame the bathroom is downstairs but there's definitely space for an en-suite*, her imagination rambled on. The views from two bedrooms overlooked the surrounding fields to the front. As she opened the door to the main bedroom at the rear of the cottage, Clara caught her breath. It revealed a large window spanning the length of the opposite wall, presenting a magnificent view out across the sea.

'Blimey!' was all she could say, mesmerised by the picturesque seascape, barely able to pull herself away from it.

She slowly inspected the cottage twice more, each time

becoming increasingly enchanted. She wasn't exactly sure when the possibility began to form in her mind, most probably it took a hold before she even realised. *What if...? No! It's impossible because..., because..., I have a home and a job and bills to pay and responsibilities and I can't just give up work, up sticks and move to Norfolk on a whim.* There, she'd said it. It would have been a lovely idea, she told herself, but it's just not practical.

She found a large solitary key attached to a frayed piece of string hanging on a metal hook next to the kitchen door. As she slipped it into the lock and turned it, Clara thought of the previous occupants and wondered how many generations of her family had lived here. She felt a strange connection to them as she opened the door and stepped into the garden, as so many of them had before her.

The land was split into sections comprising of an orchard, vegetable garden, an abandoned pigsty with a small overgrown field bordered by a decommissioned electric fence, and lawned areas on three sides which would require a ride-on mower to keep in check. There were two separate barns, one to the left of the cottage, the other closer to the pigsty. Both of their roofs had collapsed many years ago, the debris still laying among a collection of rusting farm machinery and animal food troughs.

Clara headed towards the end of the overgrown lawn, drawn by the desire to have a closer look at the view. A half-hearted attempt to cut the grass had been abandoned but a single path, flattened by prospective purchasers, led straight down to the end of the garden where Clara came to an abrupt halt.

'Oh crap!' she exclaimed out loud.

'And that's why it's being sold at auction,' a voice approaching from behind explained. William had been collecting a few garden tools from an old shed nearby. 'The owner asked me to pick them up,' he explained.

Clara could have fired a hundred questions at him, anxious to learn even a little about her cousin Michael, but as she hadn't disclosed who she was when making the appointment it didn't seem appropriate now, besides, she was enjoying the anonymity.

'A Stone's Throw! I can see why,' she declared, staring at the small avalanche that had hungrily eaten away at her inheritance. She wondered if anyone would want to buy it once they saw it. What did it matter to her? *Someone* would buy it, she'd receive a not-to-be-sniffed-at sum of money, maybe move to a bigger apartment and carry on working until she retired. *And then what?* The question she'd never really allowed herself to consider planted itself firmly in the forefront of her mind, demanding an answer. She'd half planned to retire before she was sixty. Healthy contributions to her pension pot topped up with bonus payments over the years, and a robust rainy-day savings account, had all been carefully accrued to prevent the financial hardship she had experienced as a child.

Turning to look back at the appropriately named cottage she realised that an exciting new opportunity stood before her. She could simply buy her cousin's half and move here when she retired. Meanwhile, she'd have a holiday home in Norfolk for weekends. It all made perfect sense. Looking down at the cliff edge, however, she realised that you couldn't have one without the other.

'It's quite something isn't it?' William's question surprised her. He was looking straight ahead. She allowed her gaze to follow his, and for a moment admitted to herself that if you ignored the gnawed edges of the lawn, the view of the North Norfolk coastline was breath-taking. The tranquil waters played with the light from the sky, rebounding upwards only for it to be returned down onto another gentle passing wave, like a kind of ethereal game of tennis.

'I hadn't realised it was this close,' she sighed in response to William, looking back down at the jagged edge. As she turned to look at him he smiled back at her. His blue eyes reminded her of their first encounter only a short while ago and she blushed at the memory.

Standing beside each other looking out to sea, William told Clara about the property. The cottage was structurally sound, but obviously needed updating, and the outbuildings could be converted subject to the usual planning permissions. There had been numerous viewings but no offers so far. The property wasn't mortgageable due to its proximity to the cliff-edge, so it was of no interest to developers. He told her the landslip happened two years ago during an exceptionally wet winter. The local community had been petitioning the district council and environment agency, demanding action for a number of years, and finally the sea defences had been erected earlier this year.

'So hopefully there shouldn't be any more problems,' he suggested. 'Although I obviously can't guarantee it, that's why the guide price is so low.' Clara was surprised by his openness; she was used to people hiding the truth hoping never to be found out, quick to score a point. As they stood side-by-side looking back out to sea, across the huge infantry of boulders standing to attention in defence of the shoreline, she felt herself warm to him.

Clara wasn't sure if it was the cottage, the water, or the man, but here she felt like a completely different person. Here under the vast Norfolk skies was the promise of freedom, a chance to escape the boxes in which she lived her life. *This could be a fabulous retreat. Could it become a reality?* It was a million miles away from her own life, but was that such a bad thing? She'd felt more alive here in Norfolk than she could remember in a long time. William appeared to be lost in his own thoughts too.

Clara turned and looked back along the remaining garden towards the cottage, still under its enchantment despite its depleted plot size. A gust of wind whipped off the sea, blowing her shoulder length hair into a messy heap, a look she would have quickly straightened in London, but it made her smile. She had the strongest feeling she was meant to be here, and in that moment, she made a decision she would have considered frivolous and irresponsible of others. In fact, she wondered if she ought to declare herself insane. She was going to buy 'A Stone's Throw'.

William turned to look at her and in that brief moment she felt she'd known him for a long time, there seemed to be a familiarity about him, and she wondered how she could be so comfortable in the presence of this stranger. She decided the events of the weekend must have befuddled her usual rational thoughts. The perfect moment was shattered by a loud voice in the garden.

'Oh my god I love it!' Clara and William both spun around to see a young couple walking towards them followed by an older man who the girl called out to.

'Grandpa, it's perfect.' Clara stopped breathing momentarily as she felt her whole body stiffen. The trio approached William.

'We're here for a viewing, your office said it was okay to come along. We've been inside and then spotted you from that big window,' the older man informed them. *Been inside! Been inside?* Clara screamed internally as a wave of fury swept through her. *That's my house, how dare you let yourself in and walk around inside?* It would have been a rhetorical question had she actually voiced it, instead she stood silently fuming. The older man introduced himself to William as Kenneth, his grand-daughter and her partner were Stephanie and Toby.

'I'm looking for a property for these two to doss in at weekends when they come up from London to visit. They've been staying with me but they're far too noisy for my way of life,' he joked.

Clara felt invisible. Had they not noticed she had been speaking to William when they rudely interrupted? Kenneth continued.

'Stephanie loves to paint so I'm sure these views will inspire her. I'm not worried about the landslide, I'll buy it through my company and set it off against tax, quite convenient really. By the time it falls into the sea I'll be long gone!' he joked, again.

'Oh! Grandpa you'll go on forever,' Stephanie replied gazing lovingly at him. The group all smiled at William who was as surprised at their arrival as Clara. William introduced himself as the auctioneer.

'And this is another prospective purchaser,' he said, introducing Clara. They all turned to look at her. How she longed to be invisible again.

'I like a bit of healthy competition,' Kenneth warned her. 'But beware, my pockets are deep!'

Clara was reluctant to leave but glad to get away from Kenneth who had commandeered William. She couldn't bear to stay and listen to him boasting about how he always got what he wanted and was sure he would easily be the highest bidder and win *her* cottage. Yes, it was 'her' cottage, well half of it was, she was determined to own the other half despite Kenneth's confidence.

The journey back to London began as slow and tedious until she reached the A11, where she was able to put her foot down and stay reasonably close to the speed limit. Norfolk's country roads were definitely not suited to her company car. Living in London she often wondered if having a car was even necessary. She could have joined a car club for when she visited her mother, but it was a company perk and admittedly she liked the way it turned heads when she did take it out. It was worth it, even if it was filed away in the car park for twenty-five days a month.

Her mind drifted back to A Stone's Throw, wondering exactly how deep Kenneth's pockets were. She wished she could write an alternative, satirical agent's description of the property, to deter any other interested parties:

'This detached cottage, with two dilapidated outbuildings and outside toilet complete with nauseating stench and rather unsanitary appearance, stands in approximately two acres, at the moment! Around 20 feet of it is piled up on the beach below, however, from the rear of the cottage there is a good, or not so good depending how you look at it, 193 feet remaining. To the front of the property an overgrown and unruly hedge wraps itself around a large Christmas tree a previous owner planted some fifty years ago in the spot where his beloved dog died. (William had told her this). A roughly cut pathway through the overgrown grass has recently been cleared from the driveway to the front door of the cottage to enable easier access. There are several fruit trees, their crop piled abandoned beneath them, unharvested these past two seasons. The large driveway allows for parking of several cars and winds itself around the side of the property where it meets an expanse of grass that was once a well- manicured lawn, before it fell into the sea!'

Clara laughed out loud to herself, amused at her own description. 'Despite all of that, I love it.'

The roads became busier as she left the large, open skies of Norfolk behind her and reluctantly headed back to London. Eventually pulling into the underground car park of her apartment block she stopped neatly in her allocated parking space. Sitting for a moment she paused; getting out of the car would mean stepping back into her life.

Most of the cars parked around her were either black, silver or varying shades of grey. BMW, Mercedes, Jaguar, Porsche, Tesla, Audi; a reflection of their owners, or more accurately a reflection of their careers she decided. Clara hardly saw her neighbours, occasionally voices could be heard in the hallway as people came and went but no-one seemed to have time to stop for a conversation, including Clara. Sharing the lift in awkward silence still couldn't compel them to strike up a friendly exchange, instead choosing to scroll through their mobile phones, each pretending the other didn't exist. Clara scanned the shiny, overly expensive metal boxes on wheels standing to attention. *They're probably all company cars,* she imagined. She wondered if this was who she had become. A money-making vehicle for shareholders and corporate greed. The cars were all parked neatly in their place, stagnating, gathering dust, with few opportunities to reach their full potential and little prospect of being released full throttle out onto the open road. It was if they were parked in cells, pasted into an Excel spreadsheet. Overcome by an excruciating need to escape, Clara unplugged her seatbelt, opened the car door and stepped out.

As she took the lift to her 5th floor apartment, she noticed her shoes were covered in grass and dust and the leather on the stiletto heels was ripped. Her new weekend lifestyle would require a change of footwear. She carefully removed them as she reached the front door, wondering whether to throw them away rather than clean them. Where would she start anyway? Perhaps Helen, her cleaner, would know what to do.

Her apartment in Canary Wharf had been a colossal step up from the small studio flat over a shoe shop that had been her first step onto the property ladder. It was a dream come true following a long-awaited promotion, coupled with a significant salary increase. That was fourteen years and 8 months ago. A further two more promotions and several more pay increases later, she'd been content to stay.

The spectacular view of the River Thames from the living room window and its proximity to work, the tube, restaurants and shops had appealed to Clara when she'd first viewed the show home. Twinkling lights reflecting on the Thames greeted her now as she opened the door to her apartment, but tonight she wasn't cheered by their sparkle. Looking around she noticed for the first time how bland and clinical her home looked with its white leather sofas, white kitchen units with white appliances, white walls and white bed linen. Her super king size bed stood alone in the middle of her bedroom, decorated with a large sumptuous brown faux fur throw and similarly coloured oversized cushions all precisely positioned. The apartment was convenient and useful; its open-plan layout allowed her to watch the television while decanting her ready-meal from its cardboard shell onto a plate. 'But this isn't just any ready meal,' she would say out loud, 'This is a Marks and Spencer's ready meal.' She didn't have time to cook she told herself, and at least it satisfied her mother's regular question of 'Are you eating proper meals?'

The journey home, particularly crawling through the evening London traffic, had taken Clara longer than expected and she realised she'd not eaten since leaving that morning.

'Hey Google, what time is it?' she asked her encyclopaedic flat mate.

'8:40pm' it replied, offering nothing further. Clara opened the Indian takeaway app on her iPad, ordered her favourite curry and walked through to her bedroom, discarding her clothes in a trail on the dressing room floor until she reached the en-suite. Turning on the shower, she placed a fresh soft white towel on the floor, stepped in and stood under its waterfall, humming a tune she wasn't aware she knew.

Dressed in her cosiest loungewear, she made herself comfortable on her favourite sofa, opened her laptop and typed the name of the auction house into the browser. She found the details for 'A Stone's Throw' and started to download the legal pack. She paid particular attention to the Special Conditions of Sale as William had suggested. It stated that no pre-auction bids would be accepted, advising prospective purchasers that the property had to go to auction, which meant she wouldn't be able to just purchase her cousin's half and avoid a battle with Kenneth. Tomorrow she would speak to her financial advisor and the solicitor who had written to her. She'd have to move fast, the auction was in just over three weeks' time. Next, she emailed the surveyor William had recommended, moved some money around online ready to pay the 10% deposit and quickly calculated how much of her savings she would have to liquidate. Taking into account the guide price of £160,000 - £180,000, she could easily afford half as she already owned 50%. This left her enough after fees to tidy the cottage up a bit. It would use a large amount of her savings but she could manage until her next bonus from work.

The sound of the buzzer made her jump, she'd forgotten all about food. She pressed the button to let the delivery driver into the main door downstairs, opened her apartment door in anticipation of their arrival, poured herself a glass of red wine, turned on the TV and grabbed a plate, fork and spoon in readiness. Wait! She hadn't washed her hands.

4

Startled out of the best sleep she'd had in years, Clara reached out to silence her phone as it vibrated on the bedside cabinet, its offensive buzzing a stark reminder that her life had returned to normal. Her eyes still firmly closed, arm outstretched, her finger blindly prodded the screen in search of the elusive 'stop' button. Finally, she hit the right spot and felt instant relief from the silence that resumed. On workdays her alarm was set to 5.30am, she would rise the moment it sounded and take a shower. This morning, she threw the phone to other side of the bed, turned over and pulled the duvet up under her chin. *I'll get up in a minute*, she told herself.

As her phone sprang into action for the second time that morning Clara groaned, reaching out to where she'd thrown it only moments earlier. *Who on earth would call at this time?* she wondered, answering the call sleepily.

'Hello?'

'Where *are* you?' the caller rudely enquired. It was the unmistakable voice of Freya, her boss's secretary. Clara didn't quite understand the question, where else would she be?

'It's gone 8.30am and you weren't at the morning meeting,' Freya berated her.

'Shit, I've overslept!' Clara exclaimed, untangling herself from the duvet and scrambling off the bed still half asleep. Heading for the bathroom she turned the phone off, and the shower on.

Half an hour later Clara shuffled through the revolving doors to her office building, willing them to go faster. Running towards the lifts she squeezed in through the closing doors of lift 3 and smiled at its only other occupant, a tall slim man in his thirties who began to smile at her, then stopped. The edges of his mouth turned into a grimace as he stared a little too long into her eyes. Clara mirrored his expression, uncomfortable and uncertain of what it meant. Grateful for his early exit on the sixth floor she turned to look in the mirrored walls in the lift. Her cheeks were flushed pink and her brow glistened with sweat following her quick sprint to the office, but surely that wasn't reason enough for his startled reaction to her appearance. It took a few seconds of closer inspection, and as she stared back at herself, she remembered what she'd forgotten.

In her hasty attempt to apply her mascara she had dropped the brush into the bathroom sink where it landed neatly in the blob of toothpaste that had fallen off her toothbrush a minute or two earlier. Her hurried efforts to clean the mascara brush had created a gooey mess, in an attempt to speed up the process she turned the tap just a little more, or so she'd thought. The ensuing jet stream of water hit the brush, decorating her white blouse with a splattering of grey sludge. Tearing her top off and hurriedly finding another she forgot to return to the bathroom and complete the process as she ran out the front door. This had clearly resulted in one set of lush, black, thick lashes enhanced with her new mascara that promised volume, length and stretch; while thin, naked, lifeless lashes apologetically protruded from around her left eye. Clara's mouth fell open as she realised her faux pas.

It was 9.32am when she stepped out of the lift on the 17th floor. At the far end of the office, directly opposite the lift, the door to her boss's office was open. *Damn.* He was standing in the doorway talking to Freya, and despite her attempts to sidle unnoticed towards her own corner office, he spotted Clara and beckoned her in. She wore the conspicuous glares from her silent colleagues like a heavy coat, slowing her every step as she prepared herself for the impending lecture that undoubtedly awaited her. Tardiness was not tolerated at Coopers & Leigh.

No sooner had Clara entered the room she began her apology. 'I'm so sorry I'm late...' Grant interrupted her before she could think of a reasonable excuse, which she couldn't.

'Don't worry about that,' he said. 'Shut the door.'

They had both joined Coopers and Leigh a week apart from each other almost 19 years ago and Clara had always felt the disadvantage of arriving a week behind him. She told herself over the years his rapid rise to the board room was due almost entirely to his advantage of being a man. Despite working long hours and gaining several prestigious clients Clara's rise among the ranks had been comparatively slow, but even she had to admit that she could have done more. She was a loner. The company of a good book and a carefully procured bottle of red wine usually guaranteed her an ideal weekend of solitary indulgence. Grant had gone the extra mile, entertaining clients at weekends, dutifully attending meetings and functions, even to the detriment of his own marriage. Clara had always believed Grant to be her rival; in contrast he had never once considered her to be his.

He motioned for her to sit as he walked around the desk to his own chair and sat upright, his arms resting on the arms of the leather high-backed chair. Clara wondered what could be so pressing if he was willing to overlook her late arrival.

'Chris Jaego was in the office at the weekend.' It was well known that Chris Jaego, the company CEO, only visited in exceptional circumstances. He let his statement float in the air for a few moments before continuing. Now Grant had her full attention.

'I'm going to run the Singapore office; I leave next month.'

Clara felt her jaw drop open, and by the look of Grant it seemed he'd had a similar reaction at being given the same news.

'So, you're probably wondering who's stepping into my shoes?'

She easily guessed she wasn't getting a promotion any time soon so waited to hear which of the usual 'Favourite Five' would be lording it over the London office for the foreseeable future. Henry Cochrane, James Leader, Pip Sandhurst, Samuel Schuster and Calvin Woolsenbrook made up the 'Favourite Five'. They were the golden boys of the future, all vying for the top jobs, and each would sell their granny to get it.

Grant stared at Clara, *what's wrong with her eye?*

Clara's mind had wandered off, silently considering the attributes, if any, of each of the most likely candidates.

'I thought it was a rhetorical question,' she mumbled, suddenly realising he'd fully expected a response. Biting her lip as he stared at her face. Clara held her hand over her left eye in a limp salute to hide her naked eyelashes. She hoped he hadn't noticed.

Standing up from behind his desk Grant continued as he paced the office.

'They don't have anyone. Can you believe it? I'm so irreplaceable they haven't got anyone to replace me!' Clara's eyes followed him back and forth, he was clearly agitated, and she guessed he hadn't been overjoyed at the news.

'When will your family join you?' Her question took him by surprise, and he stopped in his tracks.

'They're not coming.' Staring momentarily at the floor he walked to the door and opened it, gesturing for her to leave. 'I just thought I'd keep you up to date,' he informed her as he motioned her out of the room.

Clara was glad of her early release and quickly made her way to her office where she threw her bag onto the green sofa, hung her jacket on the back of the chair and took her place behind the desk. She stared at the array of files in front of her.

'Back to reality. Shit!' Clara realised she'd sworn more times in the last few days than the whole of last year.

Not a soul entered Clara's office that day until 5.30pm when Jordan, the latest intern, knocked quietly, gingerly opened the door and smiled at her apologetically.

'Hi Jordan,' Clara smiled back at him, he was a quiet lad, always polite, helpful and eager to learn. She was grateful for the interruption.

'Would you like to sign Freya's birthday card? We're going for drinks at The Red Lion from 5:30, do you want to come?'

Clara was taken aback at the invitation and was about to decline, as she did so often, when she uncharacteristically changed her mind.

'I'll see you there.' Jordan seemed as surprised by her response as she was.

It was quarter past seven before Clara entered The Red Lion, having first removed any trace of mascara from her right eye. The pub was a two-minute walk from the office and was often frequented by the employees of Coopers and Leigh. Although its façade dated back to the early 1900s the brewery had recently converted the inside with an open plan contemporary design, decorated with oversized sprawling plants reaching for the ceiling, panelled walls and super comfy chairs, stools and sofas.

The pub was mainly empty apart from a large group of rowdy office workers at one end, many of whom she recognised, most of whom had clearly already consumed vast amounts of alcohol.

Clara heard Teagan's familiar voice above the throng and glanced across to see if Daisy was with her. She smiled when she saw her new friend sitting quietly on a bench, sipping a glass of red wine among the loud chatter and animated gestures of her increasingly intoxicated co-workers. Daisy looked up as Clara approached, and climbed out from the group to join her. For a moment Clara considered that someone else must have walked in behind her, someone more interesting, but Daisy was heading straight for her. She was glad she'd come along after all. Together they found another table and sat chatting for the remainder of the evening about their weekend away, and the animals, then whispered as Daisy talked excitedly about her plans for next year. Feeling safe in Daisy's company Clara confided in her about A Stone's Throw. She was taken aback by Daisy's excitement and felt it rise in her chest, an emotion she hadn't allowed herself to experience, especially since Kenneth had laid down the gauntlet. They both agreed he was the one person who could put a spanner in the works.

Clara knew that asking Grant for a day off work now he was leaving wouldn't be met with his usual objections to staff disrupting the workflow. She had considered calling in sick if he refused, but it would be just her luck that Homes Under The Hammer were filming the auction and she'd be found out on national television. She'd heard how Jack in IT had been spotted on TV last year in the crowd at Wimbledon the day he'd phoned in with a high temperature and diarrhoea! The following afternoon she seized her opportunity.

'Yeah, sure. No problem.'

Clara momentarily considered asking for a raise to see if he gave the same response. Instead, she decided to take the win and returned to her office to try and finish a report she'd spent all day re-writing. Since returning from Norfolk her concentration levels had plummeted as she found herself daydreaming about the improvements she would make to the cottage. Staring at the report laying open in front of her, she picked up her mobile phone and called William.

Clara decided to come clean and tell him of her vested interest. Apologising for not being upfront she explained she had never even contemplated buying the cottage until she saw it. William laughed,

'Well, the good news is that you already own half of it, so you don't have to buy that half. Unfortunately, the special conditions of sale state it must go to auction, so you will have to bid against Kenneth. He's already been in touch and registered to bid.'

William helped Clara to register her interest and explained the process to her.

'Will you be at the auction, or do you want to bid by phone?'

Clara had already booked herself a room for the night before at the hotel where the auction was being held, she had every intention of being there, and on time. William confirmed he would make the key available to the surveyor she had instructed. He looked forward to seeing her again at the auction and wished her good bidding.

Since returning from Norfolk Clara's life was off-balance, see-sawing between two completely different worlds. Speaking with William she felt as though she was being transported back to Norfolk, to a life she suddenly craved, not wanting the conversation to end. Her heart and her mind were there, and she struggled to stay focused on the pile of work on her desk. As she pressed the red button to end the call the bubble burst. She stared around her windowless office; it was just one of the boxes in which she existed. Compared to the wide-open skies and possibilities of Norfolk Clara now felt suppressed by the confines of her life. So much had changed since she left the office last Friday afternoon. Auction day couldn't come soon enough.

Clara picked up her phone again and made the call she'd been avoiding. 'Hi mum.'

'I wondered if you'd love it darling. I went there a few times when Uncle David and his wife lived there. I used to sit at the end of the garden staring out to sea, imagining who or what was on the other side, wondering if there was someone staring back at me thinking exactly the same thing. My life was so small, I'd never been out of Norfolk, and I'd only been to Norwich once with my parents to collect David from the hospital.' Her mother's voice became silent for the shortest of moments but for once Clara didn't notice its significance.

'So, you don't mind?' Clara knew that even if her mum objected, she'd already made her decision, but it would be much easier if she didn't.

'It will do you good to get out of London at weekends and into the fresh air. Just make sure you keep up our monthly visits!' Clara smiled at her mum's request; they both knew that it wasn't in any doubt.

Clara had one close friend, Andrea, who she met on their first day at high school when they both signed up for book club. Their attendance was short-lived as they found so much more to talk about, and their friendship had remained strong all these years. Social outings were mostly planned around Andrea's busy social life and husband, Nick, a partner in a firm of solicitors in London. They had lived in Sevenoaks for many years but last year Nick had been head-hunted and offered a job in Dubai working for wealthy ex-pats. Clara and Andrea stayed in touch via Facetime and WhatsApp, but over time their conversations had become less frequent. Until now, Clara hadn't realised how lonely she'd become. Ignoring the file yet again, needing to bring her dream to life, she hit the green video button on WhatsApp.

'I can't believe you kept this from me,' Andrea feigned upset. 'You've got a secret family hidden in deepest Norfolk, your mum had a tragic childhood, was deserted by her own family and her first love - if you think a quick shag in the back of a car qualifies him for that status - a secluded cottage on the edge of a cliff and a dishy auctioneer. I can't wait for the sequel!' Clara felt the contagion of Andrea's excitement well up inside her.

'It does sound a bit Mills and Boon I suppose. I just wish I could cut out the drama and move straight on to the happy ending.'

Andrea continued, 'I do love a romance, will the girl get William in the end? Do you know if he's married C?' Clara laughed, embarrassed by her own feelings but not wanting to own up to them just yet.

'I'd rather get the cottage than a man any day!'

'Come on C, you can't stay single forever, you'll turn into a mad cat lady.' Clara realised she'd not yet told Andrea about Elsa. An hour later when she ended the call Clara was still staring at the untouched file.

Clara limped through one day at a time. She spent her birthday with her mum, as usual, who made her a birthday cake, and they took a picnic to the park. In a way Clara was glad when it was over, she was one day closer to the big day.

5

Checking her watch for the umpteenth time that day, Clara attempted to stay focused on her work. During these last weeks leading up to the auction she'd developed and almost perfected her procrastination skills; lucky for her Grant was mostly away and failed to notice the drop in her work rate and efficiency. Finally, at 5.10pm, unable to contain herself any longer, she threw the one file she'd been working on all day into the cupboard, grabbed her bag and tried her very best not to run out of the door. The lift seemed to take forever to arrive, then made seven excruciating stops on the way to the ground floor. As though it had a mind of its own, she tapped her foot frantically as if to make the lift go faster. When the door finally opened on the ground floor Clara felt the urge to run. She ran across the atrium into the revolving doors, jogging almost on the spot as they laboriously crawled forward; anyone watching might think she needed a wee, but she didn't care. The doors finally released her and she sprinted homeward. Heading straight for the car park Clara made a mental check that she'd packed everything she needed that morning. 'If I've left anything behind I'll just buy it' she decided. She'd purposely worn flat shoes to work that she could comfortably drive in, and that morning packed a bottle of water and packet of cheesy biscuits in her car for the journey. She had no intention of stopping; the sooner she got there the better. She began to sprint, the urge to run was so strong inside her she couldn't stop herself; walking was an impossibility. She knew what she was running to but had a niggling feeling she was also running away from something too.

The A11 was thankfully less congested than the previous time she made the journey to Norfolk, little did she know back then what lay ahead. Pulling into the entrance to the Manor Hall Hotel Clara felt a mixture of trepidation, excitement and anxiety. She decided to call it 'trepexciety' as there was no other word for it. The car park was half empty, *or was it half full?* she contemplated, wondering whether her viewpoint of the car park was a pessimistic or optimistic vision or premonition of what lie ahead. She wasn't usually superstitious, but she wasn't her usual level-headed self since making the life-changing decision to buy the cottage; at times wondering if she was having an out-of-body experience or a mid-life crisis at the very least.

The hotel was an imposing stately home, previously owned by several generations of a local Norfolk family. They had been forced to sell several years ago to a large conglomerate when the soaring costs to maintain and update the aging building exceeded their financial capabilities. Following an extensive refurbishment programme the interior now belied it's Elizabethan-style exterior. Sumptuous sofas of bold oranges and greens sprawled lazily in the large foyer, oversized palms sprouted from gargantuan pots and a black onyx-effect reception desk glistened under the sparkling chandeliers. Clara's room was situated on the first floor at the front of the building, overlooking the tree lined driveway. She slid aside the panes of secondary double glazing before lifting, with more than a little effort, the old sash windows. Clara breathed in the warm evening air that filled the room. It was mixed with the perfume of the wisteria that embraced the entire front of the building. She was thankful for the aromatherapy treatment that momentarily relaxed her mind and calmed her thoughts as she breathed in its sweet scent.

At dinner Clara studied the other diners suspiciously, craning her neck, attempting to eavesdrop on their conversations to gauge if they were there for the auction. An elderly couple two tables away had attended a friend's funeral that afternoon but the other guests were too far away for her to hear anything meaningful.

As she washed her London life away under the shower Clara really hoped she would get a good night's sleep. Thoughts of the cottage jostled around in her head, like one of those battery-operated bumble balls for children that wiggle and jiggle across the floor and make your teeth vibrate if you try to hold onto it. *But I need to be alert for the auction. I mustn't miss what's happening and who's bidding. Where shall I sit so I can see everything that's going on and still be seen by William?* His blue eyes floated momentarily into her mind. *I must tell him where I am so he can look out for me. I can't be near Kenneth. I want to be behind him so I can see him, but he can't see me. Perhaps I'll sit at the back. Definitely not the front, I'll seem too keen. Aaaargh, I need to sleep!* She daren't look at her watch as the night ticked by. Instead she found a relaxation playlist on her phone, plugged in her ear pods and tried to remember her most relaxing holiday. Eventually her mind gave in to exhaustion and allowed her to drift off.

As the auction didn't start until 11am Clara set the alarm for 8.30am. She was already awake when her phone lit up and filled the room with the familiar sound of tinkling bells. Laying there, but with her eyes still closed, knowing the moment she opened them the 'trepexciety' would take hold again, Clara took a deep breath. She counted to five, took another deep breath, opened her eyes, then sprang into action.

Half an hour later she entered the dining room where a young waitress took her order.

'Earl Grey tea, no milk or lemon, tea bag on the side not in the pot, two slices of white toast, golden brown both sides, butter also on the side, with peach jam please.' *Just the ticket* she thought, it was a good start to the day. Clara was particularly pleased with the peach jam, so often hotels only offered strawberry jam, or raspberry (even worse), honey (yuk!) or marmalade, which she often had to make do with and pick out the bits. Peach jam was her favourite; apricot jam was a satisfactory substitute. Would her luck continue?

At 10 o'clock Clara found her way to the room where the auction was being held. It was filled with empty chairs and a few staff from the auction house who were battling to erect the backdrop which would stand several feet high. She was surprised by the number of chairs, estimating over 200. The trepexciety kicked in again. Until now she had imagined Kenneth would be her only opponent, but the reality could be a sea of hands all vying to steal her precious cottage. Her dream of being the winning bidder began to dissolve, . She didn't have a word for that, perhaps it was plain old-fashioned 'fear'. She turned to walk out of the room and came face to face with William.

'Morning! You're bright and early, I'm glad you made it on time today.'

Clara managed half a smile but felt any brightness slowly drain out of her again. She followed William to the front of the room where a lectern had been placed.

'I'll be standing here, where will you be?'

Clara looked out at the room full of chairs before her, how would he possibly see her? She suddenly felt small and insignificant.

'If you sit at the back on the corner I'll be able to spot you. I'm assuming you'll still be bidding and you're not just here to see how much your inheritance sells for?'

'Yes, yes I'm still bidding. I wasn't expecting there to be so many people, I'm not so sure I'm going to get it now.' William looked at her for a moment, not sure whether to tell her about the 100 or so extra people who would also be standing. His auctions often attracted an audience of around 300. He decided against it and assured her that a number of vendors and their families often attend the auction to watch the process and find out first-hand how much their property sells for. Clara felt a little easier and breathed a little deeper for the first time since entering the room. At that moment William's phone rang and he excused himself. A member of his staff offered her a tea or coffee. No Earl Grey here. Thankfully she always carried some in her bag so requested a cup of hot water so she could make her own.

Clara draped her jacket over the back of the chair in the furthest corner at the back of the room as suggested by William. No sooner had she sat down she felt the urge to stand, knowing she couldn't bear to watch the room fill with her competition. A couple in their forties drifted into the room, stopping for a coffee and taking a few moments to choose a biscuit. *How can they be so calm?* Clara wondered, her stomach churning. She wondered if she might she need the loo. Should she go anyway, a precautionary wee, just in case? Deciding instead on fresh air and a change of scenery to calm her nerves she headed for the balcony leaving her jacket on the back of her seat, reminding her of last year's holiday in Menorca, when every single sunbed had been claimed by a towel by 7am, yet not one of them was occupied.

Breathing in the warm air from the balcony her thoughts drifted to Elsa who she was planning to visit this afternoon on her way back to London. It felt strangely odd that she was looking forward to seeing Tina, Lizzie and the others too, she had never felt this way about any of her own work colleagues, until Daisy. She had called Tina yesterday to check Elsa was still there, would she remember her? Clara felt her heart lurch as Tina told her a couple had applied to adopt Elsa and would be returning tomorrow to collect her. A mixture of pain and happiness engulfed Clara at the same time. Elsa deserved a forever home but Clara couldn't help but be disappointed that she'd never see her again after today.

She wasn't sure how long she'd been standing there but she jumped when she felt a tap on her shoulder. As she turned around she heard William apologising for startling her.

'It's filling up, I thought you might like to take your seat.' Clara thanked him, poured the spilt tea from her saucer back into her cup and walked back into the room.

'Bloody hell!' A man covered in dry paint turned around at her exclamation.

'You all right love?'

'Sorry, yes I'm fine, I'm .... I'm fine, thanks.' Clara made her way through the crowd, it was now standing room only and the sight of the full room made her heart sink. 'Excuse me, sorry, thank you, excuse me, just... trying to get through, thank you.' Eventually she made it back to her chair, thankfully people had noticed her jacket and it was still empty.

Whilst Clara tried to make herself comfortable, juggling her cup and saucer with her bag and the auction catalogue, William's voice rang out above the crowd. He was speaking through a microphone and she could hear his voice booming out from both sides of the room. She hadn't expected there to be so much noise, people were chattering loudly, treating it almost like a meeting place, a social club where so many of them knew each other; some of them had been attending for years. William was welcoming buyers, vendors and anyone who was attending just out of interest; advising them about health and safety, in an event of a fire etc. He informed them they ought to have done their 'due diligence' before bidding on a property and to ensure they have the funds available for the 10% deposit payable today. On the fall of the hammer contracts will be exchanged and the balance will be payable on completion 28 days later. *Goodness*, she thought, *is anyone listening to this, it's so noisy?* Clara looked around for Kenneth but all she could see were the backs of people's heads, she didn't expect he would be standing. She wondered if her cousin Michael was here too and how she would know. She realised it was a waste of time looking as she didn't have a clue what he looked like.

Clara opened the catalogue as the auction began. Lot 1 was an empty two-bedroom, Victorian terrace house in Norwich that had been lived in by the same person for over 50 years. The pictures in the catalogue showed an extremely dated interior, Clara wondered if the kitchen had been updated in 50 years, and the bathroom.... *Yuk*, she shivered at the thought of it but was careful not to blurt out her true responses yet again. The bidding started low at £80,000, and Clara was amazed at how cheap property could be bought for, she was used to extortionate London prices. She was sure that amount would just about buy a bike shed where she lived.

The bidding went up in increments of £2,000 and the price quickly increased with several bidders around the room raising their hands until it eventually slowed down. The increments reduced to £1,000 and then £500 as the two final bidders fought against each other in a duel to win the prize. The bidding stopped at £126,000. Clara looked around the room waiting to see if anyone else would bid. William had been pointing to each bidder as the price rose, and now the man on the front row was about to win. William raised his gavel.

'Are we all done then? At £126,000 for the first time, at £126,000 for the second time, at £126,000 for the third... fresh hand £126,500.' Clara gasped at how quickly it had been snatched away from the man in the front row who had clearly reached his maximum and was shaking his head. The hammer fell and the deal was done.

'Lot 2 is...' Clara wasn't listening to William as he turned his attention to the next lot. She unknotted her hands from each other where they'd been tightly clasped during the first Lot. They were clammy and her mouth was dry. Looking down she noticed tiny bits of paper on her lap where she'd picked several bits off the catalogue during the suspense of it all. She felt disappointed for the man on the front row, and wondered if he was upset, did he have his heart set on that property? A sickening doubt began to rise up inside her. The first property had sold for way over the asking price, what if the bidding for her cottage climbed beyond her means? What if five, or six, or seven people want it? Her breathing became shallow and a tear pricked at the side of her left eye, she wiped it away on her sleeve.

Lot 3 was a small, non-standard construction, semi-detached bungalow in Happisburgh, pronounced 'Haysbru' she was surprised to learn, whose tenant was entitled to live there for the rest of his life paying very little rent. *Who in their right mind would want that?* she wondered. Apparently, someone did but it only just about sold for the reserve price set by the owner. A flurry of butterflies danced in Clara's stomach; she placed her hand there to settle them. Mildly encouraged that it had sold for so little, dare she hope for such luck? Clara already felt exhausted with the emotion of it all and hoped she had the energy to concentrate when they eventually reached Lot 29. As the Lots were sold, or in some cases unsold, a number of people in the room began to leave. Many of them appeared to be builders, buying their next projects, she assumed. Others were owners who had come along to see how much their property would sell for. Plots of land seemed popular, and also garages, for reasons Clara couldn't fathom. As some properties didn't reach their reserve and remained unsold, William invited interested parties to speak to him after the auction to see if they can come to an arrangement with the vendor later that day.

By Lot 14 Clara really needed a wee and wished she hadn't had that cup of tea when she'd arrived. She was engrossed in the whole auction process but after careful consideration decided it was better to bid on an empty bladder than a full one. She didn't want to embarrass herself when she won and briefly wondered if she'd be the first person to wet herself at an auction! There were only a handful of people standing now as she quickly made her way out of the room to the toilets. There was one cubicle free, she quickly locked the door with one hand while undoing her jeans with the other. She sat down and was relieved to find there was plenty of toilet roll. She'd normally check that first as she'd been caught out in a supermarket toilet many years ago and had to call out asking someone to pass her some paper. A phone rang in the cubicle next to her interrupting her thoughts.

'Hi Grandpa, yes I'm here, I'm just in the loo. Yes, I know it's Lot 29, I'll be with you in plenty of time.' Clara held her breath, unable to breathe as she recognised Stephanie's voice speaking to Kenneth. What should she do? She wanted to get back into the auction room as quickly as she could but didn't want to come face to face with Stephanie at the hand basins. Should she wait until she had left or make a mad dash for it with a quick hand wash and dry her hands on her jeans as she walked out the door? She decided on the latter, quickly got her clothes back together, opened the cubicle door and fleetingly washed her hands. As she opened the door to leave Stephanie came out of the cubicle behind her, but Clara was gone before she had a chance to glance up.

There were less people standing now as the seats became available. Sitting back down Clara felt her heart thumping against her chest. *Goodness, if this is what I'm like just seeing Stephanie how the hell am I going to cope with bidding?* Her only consolation was she would be able to see where Kenneth was sitting when Stephanie joined him.

'Is that a bid sir?' William was asking. Clara followed his gaze across the opposite side of the room where Kenneth was waving wildly towards the back of the room at Stephanie who was scanning the sea of heads in search of him. Kenneth was completely unaware that William was currently accepting bids on a one-bedroom flat in Kings Lynn, but fortunately for him William was only joking. Kenneth turned and half-smiled at William, then gestured towards Stephanie to hurry up and sit down. A ripple of laughter swept through the room as the audience realised what had happened. Stephanie disappeared into the crowd as she took her seat.

By Lot 23 the room had thinned out enough so Clara could see Kenneth and Stephanie quite clearly. Suddenly feeling isolated, Clara realised again just how solitary her life had become. She hadn't noticed it in London, tucking herself away in her apartment, her reclusive lifestyle had suited her. The only visitor was Helen, her cleaner, now that Andrea and Nick were thousands of miles away. Clara wondered if her mother would have come to the auction if she'd asked her. It had crossed her mind briefly, but it seemed a cruel request. How ironic that she was about to bid on a property that had belonged to her own grandparents. Grandparents who hadn't wanted anything to do with her, never even acknowledged her existence. She wondered if they'd turn in their graves at the prospect of her living in *their* cottage. What would they think of David leaving half to her?

'Lot 28 is a freehold shop in Lowestoft, currently let to a hairdresser....' Clara's attention snapped back into the room, what was she doing daydreaming? There was a lot of interest in the shop, bids ping-ponged from across the room and Clara thought the battle would never end. Aware that each bid took her a step closer to Lot 29 beads of sweat began to gather at the nape of her neck then trickle down her back. She wished she'd tied her hair back but didn't want to search in her bag for a scrunchie in case she missed something, it was so close now.

She talked herself through her 'game plan' one more time. Don't make the first bid, don't bid too quickly, look calm, stay calm, make sure William can see you at all times. And DON'T bid more than you can afford. As she was co-beneficiary she wouldn't have to pay as much as the other bidders. Taking into account her total savings, she couldn't bid beyond £210,000 as there were further expenses to be budgeted for; stamp duty being a big chunk. William had suggested a guide price of £160,000 - £180,000. If it didn't reach the reserve maybe she could negotiate with Michael after the auction. They both had to agree the reserve price, communicating individually through William, and they had settled at £180,000. It felt strange entering into a financial agreement with a cousin whose very existence you had only just discovered a few weeks earlier. Apart from the envelope Michael had sent to Linda they'd had no contact from him. Clara had asked William if Michael wanted to meet her at the cottage but the answer had come back 'No, best not.' She wasn't sure if she was relieved or disappointed.

'SOLD! Next, we have Lot 29.'

Oh my God! Sweating profusely, her hear pounding and feeling more than a little overwhelmed, Clara concentrated hard to take in every single word William was saying. He briefly described the property, *her* property, *her* cottage. She sat up straight, *too straight, relax*, she sat back, crossed her legs then uncrossed them again.

'We have one telephone bidder we are waiting to connect with, are we there?' William received a thumbs up from a member of his team who held a mobile phone to his ear.

'Who will start me in the middle of the guide? £170,000.' Clara felt her top teeth biting into her lower lip as she held her breath yet again. The room seemed completely silent, she heard only William's words.

'OK, let's try the bottom of the guide, £160,000, who will start the bidding?' Clara saw Kenneth put his hand in the air. She felt herself breath again. So far she'd stuck to the plan, she hadn't made the first bid. As for staying calm... she was trying.

Her shirt stuck to her as sweat began to ooze from every pore of her body. Clara forced herself to breathe slowly as William announced they were going up in £2,000s. Her hand shot up in the air as if in agreement. She'd made a bid!

'£162,000 thank you,' William called from the rostrum, gesturing his hand in her direction. Kenneth raised his hand yet again,

'£164,000,' this time William gestured towards Kenneth. William's colleague with the mobile phone raised his hand, then Kenneth again. Back and forth like a game of tennis, William looked from one player to the other. Clara felt left out, invisible again. Within seconds the bidding was at £184,000 and Clara had only bid once. The bid was with Kenneth. William looked at his colleague on the phone who shook his head, he was out. Clara raised her hand, almost jumping out of her seat, unsure if it was to bid or a cheer that her anonymous competitor had pulled out, still she was winning at £186,000. Kenneth raised his hand again as if he didn't have a care in the world. There were clearly no other bidders in the room and Clara's next bid took her to £190,000, a full £10,000 above the top of the guide. How far would Kenneth go? She was about to find out as he waved his hand nonchalantly into the air, £192,000. Clara took a deep breath and raised her hand again but more slowly this time.

'£194,000 thank you,' William gestured towards her fleetingly. Her mouth was so dry she drank the cold dregs from the bottom of the teacup. She hated cold tea, but she didn't notice its temperature, she was just thankful for the moisture it provided, however temporary. Clara felt as though she were running up a hill of treacle, all of her efforts were in vain, she was getting nowhere fast. Kenneth had warned her that his pockets were deep, Clara was beginning to realise how naïve she'd been ignoring his threat. She'd been caught up in the romanticism of winning the cottage and spending weekends in Norfolk, but now the realisation dawned on her that he could outbid her for as long as he wanted.

'£196,000, back with you sir.'

Think Clara! Her head was scrambled, desperately trying to work out the numbers. Even though she'd gone over them a hundred times before the auction she couldn't recall them, they were a jumbled mess. No matter how hard she tried it was impossible to work out, like trying to pick up spaghetti with a spoon. She indicated to William that she would bid another £1,000 taking her to £197,000. She needed to slow the bidding down but knew Kenneth would see it as a sign of weakness. No sooner had William accepted her bid than Kenneth raised his hand again, £198,000. They were now going up in £1,000s. She couldn't let go now, she had to keep trying. She raised her hand again, £199,000. William gestured towards her with an outstretched hand, she was sure that for the briefest of moments he gave her a crooked smile that said 'I'm sorry,' as right on cue Kenneth came back with a counter bid of £208,000! A gasp echoed around the room and Clara felt every ounce of breath rip from her lungs. The reality of her defeat closed in around her like a shroud, stifling her dream, smothering any flicker of hope. She froze, stunned, not knowing what to do, yet knowing that whatever she did, he could and would do more. She couldn't win. Clara looked down at the catalogue open at the page featuring Lot 29, a picture of 'A Stone's Throw' stared back at her. She could try one more bid, but what was the point? She was sure the whole of the room felt her humiliation. She continued to stare at the catalogue, how could she raise her head? Rain began to fall on the picture of the cottage as large teardrops dripped from her cheeks. Clara knew William was looking at her, waiting for her decision. Without looking up she shook her head. It was over.

'No? Then £208,000 for the first time,' a few seconds passed. '£208,000 for the second time.' Clara was sure William was speaking slower and slower, she wished it to be over so she could get out of there.

'£208,000 for the third and final time,' a few more seconds passed, the pain was excruciating.

'... I'll take 500 if you want.' Clara waited, dreading the sound of the gavel hitting the block. In the distance she heard raised voices coming from the front of the room. She raised her eyes in time to see Stephanie running up the aisle towards the exit, Clara looked at William, confused as to what was happening. William seemed to be glaring at her.

'I'll take 500 if you want,' he urged.

As if it had a mind of its own her left arm slowly rose into the air. What had she done? She had bid another £500! Clara waited with absolute dread for the humiliation of Kenneth's counter bid. She couldn't bear to look at William, and certainly not at Kenneth. She put the catalogue in her bag and reached for her jacket on the back of her chair, ready to make a quick exit. What had she been thinking? In a few moments it would be over, the sound of the hammer falling like a starting pistol would signal her release, she would leave the blocks and run... she wasn't sure where, just far away from here. At the sound of William's voice Clara realised she would never see or hear him again, never see the cottage again, and she felt foolish to have had such a dream.

'No? £208,500 once, £208,500 twice' he was speaking quickly now. *Just get it over with please*, she silently implored him. '£208,500 for the third and final time. SOLD!' At the sound of the gavel Clara stood ready to leave. 'To the lady in the back row.'

Had she been looking at him Clara would have seen that William had a wide grin on his face, but she had stood to leave as soon as she heard the crack of the gavel. *Hang on, surely he'd got it wrong?* As she stood holding onto the back of her chair trying to make sense of what William had just said a lady from the auction house approached her.

'Congratulations, you had us all on the edge of our seats.' Clara stared at her. Her name badge said 'Mary', and Mary was smiling at her. 'Follow me, I'll take you to a cashier, you must be so excited!'

Clara wasn't sure how her legs were operating all on their own because she sure wasn't in control of them, but she managed to follow Mary to the cashiers where she had to sign the Memorandum of Sale and pay a 10% deposit. They were greeted by Erin who also congratulated her, and the reality of it began to sink in. Clara was sure Erin was speaking but Clara asked her to repeat what she'd said as she was struggling to take it all in. There was paperwork to sign, payment to be made, a completion date, solicitor's details, proof of ID, and there it was done. It was made a little more complicated by the fact that she was one of the beneficiaries, but Erin assured her they'd send her the paperwork with the final figures within the next two working days. It was all done, and she sat there looking at Erin in disbelief.

'You're free to go now!' Clara realised that was her cue to leave. The auction was still in progress and William was in full flow, she was disappointed not to have the opportunity to say goodbye. She walked unsteadily across the room in a daze, somehow making it down the stairs to the ground floor, again grateful to her legs for knowing what to do without any input from her. At the bottom of the stairs was a café, Clara walked in and headed for a window seat, a waitress was thankfully quick to take her order. 'A large cappuccino and a fruit scone please.'

Clara stared out of the window. This wasn't at all how she visualised it would be when she'd dreamt about how the auction would go. In her imagination Clara had outbid Kenneth as he realised how much the cottage meant to her. It was an unrealistic romantic misperception, an idea that until a few weeks ago she would never have considered herself capable of. How had she never contemplated the possibility of not winning? Clara felt wrung out and hollow, shouldn't she be jumping for joy? She was unaware of the lady approaching her until she was at the table.

'Excuse me.' Her voice broke the spell, causing Clara to jump a little. 'Oh! I'm sorry, I didn't mean to startle you, you've had quite a day already.' She introduced herself. Rachel, it turned out, had been sitting next to Kenneth before and during the auction. They had chatted about why they were there. She was the owner of Lot 3, the semi-detached bungalow in Happisburgh with the tenant. It had been left to her by her late mother, but in her will Rachel's step-father was able to stay in the property virtually rent free until he passed away or chose to move out. He was ten years younger than her mother and in the best of health. He'd already become well acquainted with a woman half his age and was 'living the good life,' she told her. Rachel decided selling up and enjoying the money while she was relatively young and healthy was better than becoming embroiled in the complications of his mid-life crisis. He and her mother had only been married for two years before she died.

'Cut and run. That's what I decided.' Clara knew she'd be pretty p'd off if it happened to her.

'How come you stuck around?' Clara asked her.

'I'd enjoyed chatting to Kenneth and so I decided to stay to celebrate him winning Lot 29. I didn't have anywhere else to be and it was so exciting in the auction room, better than Homes Under The Hammer! Kenneth had told me all about Stephanie and Toby, how they'd been together for almost 5 years and spent many weekends staying with him in Burnham Market. He idolises that girl, seems she has her grandpa wrapped around her little finger. He was so excited when she eventually arrived that he jumped up and started waving at her, I was trying to get him to sit down in case the auctioneer thought he was bidding! She was very quiet when she got there, not at all how I thought she'd be considering her grandpa was about to buy her a cottage. Anyway, as Kenneth started to bid Stephanie kept saying, 'That's enough grandpa, don't worry if we don't get it.' Kenneth was determined, he'd told her he was going to buy it for her and he was a man of his word. But when he increased his bid to £208,000 she whispered loudly 'Grandpa, no!' That's when she told him that she wasn't with Toby anymore and she was going to live in the South of France with her grandma, Kenneth's ex-wife. Well, I thought if he goes any redder he'll launch like a rocket he was so furious. It seems he's not so keen on his ex-wife and he told Stephanie not to expect to see him again if she went. So she left. I felt sorry for him, so we came in here for a cup of tea, poor man, he didn't stay long, he's devastated.'

Clara listened as Rachel revealed what had happened. She realised now that William must have noticed something was wrong so gave her the opportunity to bid again. For a moment she felt sorry for Kenneth, he was clearly devoted to Stephanie. Then Clara remembered he'd not shown any compassion to her, showing off to his granddaughter and throwing his money around. He'd have continued to outbid her if Stephanie hadn't dropped her bombshell.

After Rachel returned to her own table Clara stared out the window at nothing in particular. She was sure she was traumatised, that's how she would have described herself if anyone had asked how she felt. She picked up her phone and dialled the one person she could always count on in times of trouble. 'Hi mum.'

Despite desperately wanting to visit the cottage and perform a congratulatory lap of honour around the garden Clara remembered Elsa. She looked at her watch, paid the bill, waved at Rachel who clearly didn't have anywhere else to be, and set off for Heathfield. As she pulled out of the entrance of Manor Hall, the realisation of what had happened hit her.

'Flippin', bloomin', blinkin', blimey, bloody, bum, poo, crap, damn, shit I've only gone and done it!' she shouted.

6

Pulling into Heathfield Animal Sanctuary Clara felt a familiar rise of excitement. As she stepped into the office she was greeted like a long-lost friend. Tina was in the kennels and was expecting her.

'I hope you've got your walking shoes,' Lizzie motioned at Clara's black suede shoes. 'You look like you're going to see a solicitor rather than going dog walking.' Clara realised that once again she was wearing inappropriate footwear. She could have gone back to the car and changed them but at that moment she didn't care, she wanted to see Elsa as soon as possible. Tina was hosing down a large black Labrador when Clara reached the kennels.

'Hi, so glad you're here, I've got some news for you.' Clara wondered if it was good or bad, or whether good was bad, or bad was good. It was surely about Elsa, she had mixed emotions about her being adopted.

'Can you grab me a couple of dry towels from that pile please?' Tina tilted her head over to a table just outside her office.

'This one found a pile of fox poo to roll in and he absolutely stinks. Don't you, you stinky, smelly boy?' Tina ruffled the dog's face and neck as she bent and pulled his face close to hers, as if he would understand her special 'I love you really' language.

Tina stood up and looked at Clara. Tina was soaking wet but didn't appear to notice.

'That couple came back today and it all went well so she has a new home. Isn't that fantastic?' Tina's face was beaming as she told Clara Elsa's good news.

'Wow, that's great,' Clara managed in her best 'feigned excitement' voice, trying to match Tina's smile, knowing that saying goodbye would be hard.

'Where is she, I need to wish her luck?'

'Oh, she's gone. They took her with them shortly before lunchtime, they came a day earlier than planned as they were so excited.'

Not for the first time that day Clara found it difficult to breathe. She felt herself gasp in, but she couldn't breathe out. Gone? Just like that. Clara felt a pang deep in her chest and instinctively held a hand to her heart in an attempt to soothe it. But hadn't she come to say goodbye? No. She'd come to say hello.

Tina sensed Clara's disappointment and handed her the hose pipe to spray Dodge the black Labrador while she rinsed the soap off him.

'They said they'll be in touch and let us know how she's doing. I'll message Daisy and she can update you.'

Tina's words were of no consolation to Clara. She pictured Elsa, with her silky ears that you just *had* to stroke, her long tail, the sensation of her tongue as she had licked her tears away. She fought back the tears now and was glad of the excuse to wipe her face when Dodge gave an almighty shake and covered them both with water.

'Shall we have a cuppa and a Kitkat?' Tina offered as she dried Dodge briskly with a towel, 'I think I've earned it. What about you?'

'Actually, that's exactly what I need,' Clara replied as she took the wet towels from Tina who returned a damp Dodge to his kennel.

'It's a shame you weren't in a position to have her, she'd have loved being with you.'

Tina was excited to hear Clara's news and sat on the edge of her seat, Kitkat half-way to her open mouth as Clara relayed those last few moments at the auction.

'So didn't you realise you'd won?'

'Not straight away. Not until a lady with a clipboard came and congratulated me. I was so desperate to get out of there at that stage I didn't notice Kenneth hadn't increased his bid.'

Tina took a huge bite of her Kitkat, her eyes wide open as she stared at Clara. 'That's fantastic,' she managed to say even though her mouth was full, she wiped away a slither of melted chocolate that had escaped and was dribbling down her chin. They both laughed,

'I know,' Clara could feel the excitement rising in her again. 'I can't quite believe it.'

Tina raised her mug, 'Well done you, cheers!' They tapped their mugs together and Clara explained how she was planning to come to Norfolk most weekends, except those when she saw her mum.

'Will she be visiting you up here?' Tina asked. Clara hesitated for a moment, remembering her mother's childhood in Norfolk.

'Probably not,' she replied. 'It's easier for me to go to Tonbridge.'

Tina asked Clara if she'd take a new guest for a walk. A little dog whose owner was in hospital so he was boarding temporarily.

'We don't normally take in boarders but his owner is one of our regular dog walkers.' Clara followed Tina to a kennel where a small black fluffy dog with a very waggy tail greeted them.

'His name is Gus and he's a cross between a Havanese and a poodle. In other words, he's a Havapoo!'

It took a moment for Clara to see the funny side then they both burst out laughing. Until that moment Clara hadn't realised how much she needed to laugh. She changed into a pair of flat shoes from the car while Tina got Gus from his kennel.

He was a jolly little chap, walked beautifully on the lead and every time Clara stopped to pet him she was sure he smiled at her. As they crossed the field, into the woods, Gus trotted obediently beside her, looking up for treats and getting over excited whenever she gave him one of the little biscuits Tina had put in a bag. He made her smile. Clara thought of Elsa and hoped she was happy in her new home.

It was getting dark, Clara knew it was time to go but it was so difficult to leave. She loved being here, away from London, from work, from her life. She felt at home in Norfolk. She grudgingly said her goodbyes and gave Gus a last little tickle behind his ears before changing her muddy shoes for an old pair of trainers she'd also put in her car. She was learning fast that she needed a boot full of old shoes when she was in Norfolk.

'What a day!' Clara exclaimed to herself as her car pulled out of Heathfield, starting the long journey home. As she reached across to the glove compartment for the bottle of sanitiser she changed her mind. She wasn't ready to eliminate the smell of Norfolk and Gus from her hands. For once she didn't mind the slow crawl of traffic through London that delayed her return.

7

The days dragged far more than usual as Clara continued to struggle with focusing on her work. She'd let things slip running up to the auction but now she absolutely must knuckle down. Grant was in the office less and less. *Lucky him*, she thought. His secretary, Freya, had become a frequent visitor to Clara's office, dropping in around 3 o'clock for a tea break each day as her boss was absent more often than not. Clara looked up as Freya tapped on her door with two mugs in her hands.

'Fancy a cup of tea?'

The first time they shared a cuppa Clara arrived in the kitchen while Freya was waiting for the kettle to boil.

'You'd think they'd install a water boiler, it would save so much time,' Freya declared. Clara was thankful Freya had filled that awkward moment when you don't know what to say to someone you kind of know and you're stuck in the same space together.

'I'd have thought you had loads of time since Grant is hardly here these days.' Clara wondered if she sounded too abrupt but Freya surprised her.

'You're absolutely right, I've got all the time in the world. I could stand here with a candle under this mug and still not miss a deadline by the time it boiled!' Clara laughed and they started to chat as they made their drinks. She surprised herself by inviting Freya into her office.

'Come and sit on the sofa, I need a break from working on the Smithson file for hours on end.' They chatted about having too much work to do, not having enough work to do and debated which was worse until Freya decided she ought to at least return to her desk. She was bored to tears. Grant's replacement still hadn't been appointed and Freya had been left in limbo waiting to find out if they would bring their own assistant with them.

A couple of days passed before they arrived in the kitchen at the same time again. With their drinks made, Clara motioned for Freya to follow her back to her office, and so their routine began. Clara would never have believed she and Freya had so much to talk about. She had recently become a member of the same category as Clara, 'divorced no boyfriend', although her marriage had lasted for over 20 years. By the second week Freya confided in her the reason why they divorced. They had married young but had not been able to have children.

'Daryl said he didn't mind. We had fabulous holidays, top of the range cars, focused on our careers and developed our own interests. One day last year he came home from work, looked at me and started crying! He said he loved me but he wanted a child of his own. We'd talked about adoption years ago but both agreed we didn't want to. I was stunned, I couldn't understand what he was saying to start with. He wanted a child, he said he wanted me too but he couldn't have both. I suggested we find out about a surrogate but he said he wanted to have a relationship with the mother of his child.' Clara sat in silence as Freya poured out the details of her private life.

'I asked him if he had someone else, but he said he didn't. At the time that was true. He's recently met someone so he told me before anyone else did. It's so sad. I could do with being busy at work to take my mind off it all.' Clara wasn't sure what to say, she wasn't used to people confiding in her. First Daisy, then Freya. Did that make them friends?

Clara was counting down the days until she completed on the cottage. She had printed a 28 day calendar and stuck it to the door of her freezer, ticking off each day as it passed. With just 6 days to go she forwarded the remaining funds to her solicitor and planned her 3 days off work for a long weekend in Norfolk. Grant said yes to almost anything he was asked these days.

Clara confided to Freya during their tea break about A Stone's Throw and her weekend in Norfolk with the marketing department.

'Can you imagine if you'd never got stuck in the lift with Teagan and Daisy? You'd probably never have gone to see it.'

Clara had always believed in destiny. Not that she thought she'd ever encountered it in a good way, until now maybe, but she guessed that as so many books and films made millions from the concept it was a good chance there might be something in it.

The day before completion she'd planned to have an early night so she could leave early and beat the worst of the traffic the following morning. Her solicitor advised her the monies might go through at around midday, so she scheduled to stop along the way for brunch and a supermarket shop for a few essentials – milk, biscuits and a Mars Bar. The new microwave and kettle she'd bought yesterday was already in the boot of her car along with suitable clothing and a few DIY tools for the weekend. Annoyingly, Grant's leaving party was arranged for that evening and so scuppered her plans. As an Associate Director she would be expected to stay for the whole of the evening.

Making her way to The Red Lion Clara realised she hadn't seen Grant for ages, he'd been working in the Singapore office for most of these past three weeks but had flown in this afternoon via New York. She was surprised to find the pub almost full as she pushed open the doors. Were all these people here to congratulate him, she wondered, or pleased to see him go? She briefly considered if anyone would show up for her leaving drinks, then decided it would depend on who was buying them. She was sure there would be a full house if the drinks were free.

Daisy waved to her from the far corner of the pub, but she was hemmed in by the rest of the marketing department. Clara found Freya who had a glass of red wine waiting for her.

'You're just in time for his speech.' Freya rolled her eyes. Grant was not the sort of person to leave quietly.

'Thank you for coming everyone. I felt it was important to fly back especially to say goodbye to you all, and celebrate my exciting new venture with you,' he announced, clapping himself. People around him who had been drinking since 5.30pm joined in. Clara and Freya looked at each other and shrugged in that 'I can't believe he's clapping himself' kind of way.

'Whoopee!' Teagan's sarcasm could be heard above the crowd, but Grant chose to ignore it and began listing his many achievements since he'd joined Coopers & Leigh.

'... as a young, handsome chap I was ambitious and creative, with the foresight to see opportunities and make them happen. So, listen all you young wannabees, learn from me and work, work, work! Thank you.' Freya took a large mouthful of her red wine, finishing the glass.

'I wish he had the foresight to stop blowing his own trumpet and sod off and leave.'

'And now,' Grant continued as a few groans rumbled around the pub. 'Without further ado, I have the great pleasure of introducing you to your new CEO of Coopers & Leigh London.' Clara looked at Freya who shrugged.

'I have no idea, he didn't tell *me*.'

'He's flown with me all the way from New York just to be with you this evening to say hello. He'll be taking over my office from next week. Please welcome...' The room was suddenly silent, all eyes were on Grant and then at the back of the room as he pointed. '…Mr Dan Sayer.'

Clara froze, her glass halfway to her mouth. Had she heard correctly? Surely it wasn't? Her chest constricted and she stood frozen in time. Clara was sure her soul left her body and floated above the crowd, looking down at her static self, immobilised by the sound of his name. The sound of glass breaking and someone pushing past her brought her back to life, back to breathing. She had to get out, unseen. With her glass still in her hand she turned towards the ladies' toilets, she'd be safe there. She threw open the door, three of the four cubicles were free. Clara headed for the closest one. Locking the door behind her she leaned back against it. Her wine glass shook in her hand, her mind still reeling from the sound of his name. It was as though someone had set off a firework in her head, its sparks searing her nerve endings, sending electric shocks to her brain. She closed her eyes, her head resting back on the door.

'Jesus Christ what am I going to do?' They could have been Clara's exact words, but the whisper and quiet gasps came from the next cubicle. Listening carefully Clara could hear someone having what seemed like a panic attack. What if they were having a heart attack, what should she do? Anything seemed possible at that moment. Ten minutes ago she was desperate to leave so she could make an early start to Norfolk. Now she had to get out of there without being seen, she had to be... safe.

Clara heard the latch on the next cubicle open and someone turn on the tap. She'd wait for them to leave before getting out, but they weren't leaving. Then she heard their phone ring. It was the unmistakable ring tone of Freya's phone. She loved 'Lifted' by The Lighthouse Family and usually sang along to it whenever it rang, but not this evening. Realising it was Freya, Clara opened the cubicle door. She was leaning against the basin, staring straight ahead, ignoring the call. Clara could see her reflection in the mirror; mascara streamed from her bloodshot eyes and across her face where she had rubbed them. She was clinging to the basin with both hands.

'Are you OK?' Clara approached her slowly, not understanding why Freya would be so distressed. Freya looked back at her in the mirror,

'I'm so glad it's you. I can't go back in there.' Clara was confused, why couldn't *Freya* go back in there?

'What happened, what's wrong? Are you ill?'

'Oh Clara, I can't go out there, not while *he's* there.' Still looking in the mirror Clara asked who she was talking about.

'Dan Sayer. I can't look at him, I can't be in the same room as him. I sure won't fucking work for him.' Clara was taken aback, struggling to work out why Freya would have such a reaction to *him*.

'I don't understand. Why can't you?' Freya turned to look at Clara as the door opened and someone tried to enter.

'You can't come in!' Clara shouted and pushed the door closed. She turned back to Freya. 'What's going on?' Freya turned and leant against the basin, staring ahead at the cubicle door.

'About three years ago I was invited on a business trip to the states with Grant. On the last day he got drunk at lunch and went to bed early, so that evening I sat in the hotel restaurant with my Kindle and a bottle of wine. Dan Sayer was staying there too. He said it was because his wife didn't like him coming home late and disturbing her sleep. He ordered another bottle of wine and we talked. He was rather funny and another bottle of wine later we got a bit flirty. Nothing happened, just laughing and touching a knee or an arm. When I said I needed to go to bed because I had an early flight he said his room was on the same floor as mine. We got in the lift and I pressed the button. I'd had a lot to drink, it was a high-speed lift, I felt a bit woozy and stumbled a bit. Dan caught me. Nothing happened but he said he'd see me to my room to make sure I was OK. I let myself in... and... when I ... turned to say... goodnight. He... he erm, he pushed his way into my room and grabbed me. He pulled me to him, and he, he said I'd been wanting him all night. He said I'd been flirting and giving him signals. I kept saying I hadn't. He'd got it wrong. We'd had a lovely evening but that's it, nothing else. He said I was playing hard to get. He said I made him hard and he was going to get what I'd been offering. He was forcing me towards the bed. I said I hadn't offered anything, please, leave. I apologised if I'd given him the wrong idea, I hadn't meant to, I was only being friendly.'

Freya turned around, holding back onto the basin, her head bowed. Clara guessed what was coming next. 'And then he raped me.'

Clara pushed Freya's bag into her arms and held out her hand to her. 'Come with me.'

Freya complied without question, her head still bowed. Opening the door Clara pulled her through the crowd, not looking at anyone she headed straight for the door and into the fresh air. Clara saw the yellow light of a black cab and stuck out her arm. It may only be a ten minute walk she thought, but we need to get home now.

Closing the door to her flat behind her Clara walked into the kitchen to put the kettle on. 'Make yourself at home.'

Freya sat on the edge of the sofa facing the view of The Thames with its bright lights and sparkling reflections.

'Tea or coffee?' Although Clara had her own dark secret she wasn't sure she was ready to reveal it, she had never told anyone, even Andrea. Maybe it was time. Clara handed Freya a mug and sat on the edge of the armchair.

'I am so sorry you went through that. It must have been extremely difficult to tell me. Did you go to the police?' Freya cradled her cup in her hands and stared out at the lights.

'No. I suppose I thought I was partly to blame. I *had* flirted. I know I didn't deserve it, but I felt so, ...*dirty*. I didn't want anyone else touching me, I wanted to curl up and pretend it hadn't happened. When I got home Daryl was away on a rugby trip. By the time he got back I'd found a way to cope, and I didn't want to undo that. We hadn't made love for years so that was never going to be an issue.' Freya looked straight at Clara.

'I can't be in the same office as him. I can't work for him. I'll have to leave, get another job. What if he comes into the office tomorrow?' Frightened and confused Freya stood up to leave.

'I should go home. You have an early start tomorrow and need a good night's sleep. It's an exciting day for you.' Clara stood and met her gaze.

'Come with me. Come with me to Norfolk tomorrow. Stay here tonight in the spare room. We'll go to yours in the morning and pack a bag, phone in sick, get away from here.'

Grateful for the opportunity, Freya accepted without hesitation.

8

By 8.30am they were on their way, leaving London behind them as quickly as the traffic would allow. They sat in silence, each deep in their thoughts. Freya broke the silence.

'Thank you. This is the best thing for me right now. I need to get away, run away, and get my head straight.' They had at least a two-hour journey ahead of them. Clara braced herself. It was time to let it out.

'Actually, I've got something to tell you. I didn't want to tell you last night. I *couldn't* tell you last night. He used to work in the London office many years ago. That's how I came to apply there. We went out together for eighteen months.' Clara saw Freya turn to look at her, eyes staring in disbelief. Clara kept *her* eyes on the road ahead.

'He used to play football, so we'd mainly go out with a group of people, we hardly went out alone. We got on OK in a crowd, but I'd not experienced relationships as my mum brought me up on her own, so I didn't know what to expect. One night, after about six months, we'd been to an 'end of season' party. I was so tired when we got back to his flat and wanted to go to sleep. But he had other ideas. I kept saying 'no', but he wouldn't let me sleep. Then he got a bit rough, then he got angry when I said 'no' again. I couldn't stop him. He said he was my boyfriend and he had 'conjugal rights'. The next day he carried on as if nothing had happened. I began to wonder if I'd imagined it. Apart from the discomfort 'down there', I was so confused. Nothing else happened until about four months later. Then it was weekly. We were working together so it was difficult to get away from him. He said no-one else would put up with me. He called me 'Billy No Mates', all my friends were his friends and he said no-one would believe me. By then I was so scared I couldn't think what to do. So, I didn't do anything, until we were at a party. He was standing in the kitchen for ages talking to someone, I was dancing in the living room. I went upstairs to the toilet and he followed me. He dragged me into a bedroom and pushed me up against a wall. I don't know where he got it from but he held a razor blade to my throat. His face was inches from mine, I could smell the alcohol on his breath. He accused me of deserting him at the party, leaving him in the kitchen while I had a good time. His eyes burned into mine, I froze. I could feel the cold of the blade against my neck. Then suddenly he let go of me, left the room and disappeared downstairs. I stood against the wall trying to catch my breath. What had just happened? My head was scrambled, I felt worthless. Anything I'd still felt for him drained away at that moment. Outside, he punched a wall then walked up the road. I knew then I had to get myself out of the relationship, but I was scared.' Clara heard Freya's sharp intake of breath as she told her about the razor blade.

'Then a miracle happened. He got transferred to New York on a fast-track management scheme, for up and coming 'Directors-in-waiting'. It took 3 months for the work visa to come through so I stuck it out until then. I've never seen him since. Until last night. I ran into the toilets. I needed to get out of there too.'

Clara and Freya both sat in silence for a few moments. Clara pushed her foot down on the accelerator, the car burst forward, they had to get away and leave London behind. Leave *him* behind.

Clara felt the soft touch of Freya's hand on hers for a few seconds. Nothing needed to be said. A single tear slowly descended down Clara's face and rested on the side of her mouth. She licked it away, tasting the saltiness. It reminded her of Elsa.

'It's time for a fresh start,' she suddenly announced to Freya, making her jump. If Elsa could do it, so could she.

'We need a plan of action.'

They both agreed they could not possibly work with *him*. Freya had called in sick that morning, saying she had a migraine, which would give her a couple of days to think. They were both due back in the office on Monday, *his* first day. They hadn't stuck around long enough last night to discover if he was bringing his own assistant. That gave Clara an idea.

'He's bound to bring his PA with him, he knew you worked for Grant. He *has* to make you redundant. If your position no longer exists and there's no "suitable alternative," as he can't risk having you around to tell everyone what he did, he'll have to pay you off.'

Freya sat up straight in the leather bucket seat, relieved at the possibility of having a way out.

'What if he refuses to? And what about you? Your job isn't redundant.'

Clara realised she only had half a plan.

'We've got 'til Sunday, we'll have it sussed by then.' She turned on the radio and tuned into Radio Norfolk in time to hear the end of the song 'Our House' by Madness. They both laughed.

'Let's go get your new house,' Freya cheered.

They stopped for brunch and a quick loo break at a pub William had told Clara about that served great food. They had time before they collected the key around mid-day, so it was an ideal stop-off point. As they walked through the doors of the 16th Century coaching inn they were taken back in time.

'Bloomin' hell!' Clara led the way towards the bar, past chunky mahogany tables, and chairs with faded floral upholstery. Tassled lamp shades adorned the walls where heavily patterned floral wallpaper had hung steadfast these past decades. 'What century are we in?' she whispered to Freya.

An hour and a quarter later they sat back in the car, stuffed with far too many slices of toast, an extra sausage and three more cups of tea neither of them had needed.

'Well that was a good old-fashioned breakfast. I'm not sure my seat belt is going to fit now!' Freya laughed. Clara started the car, programmed the location of the auction house into the sat nav and set off towards Norwich. The traffic news from Radio Norfolk reported traffic was moving slowly but freely through roadworks near Wymondham, but neither of them minded, they felt a million miles away from London.

Clara's phone ringing burst through the audio system of the car, interrupting their sing-a-long to Lady Gaga's 'Shallow'. The display revealed it was her solicitor's office.

'Oh my God! Quick, answer it.' Freya was almost as excited as Clara. The purchase had completed. Clara clicked the button on the steering wheel to finish the call.

'Wooo hoo!' they shouted. The radio came back on again. The call had been so brief they were able to continue singing along, but much louder this time, and with a slight squeal as they attempted to reach the high notes.

Clara was disappointed that William was out of the office when she collected the keys. She waved them at Freya as she walked back to the car. A shiny black Audi Estate pulled into the parking space behind them as Clara opened her car door.

'Hey! Aren't you going to wave them at me too?'

William stood smiling as she turned in his direction. He was wearing a dark tailored suit, shirt and tie and shiny black shoes that matched his car.

'Congratulations, you are now the proud new owner of a set of old keys. I hope you enjoy them.'

'Wasn't that old car yours at A Stone's Throw when I viewed?' Clara recalled.

'No, well yes, it's sort of a family car. My car was in the garage so I'm embarrassed to say I thought that would be an acceptable alternative. Which it probably wasn't because now you think I'm a dusty old man. Emphasis on the 'dusty' obviously.' He could feel himself being swallowed deeper into the hole he was digging. In truth it belonged to his father who lived on a nearby farm, hence the dusty car and his very dusty shoes. Why was he trying to impress her?

William recollected the sight of her reeling from the smell of the compost toilet. He could have kicked himself for not changing out of his old clothes as she'd stood before him. She was so… beautiful.

Clara's smile faded. So he had a family. She wondered who the real William was, the dusty one or the shiny one, but it didn't matter because she would probably never see him again.

'If you're ever in the area you're very welcome to come and visit the keys.' *What the hell did I say that for? Damn, smile, you've said it now. He must think I'm some kind of idiot.* 'Thanks for all your help. Bye.' Clara quickly jumped back in the car, hoping he hadn't seen her face turn scarlet.

'Oooo, who's that?' Freya enquired, looking back over her shoulder as Clara put her foot down and drove off at speed in an attempt to leave her embarrassment behind her.

Clara felt a flush of excitement rising in her stomach as they reached the lane. She lowered the car window to reduce the heat in the car and lower her blood pressure, as she slowly manoeuvred around the pot-holes until they reached the old wooden sign, 'A Stone's Throw'.

'I can't quite believe this is happening,' she confided to Freya.

As they pulled into the drive Freya sat forward in her seat, leaning towards the windscreen, anxious to take it all in as much as she could. The driveway was empty, looking larger than before, Clara was disappointed the dusty old car had gone. *No chance of seeing William again now.* The thought of never seeing him again felt too great to consider.

The grass had grown and the previously well-trodden pathway to the front door was barely visible. Clara stopped the car.

'Where shall we park?' With the old car gone there didn't seem an obvious parking place.

'Anywhere you like!' Freya replied, 'It's huge.'

She decided to leave the car in the middle of the drive, just because she could. *No computer cells for parking spaces here.* They stepped out onto the gravel to the sound of birdsong and a soft, warm, gentle breeze that seemed to welcome them to 'A Stone's Throw.'

Clara slowly turned around, taking in the panoramic view. She wanted to see and breathe it all in and remember this moment, creating a permanent picture in her mind. She took out her mobile phone.

'How about a selfie?' Clara held the camera so she and Freya could pose and make a range of amusing faces. 'Let's take one by the outside loo,' she laughed, grateful to have a friend to share the moment with.

'Come on, I want to show you inside.' As she turned the key in the lock Clara's hand trembled slightly as she realised the enormity of what she'd taken on. The heavy wooden door swung open into the hallway and she stepped across the threshold, *her* threshold, *her* cottage.

Clara turned right and showed Freya a square room with windows to the front and side. 'I'm not sure what I'm going to use this room for yet, I don't think I need a dining room. Then out of here the door opposite is the living room, I just love that open fireplace, I've always wanted one. And I can see out the front and the side, it's so light and bright in here, then I can wander through here into the kitchen. I was planning to give it a good scrub for the time being. Don't you just *love* that view down the garden? Here's the bathroom, that's on the list to be scrubbed too! I know, sage green, what were they thinking? Then, back into the hallway and up the stairs, you can sleep in one of these rooms at the front when you stay, I'll let you choose. I think they're both the same size. And this is my room.'

Freya had followed Clara around, letting out intermittent sounds of 'Oooo', 'oh!', 'yes' and 'lovely!' Clara opened the door to her bedroom.

'Wow! Just wow, that is bloody fabulous.' Freya walked over to the window looking out across to the sea. Fluffy white clouds filled the sky, all the way to the horizon. They both stared out for several seconds after which Freya turned to Clara.

'I love it. I will definitely be visiting you, regularly!'

They made their way back outside, at first inspecting the enormous Christmas tree where Clara told Freya the story of how a family dog had sadly been killed along this road and the family planted a Christmas tree in her memory as her name had been 'Holly'. They walked around the perimeter of the garden until they finally reached the cliff edge, stopping to breathe in the air and gaze at the sea. They continued along the top to the far end, staying away from the edge of the landslide, wading through the long grass. Back at the car they unpacked the new kettle, mugs, cutlery, crockery, microwave, cleaning equipment and rubber gloves Clara had begun to store in her car a week ago, and carried them into the kitchen. They threw open all the windows and doors to let the air blow through, then Freya put the kettle on and made them both a large mug of coffee.

'Just the ticket,' she handed a mug to Clara, who offered her a shortbread biscuit. They sat on the stairs in silence, listening to the sound of the birds and the sea as the warm breeze swept through the cottage.

'I hope you're planning on getting some furniture, my bum's killing me sitting on these stairs!' Freya joked.

They set about removing the old carpets which they estimated had been there since around 1970. Cutting them into manageable pieces they dragged them outside and piled them by the old greenhouse. Clara had brought a speaker and found a playlist of 1970s hits on Spotify to get them in the right mood. Singing along to the tunes of Abba, Candi Staton, Johnny Nash and Stevie Wonder eased the pain of the job in hand and they were surprised how many songs they knew the words to.

At five o'clock they stood in the kitchen, dusty, dishevelled and exhausted. They decided to call it a day and made their way to the hotel Clara had booked a month ago. Thankfully, when she called this morning they'd been able to change her room to a twin. It was only a short drive to the Country House Hotel in Sheringham. As they entered the room Freya opened the doors onto their own private terrace and looked out over the gardens.

'I feel like I'm on holiday,' she declared. 'Bollocks to Dan Sayer!' She breathed in the sea air. 'Fancy a swim?'

Once in the pool the warm water soothed away any thoughts of *him*. Their chatter echoed around the pool area as they enjoyed it all to themselves. An hour later they washed and dressed for dinner. Clara planned to celebrate her new home in style and had booked a table in the formal restaurant for the first evening. They ordered from the À la Carte Menu and shared a bottle of Champagne, toasting new beginnings and good times in Norfolk.

They both slept deeply and late into the next morning. Clara awoke first, Freya was right, it was just like being on holiday. Something else was different too. The knotted ball that had resided in her stomach these past twenty or so years, creating a hard shell to keep people at a distance, somehow felt smaller and softer. Perhaps she'd been wrong to keep her secret for all this time, would it have been better to let it out? She certainly felt better for it today, she decided.

9

After breakfast they drove to the Georgian market town of Holt. Daisy had told Clara of a charity that sold second hand furniture to support their work with vulnerable young people and families. Clara chose a large coffee table for the living room, a pine kitchen table with four chairs and matching dresser, which would fit one end of the kitchen, a washing machine and a fridge freezer. They were amazed to find they could be delivered the following day for a reasonable fee. Clara was delighted with her bargains and her first pieces of furniture. The new bed she had ordered online wasn't due for another four weeks, and until it arrived, she planned to use an inflatable bed when she visited. She was looking forward to camping at her weekend hideaway. Clara smiled to herself as she remembered the painstaking process of selecting furniture for her London apartment. Did that belong to another person? Another version of her?

Clara was glad to have had Freya's help. It had taken her hours to scrub the bathroom floor and attempt to remove an unsightly stain from around the inside of the toilet. Freya had cleaned the insides of all the windows and made the kitchen sink and taps almost respectable. They'd bleached all the kitchen cabinets and worktops, and Freya had cleaned the oven. Clara was sure she wouldn't have managed all of it on her own. The furniture arrived as promised and they spent almost a whole afternoon arranging and re-arranging the kitchen table and chairs, and they'd moved dresser five times.

Another tour around the gardens revealed a dilapidated red tractor, rusting in a rickety old stone barn whose roof lay on top of the tractor. The word 'Tinker', painted on the side of it, was barely visible beneath the debris. Clara wasn't sure why Michael hadn't removed it but it looked like it had been there several years so probably didn't work. She didn't mind a bit of rustic charm.

The days passed by too quickly, Sunday morning came all too soon, and it was time for them to leave. They decided on a last swim in the hotel pool before breakfast then loaded their bags into the car. Both were reluctant to leave Norfolk and return to London, so Clara took Freya to Heathfield to walk the dogs. Gus was still there as his owner hadn't recovered enough to return home. Clara was sure he remembered her when he wagged his tail as she approached his kennel. She couldn't resist taking him for a walk. Freya was matched with 'Stan', whose forefathers and mothers would remain a mystery for all time. Tina made Clara promise to visit regularly now she almost lived in Norfolk.

Reaching Clara's apartment late in the day, they each sat with a coffee looking out at The Thames, trying hard to think of a solution to their immediate problem. Clara opened her work laptop to check her emails. Freya asked to sign in to her account.

'Oh shit!' Clara turned to look at Freya, desperate to know what she'd seen.

'Grant's sent me an email thanking me for all my hard work over the years, what a pleasure it's been, blah, blah blah.'

'So?' Clara was confused. 'Was that it?'

'No. There's an email from *him*.'

Clara took a sharp intake of breath. 'What does it say?'

Freya looked at her, fear in her eyes. 'I haven't opened it yet.' She looked visibly shaken. 'I'm not sure I want to.'

Clara moved to sit next to her. 'Do you want me to open it?' She was surprised how brave she felt. Freya turned the laptop in her direction. Clara took a deep breath. Perhaps she wasn't so brave after all, but she had to be for Freya's sake. She took another deep breath, clicked the mouse and read out the brief and concise communication.

'Dear Freya, following a change of personnel at the head of the department your position of Personal Assistant no longer exists and a suitable alternative position within the company is not available. Therefore, you are being made redundant with immediate effect. You will no longer have access to the office building, please arrange for someone to collect your personal belongings. A representative from Human Resources will be in touch with you on Monday to discuss your remuneration package.

Regards, Dan Sayer

'Well! We certainly talked that one up.' Clara handed the laptop to Freya to read.

'I hope it's a pretty hefty sum; he obviously can't face you either.'

Freya read it for herself then firmly closed the laptop shut. They both sat in silence for a few moments digesting the contents of the email.

'Well, he's done me a favour and I'm relieved.' Freya stood and took a closer look out of the window. 'I think bringing his own PA was one of his conditions for coming over, he couldn't chance me telling everyone what he did.' Freya stared out of the window, mesmerised by the water below. Snapping herself out of it she turned to look at Clara.

'I'm sure I can get another job soon, even temp for a while. I can downsize my apartment if I have to, the lease is up in two months anyway.' Freya forced a wide smile, but Clara didn't believe her bravado for one minute. Even if she didn't have to see him his appearance had prized open old wounds, for both of them.

'But what about you?' It was Clara's turn to look out of the window. She stared at the lights on the water which usually brought her peace and solace, but this evening their gleam couldn't refract her thoughts.

'I'll be fine. I haven't worked out what I'm going to do yet though. Come for dinner tomorrow evening, I'll ask Daisy to bring your things.'

Alone once again, Clara tried to push Dan Sayer out of her mind. She hadn't seen him for so many years, she felt she ought to have forgotten him. Her bravery that afternoon, so blasé, reading his email as if he couldn't touch her, diminished now with each breath as the memories resurfaced once again.

After that first time she was shocked and confused. Bruised and hurting she lay still until long after he left. He'd called out 'bye' as he walked out the door, but she didn't answer. Later, she stood in the shower until the water ran cold, not even noticing it at first. From then on, no matter how hard she tried, she couldn't wash away the fear, the smell of him, the shame, and no amount of scrubbing would truly purify her. The more she washed, the more she needed to wash, scrubbing her hands while counting to twenty, then counting to twenty again, several times a day. Even after he left for New York she could feel him on her, permeating her skin. How could she work with him now? She had tolerated him before. She remembered how she would freeze when they were together, when he…, until he thankfully left. Somewhere inside, in that place where nightmares linger, she'd buried his smell, his touch, his breath, the pain, the tears. She'd built a life where he didn't exist, if you didn't look too hard. She was trying to be brave for Freya but the cracks were already starting to show. She could feel their crooked hands around her throat, stifling her breath, tightening their hold. She curled up into a ball on the sofa and pulled the oversized crochet blanket around her. Could she work with him? No. She wouldn't, couldn't let him in. She opened her laptop once again and marked herself as 'working from home' in the office diary.

Monday morning arrived without any resolutions, calm or clarity of mind. Ignoring the rest of the previous evening's emails she messaged Daisy asking her if she minded clearing Freya's desk and bringing her belongings to her apartment that evening. 'Come for dinner, Freya will be here too.'

Clara spent the morning researching wi-fi options for the cottage and organising the contents of her wardrobes into 'work', 'Norfolk' and 'other'. *I must look exactly the same everyday,* she decided as she stared at a wardrobe almost full of black or grey suits and white or cream blouses. The 12 pairs of blue jeans and 27 jumpers, most of which were varying shades of blue, grey or green were equally uninspiring. *When did I become so bland?* Looking around at her whitewashed apartment she suddenly yearned for some colour in her life.

Back online she looked on Rightmove, apartments sold quickly in her block, she wondered what the current market value was and how quickly it would sell, *if* she wanted to. Apartments with a great view were highly sought after. She called two estate agents who had recently sold in her block and made appointments for valuations that Wednesday.

Freya arrived late afternoon, weary from updating her cv and applying for jobs online.

'I've put in a full day's work and not earnt a penny. I can't believe how many people are applying for the same job, it's like a lottery out there. Can we have Indian? I'm starving, I haven't eaten all day. I've brought a change of clothes; do you mind if I stay?' She dropped onto the sofa and hugged a cushion tight to her chest. 'Pleeease?' she implored. Clara loved how their friendship had become so easy. The intercom rang, breaking her thoughts - it was Daisy. *You wait years for a friend to come along and then two come along together,* she smiled as she pressed the button to let Daisy in. She couldn't remember the last time she felt so connected to anyone other than her mum.

Daisy deposited two large carrier bags full of Freya's belongings in the hallway. The taxi driver had left two more bags and a box by the entrance to the building, so Freya went down with Daisy to collect them. Clara poured 3 glasses of wine, pulled up the Indian takeaway menu on her iPad and set the table. She couldn't remember the last time she'd used the table to eat, usually a tray in front of the telly made do.

She heard the 'ping' of the lift through the open flat door and watched her friends struggle in with the personal contents of Freya's office desk and cupboards. 'How many pairs of shoes are there for God's sake?'

'There was almost one less because I *love* these Jimmy Choos but they didn't fit!' Daisy held one to her chest then quickly threw it back on the pile holding her nose, 'And they smell!'

'Bloody cheek, my shoes don't smell,' Freya retrieved the discarded shoe, stroking it.

'I see you didn't stick it under *your* nose,' Daisy laughed.

Clara ordered their food as they sat at the table and quickly finished the first bottle of wine. Daisy was keen to talk about the new boss.

'What a prat that Dan Sayer is. He went 'round to everyone introducing himself and shaking their hand. *'Hi, Dan Sayer, what's your name? Great. Looking forward to working with you.'* He repeated the same thing over and over, *and* his hands were sweaty!

'Aaaaaaargh, yuk!' Clara and Freya both simultaneously feigned vomiting into their wine glasses. Daisy continued.

'He's brought his American PA with him, Marcie, I felt so sorry for her. She obviously knew you'd been elbowed out Freya, she kept apologising as I was emptying your desk.'

Eager to change the subject Freya sat upright, picked up a fork and tapped the side of her glass to get their attention.

'Now we're all here I've got something to tell you both. Christine from Personnel called me today about my remuneration package.' Clara and Daisy turned their whole attention to her. 'She told me I was entitled to one week's salary for every year I've worked there.'

'No! Boo!' Clara and Daisy exclaimed in unison.

'But…,' Freya continued, 'the company wanted to recognise my contribution in supporting Grant and his predecessor over the years and 'are delighted to award me' with a whole year's salary, in addition to statutory redundancy, *plus* a year's worth of holiday pay *and* they're going to pay me this year's bonus!'

'Yes! So they bloody well should,' Clara declared.

Daisy raised her glass. 'Good for you. You can buy a new pair of Jimmy Choos that don't stink now!'

Freya pretended to throw her glass of wine at Daisy. They all laughed and raised their glasses in a toast.

'Cheers!'

After Daisy left, Freya helped Clara to clear away their plates and glasses.

'What are you going to do tomorrow? You can't work from home until you retire!'

'No, but I'm going to phone in sick for a couple of days until I get it clear in my head.' Clara filled the kettle and switched it on. 'I want him to make *me* redundant. I can't work with him, I really need get him out of my head and out of my life, I don't want to think about him anymore. During the day I can keep busy, but I've had nightmares about him every night since he walked into the pub. I don't want to live like that. It's like he's haunting me.' Clara filled the cafetière with hot water and twisted a spoon in her fingers as if mesmerised by it. Freya took 2 mugs from the shelf and finished making the drinks, she had half an idea, but she was clutching at straws.

'You can tell him you know what he did to me. Threaten to tell the Directors. He can't hurt me anymore.' Clara was grateful for the offer, but she knew there must be another way.

'Thanks, but I can't drag you into it. I'm sure I'll think of something.' Neither of them was convinced she would but they changed the subject and talked about her plans for the cottage while they drank their coffee.

Clara hadn't had a single day off sick in the past 8 years at Coopers & Leigh but she felt guilty lying to Lois in HR. Having considered her options; stomach bug, period pains, migraine, toothache, haemorrhoids, smallpox, abusive ex-boyfriend, she decided on feigning a bad back as it could potentially give her a longer amount of time, if necessary.

By the end of the day she had arranged for the internet to be connected at the cottage, employed a gardener to cut the lawns, spoken to her mother and read several chapters of Pride and Prejudice, having begun it yet again for the umpteenth time. It was her comfort blanket, and although she knew a Mr Darcy wouldn't step into her life, she immersed herself in the character of Elizabeth Bennet and delighted in their interactions. By 9.30pm she was exhausted from not doing very much at all and decided on an early night. Falling asleep only a few brief moments after nestling into her pillow she didn't hear the 'ping' of an email from her laptop which she'd left open in the living room. Had she heard it, and read the email, sleep wouldn't have come so easily.

The sound of heavy rain against the bedroom window teased her from a light slumber. She could sense it was daylight through her closed eyes but as there was no need to get up she drifted in and out of a gentle drowsiness, not waking again until 10:05am. For the first time in her adult life Clara had no desire to go to work, and as she lay considering her options, she also wondered for the first time ever if London was the right place for her to be. She took her time in the shower and getting dressed, enjoying the leisurely pace.

'I haven't got a rush in me,' she informed her reflection in the bedroom mirror, who stared back at her, devoid of emotion.

Clara and her cleaner were both momentarily startled when they encountered each other in the kitchen at 11.01am. Neither of them had expected to see the other, and as their paths hadn't crossed in the two years Helen had been working for her, both thought for a split-second they'd come face to face with an intruder. Both were irritated by the other's presence. Helen because she would usually bluetooth her music playlist loudly through Clara's smart speaker to alleviate the monotony of the job she secretly hated. Grudgingly she quietly dusted, hoovered, wiped, mopped, ironed, changed the bed covers and tidied. In all the time she'd worked for Clara, Helen had never had to tidy a thing. This morning there was a cup on the bedside cabinet, a towel on the bathroom floor, dirty shoes in the hallway, crumbs on the kitchen worktop and even a wardrobe door left open. *Is she ill? She's very quiet,* she wondered. Helen worked silently, hoping this was a one off and wouldn't happen again.

Clara had completely forgotten Tuesday was the day Helen cleaned, and begrudged having her space invaded. She wasn't sure where best to put herself as Helen bustled quietly around the flat which suddenly felt too small. Clara sat awkwardly in silence for two hours until Helen eventually said goodbye and closed the door behind her.

'Thank goodness for that,' Clara exclaimed out loud and made a mental note to make sure it didn't happen again. Despite them both having spent the last two hours in silence, apart from the hoover, the quiet that followed filled Clara with a growing sense of isolation and loneliness.

An old emotion she recognised from the past began to stir inside her. For most of her adulthood she had carefully sculpted a lifestyle where she existed in confined spaces, safe spaces; home, work and Tonbridge. But now he was back, she felt vulnerable again. Desperate to avoid it taking hold she emptied the contents of a kitchen cupboard and wiped each item meticulously, before carefully returning it to the exact spot where it had stood, making the tiniest of adjustments to its position until she was momentarily satisfied. The compulsion to purge the entire kitchen flowed through her veins; was it starting all over again?

From deep inside Clara heard her counsellor's voice – "where's your safe place?" Clara called her mum.

The sound of Linda's voice restored some calm in her. They agreed arrangements for Clara's visit the following weekend. As usual she would pick up any shopping they needed on the way, and they would have a day out on Saturday. Chartwell, where Winston Churchill lived for over forty years, was a favourite of theirs. Clara made every effort to be her usual self, but Linda sensed her unease.

'Are you OK my darling? Is everything alright?'

'Sure mum, I'm fine,' Clara lied. Linda knew better than to force the issue and as she put the phone down she made a mental note to check in with her in a few days, just to be sure.

An afternoon binge-watching Dynasty on Netflix provided a necessary distraction, was surprisingly more fulfilling and satisfying than Clara had imagined and not a pang of guilt plagued her. It was almost 9pm before she realised she'd hardly eaten all day. After putting her Marks and Spencer ready meal in the microwave and pouring a large glass of red wine she opened her laptop. She ought to check her work emails in case she felt compelled to deal with any of her clients' queries. Thirty-nine emails that had been sitting patiently waiting since yesterday, greeted her. She poured her reconstituted dinner onto a plate, grabbed a fork and scrolled down to the first one, working backwards towards the top. Her eyes froze as she read the sender of email number eleven – *dan.sayer@coopersandleigh.com.* The subject simply read 'Hi.' Clara slammed the laptop closed as if trapping him inside, then quickly slid it under the sofa. He could wait. She finished her glass of wine, poured another and sat on the sofa with her dinner balanced on a tray. She turned on the TV again hoping it would take her mind off him, but he chipped away at her concentration as she channel-hopped through her meal. She knew that she wouldn't be able to settle until she read that email.

Clara retrieved the laptop from under the sofa. How dare he enter her home uninvited, even if it was virtually.

Hi Clara, sorry if I gave you a bit of a shock in the pub but it was all a bit last minute as I wasn't sure I was ready to come back to the UK, it's been so long. Anyway, the bosses made me a very generous offer I couldn't refuse so here I am.
My wife, Shelley – my third wife actually – won't be here for a couple of months as she has some loose ends to tie up in the States. She's a bit younger than me and doesn't want to leave her friends so she'll probably hop backwards and forwards across the Atlantic until we know whether I'm here long term.
I've got four kids, three strapping boys and a girl. The boys are from my first marriage and the girl from my second. The boys are teenagers now, so I don't see them, they have their own lives to lead. The girl's mum won't let me see her, she's hell bent on paying me back for realising our relationship wasn't working. I left so we could both find someone that suited us better, I just found Shelley real quick and Gracie didn't like it.
Anyway, it'll be good to see you again. I noticed you were working from home today, let's grab a coffee soon and talk about old times.
Dan

Clara snapped the laptop shut again, this time throwing it on the sofa. 'Well I don't want to see you again, EVER!' she shouted at the laptop. She wouldn't let him violate her again, even if it was by email. How dare he boast of his three wives and offspring? She wasn't surprised his children wanted nothing to do with him, she briefly wondered what kind of life he'd given them. He'd clearly climbed the ladder at work. Yes, he could be charming when he wanted to, he could weasel his way in, catching you off guard until…anything to get his own way. So now as a middle-aged man he had a new, young wife. What a cliché! What an arse!

He clearly hadn't grasped the knack of maintaining a relationship. But neither had Clara.

Her apartment felt stuffy, the air stale, Clara stood up and walked to the window, how she wished she could throw it wide open and let the London air blast through her apartment to blow any thoughts of Dan Sayer away. Better still, she wished she could push him through it! Initially, another glass of wine and her 'Enya' playlist seemed like the ideal antidote, but as the singer's haunting vocals infiltrated her apartment and mind, Clara let angry tears flow down her cheeks. She took another large gulp of the Chateau Petit Bocq, but for once the flavours of Cabernet Sauvignon, Merlot and Petit Verdot grapes, mixed with the savoury notes of nutmeg and liquorice, were lost on her. The poignancy of the lyrics surged to the place in her heart where she'd long ago buried the possibility of ever meeting that 'someone special'. Enya sang to her, reminding her just how lonely she'd been, for so long.

'Alexa, stop!' Alexa obeyed instantly. If only she could switch off her mind that easily. *Why doesn't someone invent an Alexa for the brain? They'd make a fortune.* Clara replaced the cork in the wine bottle, deciding she would probably appreciate a good night's sleep in the morning more than a hangover. Hopefully tomorrow would be a better day.

She awoke early, remembering the estate agents were due today. Hurriedly she cleared away the evidence of last night's meal and wine and put her laptop in a cupboard, shutting *him* away. After the last agent had left, Clara grabbed her bag and took the lift down to the ground floor, she needed fresh air and space to think. Deciding on an early lunch she stopped by her favourite sandwich shop and ordered a skinny latte, smoked salmon on rye sandwich and headed for the boardwalk by the river. She'd often come here at weekends, spending hours people-watching, some would stop and chat, it was a time-consuming pastime. But today was a weekday and the mood was distinctively different. Passers-by passed-by, bypassing each other, hurrying, in straight lines, heads down, texting, talking to an invisible somebody, connected yet disconnected to their surroundings and each other. Today no-one seemed to *notice* anyone. Clara had always loved the cosmopolitan feel of Canary Wharf, the buzz, the noise, so many choices, the convenience of having all the amenities she could want within walking distance. Norfolk seemed like another world. Which one did she belong to?

The two agents' valuations had been roughly the same, give or take £5,000, and exactly what Clara had expected. Two-bedroom apartments were pretty much the same and attracted the same types of buyers at the same price. A decision needed to be made soon, she couldn't stay off sick for much longer. Having used most of her savings to buy the cottage, she couldn't afford not to work *and* keep her apartment. She had paid most of her mortgage off over the years with bonus payments, so she could invest most of the proceeds from the sale, use some to improve the cottage and not have to work full time. It was all happening too fast. Her thoughts turned to the cottage, the gardens, the sea view, Heathfields. *What am I doing sitting here?* The realisation dawned on her. *I can be off sick in Norfolk!* Clara almost sprinted home, weaving through the automaton blue-collar workers, trailing along like ants, but far less industrious.

It didn't take her long to pack two large bags with her 'Norfolk' clothes. A sudden burst of energy made waiting for the lift impossible, she was sure she'd explode if she stood still. Thankfully no-one encountered Clara charging down the stairwell with a bag swinging in each hand.

Once on the A11, leaving her London dilemmas behind her,

she turned on Smooth radio and sang enthusiastically to some great blast-from-the-past songs. She decided to stop off at Heathfields to see Gus, Tina and the others, really hoping Gus would still be there. She headed straight for the kennels and found Tina making a cup of tea.

'I'll have a biscuit with mine.' Clara called out.

'Hey! What a lovely surprise, you just can't keep away can you? Come and have a cuppa.'

Clara told Tina she'd taken more time off work; she wasn't sure why she didn't tell her she was feigning a bad back. Maybe she didn't want to be judged.

'I thought I might take Gus for a quick walk while I'm here.' Something in Tina's expression made Clara anxious.

'What's wrong? Has he gone back home?' Tina picked up on the disappointment in Clara's voice and was quick to reassure her.

'No, he's not going back home. Unfortunately, his owner passed away last night, we've been asked to rehome him.'

'Oh, that's so sad.' Clara had become quite attached to Gus, she was sad that he had lost his owner, but more than that she was upset at the prospect of never seeing his cute little face again. She knew he would find a new home in no time, he was so lovely, just like Elsa. Tina seemed to read her mind.

'It's a shame you can't have him; he'd love to be with you in your cottage. Can't you move up here permanently?'

Funny you should say that, Clara thought, but she wasn't ready to admit it out loud yet.

'It will take a while for the family to complete the paperwork, why don't I let you know when they've been in, maybe you'll be able to say goodbye to him before he goes.' Clara nodded and took a large mouthful of tea, wishing she hadn't grown so attached to him. It would be hard to say goodbye.

Gus greeted Clara with his usual enthusiasm, she was delighted to see how excited he was to see her. He trotted alongside her as they walked around the field.

'Sorry, no time for the woods today Gus I'm afraid,' she apologised to him as he tried with all his might to pull her towards the trees. Clara had to pinch herself, only two and a half hours ago she was sitting on a bench in Canary Wharf overlooking the River Thames living her London life.

Pulling into the drive of the cottage Clara parked and sat for a few moments to enjoy the quiet and take in her surroundings. It still seemed too good to be true. The early evening sun was warm against the windscreen, she opened the car door to let in some air. The sound of birdsong filled the car, and the stillness around her was reassuring, comforting, she felt safe. He'd never find her here.

Clara stepped onto the drive and made her way down the side of the cottage and through the overgrown grass to the edge of the garden. She stopped a few feet short of the sheer drop below where the wind hurled the sea against the rocks and its spray exploded into the air. Taking a deep breath she surprised herself and a passing sea gull by screaming at the top of her voice. Looking out to sea she let the wind buffer against her and swirl her hair into a tangled mess. Inhaling the sea air she realised she was standing in almost the exact spot where she'd fallen in love with the cottage and made what seemed like a mad decision to buy it, just a few weeks ago. The last few days had taken its toll on her. Overcome with exhaustion she lay down in the long grass, looking up at the blue sky punctuated by whisps of white clouds. Clara closed her eyes and listened to the sound of the wind blowing and waves crashing. *How can life change so drastically within a short space of time,* she wondered in her semi-sleepy state. How true that was for her right now. She wasn't sure how long she slept for, but she didn't mind and it didn't matter. The evening sun was slipping into the horizon as she rose from the grass and made her way back to the cottage.

An inflatable bed had seemed like an easy solution whilst she waited for her proper bed to arrive, but Clara soon began to curse buying a foot pump rather than the more expensive plug-in kind. Within a minute she was wiping away beads of sweat from her forehead, and her quadriceps were screaming at her to stop.

'Blow-up bed? My bloomin' lungs are going to blow up in a minute,' she puffed, eventually falling onto the not-quite-fully-inflated bed and deeming it 'good enough'.

Clara managed a shower, micro-wave dinner and half a Netflix film on her iPad before her eyes began to water and lost the ability to remain open on their own. She triple-checked the doors and windows were locked then climbed the stairs, the reality of her first night sleeping in the cottage dawning on her. There were no streetlights or neighbours, nor the familiar sound of distant sirens that accompanied her usual bedtime routine. As she lay in the quiet darkness she wondered if she'd made a mistake. *I'm in the middle of Norfolk, well more precisely the edge of Norfolk, I don't know anyone… and my mum is miles away.* Clara was surprised that her mum came to mind. The last time she'd wanted her mum was when she'd been invited for a sleep-over party at Pauline Davis' house for her tenth birthday. The other girls had fallen asleep easily, but Clara spent most of the night longing to be home, in her own bed, with her mum across the hallway with the night-light on so she could find her. Clara made a mental note to buy a night-light, the thought of its warm glow began to quieten the tireless chatter in her mind. Sleep eventually overcame her as she imagined the generations of her family who had lived here before;

children running around, growing into teenagers, parents turning into grandparents, large family Christmases with lots of noise. Now as its solitary resident, she wondered how she could possibly add to its history.

She woke late in the morning and slowly opened her eyes. The wide uninterrupted sky beckoned her to the window to take in its spectacular view. She opened the windows to be greeted by the sound of the sea and sight of the birds drifting along on the currents of warm air.

Was she still dreaming? She pinched herself to be sure. It was a trick she'd learnt from one of her favourite childhood books; Enid Blyton's 'Mr Meddle' series. They had belonged to her mother who read them to her as a child. They were first published in the 1940s and '50s but Clara had loved them. In 'Mr Meddle and the Kangaroo' he asks a farmer to 'Pinch me please, you can't feel pinches in dreams.' Clara had never forgotten it and somehow been able to use the trick herself while asleep. Satisfied she was wide awake, having felt the pinch on her arm, Clara headed downstairs to the kitchen, turned on the kettle, opened the kitchen door with the big metal key and stepped out onto the sunlit patio where she pinched herself again. Yes, this was definitely the right place for her to be.

After a breakfast of tea and croissants Clara headed for the front garden still wearing her pyjamas to look at the broken greenhouse. It was the first thing she remembered about viewing the cottage and despite the rest of the garden being overgrown she felt it detracted from the character of the place. Staring at the shards of glass littering the grass and gravel she looked for the rubbish bins and found them behind the outside toilet. Dragging the recycling bin across the gravel she began picking up pieces of glass and dropping them into the empty bin, taking care not to catch her fingers.

'Hello!' Clara turned to see who had caught her wearing her pyjamas outside in the middle of the morning. At the end of the drive stood a man and lady, probably in their 60s she estimated, both wearing walking boots and backpacks, smiling at her apologetically.

'I'm so sorry to disturb you,' the lady called as Clara walked towards her. 'We often walk this way, and we've always used the toilet there when the other people lived here. When they moved out we just kept using it I'm afraid, which was a bit cheeky. We didn't realise someone had moved in as its been empty for so long; do you mind if we use it this once, we won't bother you again.' The man stood slightly behind his wife, visibly embarrassed by the need to advertise their 'need' to use the toilet.

'Of course, it's fine,' Clara found herself saying, although not altogether sure *how* they would cope with the smell. Should she expect a steady stream of ramblers using her facilities? Should she put an air freshener in there? The man stood awkwardly waiting for his wife to reappear. Clara wasn't sure whether to return to the greenhouse or attempt to make polite conversation. He saved her the dilemma.

'We've been walking here every month for twenty odd years. The garden was immaculate for a long time, but the people living here last obviously weren't gardeners!' He smiled at his polite criticism. Clara realised this was her first insight into her cousin's life. Had he lived here? Had she hijacked his home?

'I'm waiting for a gardener to come and tidy it up, then I'll decide what to do with it,' she replied, feeling awkward in her pyjamas that read '*I could sleep all day*' on the front. The man was trying hard to refrain from reading the writing as it would mean looking at her chest. He stared straight at her face. Their awkwardness was broken by the welcome appearance of his wife from the outside loo.

'I'm so sorry but thank you. We'll make other arrangements in future.' Clara momentarily wondered if she ought to offer an open invitation to use the facilities, but something stopped her. A Stone's Throw was now her safe space. She smiled at them and walked back to the cottage for a wash and to get dressed before any more incontinent ramblers appeared.

The antiquated shower surprisingly worked a treat. Invigorated by the rush of hot water Clara sorted through her Norfolk clothes and chose a pair of black jeans she'd been about to take to the charity shop as they had faded in the wash, and an oversized t-shirt she'd found in the bottom of the wardrobe that had seen better days. They were just the thing for gardening she decided.

Since leaving her childhood home Clara hadn't had her own garden. Her work / life balance had consisted of work, and her evenings were mainly spent watching TV, reading and drinking red wine. Her monthly visits to Linda in Kent were mainly her only encounter with the outside world. She occasionally enjoyed the theatre and listening to live music, all of which didn't involve much conversation, and she was happy to attend on her own. She had never cared much for socialising, which had caused problems within her marriage. Joe had wanted to go out to discos and parties, he had a large group of friends, all of whom seemed to have a lot to say, generally all at once. Coming from a family of two Clara found the noise confusing and overwhelming, preferring a quiet meal for two, a show, then home for a glass of wine before bed. After he left, Clara bought Joe's share of the flat and never saw him again. Many years later she heard he'd gone on to marry again and have two children. Clara had remained firmly single; it was simpler that way.

At the cottage Clara fell into a pattern over the next few days, never tiring of waking to the wonderful view, then breakfasting and eating lunch on the patio. The local garden centre had offered next day delivery on a garden table and chairs, several colourful flowering arrangements in large pots, two bird feeders, a selection of gardening tools and a companion set for the fireplace. Clara set the plants and furniture at the end of the patio, arranging and rearranging them several times until she was satisfied she had created the best view from the kitchen window. She put the tools in the woodshed just across from the patio, they were clean and shiny and she didn't want them to leave them outside to get dirty. The bird feeders attracted a myriad of birds and some very cheeky squirrels, but Clara didn't mind who she fed. By Sunday morning she had cleared the greenhouse glass and taken down the framework, transferring it to the barn housing the old tractor, and pulled out a large section of weeds on the gravel driveway. After breakfast she stood at the end of the garden, looking across the grey expanse of sea. As the salty breeze that had skimmed the sea danced around her, she realised she couldn't run away any longer. She had to face him.

10

Clara stopped off at Heathfields to see Gus one last time on her way back to London. She'd regretted not being able to say goodbye to Elsa, and although it would be tough, she needed to wish him good luck. Three people who had seen his picture on the website had made appointments to see visit later that week, she wasn't surprised, he'd have a new home very soon. They headed straight for the woods, where Clara found the same fallen tree she'd sat on with Elsa.

'I guess this is goodbye Gus, you're going to make someone very happy, I just wish it could have been me. Maybe one day I'll sort my life out, maybe this God-awful mess will go away.'

Gus sniffed through the leaves around them then looked at her as if to say, 'What are you sitting down for? Let's go!'

'OK Gus! I get it. You're not interested in my dramas!' They spent an hour chasing smells until Clara admitted to herself she was just putting off the inevitable. It was time to go back, to London. She said a tearful goodbye to Gus, promising to never forget him, and took a selfie of them together; his pink tongue lolling out of his mouth after their excursion.

Clara drove home in complete silence. There was nothing to look forward to heading in this direction. Running the shower she stepped out of her Norfolk clothes. As she picked them up from the floor she smiled as bits of grass and dirt lay on her carpet. She needn't bother pinching herself, being in London definitely wasn't a dream.

Not even her power shower could expel the dread she felt for the next day. Calling in sick wasn't an option anymore, she had to face him, but not at work. Uncorking a bottle of wine she opened her laptop and sent him an email asking him to meet with her before work the next day, at 7am. To her surprise he messaged straight back, suggesting they meet this evening for a drink. He was staying close by, how about her local pub in half an hour? Clara stared at the screen. The thought of conversing with him, even through the ether, made her feel sick. She hesitated. What should she do? She wasn't sure exactly what she was going to say to him, her hair was still wet from her shower, she wasn't wearing any make-up, she was petrified of being in his company. Would he want to kiss her hello? Should she dress up to feel more powerful, or dress casually to show she didn't care? But she did care. She cared that he'd dared to resurface in her life, bringing all the hell back with him. She had to be brave. She messaged Freya to tell her where she was going and why. No more than twelve seconds passed after she'd pressed the send button Freya called.

'Just call me if you need me. I can meet you there afterwards and come back to yours if you want.' Clara was about to say 'No, I'll be fine,' when she realised she probably wouldn't.

'Yes please. Stay at mine tonight?'

Clara took a deep breath and pushed open the heavy door to the pub. She'd decided to go for the 'I don't care look', wearing jeans and a shirt, her face make-up free, her hair loose and still slightly damp. He was sitting straight in front of her at the bar, looking right at her. *Great.* She hated how he had the upper hand yet again. Dan stood up to greet her, but she side-stepped him and sat on a bar stool, putting her bag and jacket on her lap.

'What can I get you to drink?' he offered.

'Red wine.' She couldn't even bring herself to say please. Determined to take control she stood as the barman handed her the glass.

'Let's sit at a table.' The pub was unusually quiet, the workers would return tomorrow and fill it with laughter and merriment. This evening it was a sober environment. Dan followed her to the table, she could hear him saying how lovely it was to see her, she hadn't changed a bit, she was exactly how he remembered her. Clara sat down and waited for him to stop talking. Their eyes caught each other's momentarily, but each told a different story. She was about to tell him hers.

'I'll come straight to the point.' Clara planned to spend as little time as possible in his presence. 'I can't work with you.' Her abruptness caught him off-guard. She was sure he visibly sank a little into the chair as she felt the shift of power turn in her favour. She sat upright. It was time to confront him; he couldn't touch her now, she was safe. There were no consequences to face. She had nothing planned but needn't have worried as she threw years of suppressed fear, pain, anger and shame at him.

'Our relationship was an absolute nightmare for me. You belittled me, you bullied me, you dragged me down.' She took a deep breath. 'You raped me.' Dan opened his mouth to object, his eyes open wide, startled, but Clara hadn't finished. 'You thought you had the right to do whatever you wanted to me. You didn't care if I cried, and you didn't care if I said no, time and time again. You didn't care about me. You only cared about what you wanted. You are a rapist. You are a nasty bastard and I will NOT work with you! You had better find a way to make me redundant or I will tell the truth as to why I'm permanently off sick. So stay away from me. I don't ever want to see you again.'

Without giving him time to respond she picked up her jacket and bag, left her drink untouched and strode towards the door, her heart thumping, head pounding, her mouth so dry her lips stuck to her teeth. Trembling, and trying with all her might to walk in a straight line, Clara opened the pub door, desperate to escape. As she stepped over the threshold she let out a silent sob. From nowhere she felt a hand grab her arm, she flinched in fear. He'd followed her. Clara span around, ready to hit out, only to see with relief that it was Freya. She put her arm through Clara's and they walked back to her apartment in silence. Once inside Clara sat on the sofa, pulled a cushion into her arms and screamed into it. Freya made them both a cup of strong coffee and waited until Clara was ready to talk.

'I swore at him! Oh my God, I can't believe I said all that.' Freya held up her coffee mug towards her.

'Here's to you. He deserved it all, and more.'

Clara looked straight at her. 'Thank you for being there, you're a good friend.'

They sat up until late that night, the adrenalin coursing through Clara's blood too fast to enable sleep. Freya had been for a couple of interviews and called back for a second interview for the one she really liked the sound of, which was this Tuesday morning.

'The salary isn't as high as at Coopers and Leigh and I'll have to rent an apartment further out of London, but there's less pressure and they finish at 2pm on Fridays. What's not to like?' she declared. For the first time Clara found herself agreeing that work wasn't the be all and end all.

Freya picked up the cold coffee cups and put them in the dishwasher.

'I take it you're not going to the office tomorrow, are you calling in sick?' Amid all the haze Clara felt a moment of clarity.

'No. I'm going back to Norfolk. *He'll* have to explain why I'm not at work. I'm going back to Norfolk and I'm staying there. I'll either sell this or rent it. I'm leaving in the morning and I'm going to get Gus.' Freya stared at Clara.

'You're going to leave London and live in Norfolk permanently?'

'Yep,' she replied, more certain than ever. 'I'm going back tomorrow.'

True to her word and with even more determination, Clara spent Monday morning packing more clothes, toiletries, books and plants into her car. Freya left after breakfast, she'd offered to help but had a hair appointment at 10am, she wanted to make an effort for her second interview.

Clara pulled out of the car park shortly after midday, her car laden with what felt like most of her belongings. When she reached the A11 she instructed Siri to call Heathfields then asked to be put through to Tina.

'Tina, hi, it's Clara. Listen, I'm moving to Norfolk permanently and I want Gus. I'm on my way up from London now, can I come and fill in the paperwork?' Tina's voice squealed through the audio of the car.

'Wow! That's brilliant news, I'll have everything waiting for you. Safe journey. See you in a bit.'

Clara made another call.

'Hi mum, do you mind if I make a couple of changes to my visit? Firstly, I'm not working next week, so can I come on Monday? Secondly, can I bring a friend?' Linda was intrigued.

'Is it a man?'

'Kind of, his name is Gus, but he's got four legs!' Clara wasn't ready to tell her mum about her life-changing decision, that was a conversation she knew was best to tell her face to face.

Although they were close, she had never disclosed what had happened with Dan and she wasn't about to now. Her mum didn't really need those thoughts in her head, so she decided just to tell her about moving to Norfolk when she saw her.

Tina and Gus were both excited to see her. Clara filled out the adoption forms and Tina promised someone would be in touch for a home check that week.

'I was hoping he could come home by the weekend,' she told Tina.

'I can't promise, but I'll see what I can do.'

Next, Clara paid a visit to the charity furniture shop again. She'd need something more comfortable to sit on than the kitchen chairs. She chose a sofa with matching armchair; it would suit her and Gus for the time being. They could deliver it the next day.

Exhausted, and more than ready for a coffee, Clara pulled into the driveway of the cottage and sat for a moment, looking at her new home. Would she ever get used to it? Her two-bed apartment in Canary Wharf with no outside space may have had all mod cons but Clara loved the quirkiness and remote setting of the cottage.

The next day Freya called to say she'd been successful at the second interview, and they'd offered her the job starting Monday.

'Why don't you come up here for a few days? Have a bit of a holiday before you get back to the grind!' They agreed she would travel up tomorrow and go home Saturday. She was also excited at the prospect of Gus moving in with Clara.

'He'll love it there; you'll have to clear all those fallen apples though, otherwise he'll get belly ache!' Clara hadn't considered that, perhaps she ought to build him a run to stop him getting into mischief. She'd look into it tomorrow.

11

The furniture arrived after lunchtime, closely followed by Freya who presented Clara with a cast iron bird bath.

'It's a new home present. It's pretty hefty though, I got it from a reclamation yard and the man had to put it in the car for me.' Between them they struggled to carry it around the back of the cottage and placed it at the end of the patio, close to the feeders.

'All you need is a bird house and it'll be like an avian air bnb!' Freya joked. She went upstairs to her bedroom, carrying an inflatable mattress, duvet and pillows, all bundled in her arms. She was going to love visiting here.

That evening Freya broached the subject they'd been avoiding all afternoon.

'Have you heard anything?' Clara knew exactly what she was referring to.

'No,' she answered nonchalantly, 'but I'm sure he's stewing on it.' No more was said.

The next morning Clara received a call from Shirley the home check co-ordinator, they could send someone around that afternoon about 2pm. A flutter of butterflies churned her stomach, she hadn't considered she would be vetted to see if she was good enough to have Gus. She'd presumed it was like buying a new car - they'd had a few test drives and now she was ready to sign on the dotted line.

She needn't have worried as Carl, the home checker, declared it was a fabulous space for Gus. She showed him where Gus would sleep and where she would have a run built for him. Carl suggested she have a gate fitted across the front of the driveway and to keep him on a long lead while he was outside until the run was built. He also suggested showing him the drop at the end of the garden so he knew it was there. Apart from that she could collect him Friday afternoon.

Clara and Freya jumped in the car as soon as Carl's car had disappeared from view and headed for the nearest pet superstore. Clara chose a tartan bed, a bright red collar with matching lead, a long training lead and an assortment of toys. Freya insisted on buying his food and water bowl as a gift from his Auntie Freya. Clara texted Tina to ask which food she should buy. Tina suggested she buy it in bulk from Heathfields, it was cheaper, and it would give her an excuse to bring Gus back for a visit. At the counter they chose a sweet little bone-shaped identity disc and had her mobile number engraved on both sides. As they emptied their purchases into the boot of her car Clara suddenly called out 'poo bags!' and disappeared back inside the store.

Standing in the queue again she perused the items on display, the ones that you definitely don't need but are put there to tempt you while you wait to be served. Clara picked up four packets of treats of various flavours.

'You must be *very* hungry,' a male voice behind her declared. Clara stood for a moment, wondering if he was speaking to her. She recognised the familiar voice, could it really be him? She turned around to see William smiling at her and felt her heart thump against the walls of her chest. He was holding a pretty, black Labrador puppy in his arms.

'Oh, she is gorgeous,' Clara exclaimed in an excited voice that was probably a bit too high. She quickly diverted her enthusiasm towards the puppy, hoping William didn't notice it was really for him. It seemed to work.

'This is Lottie, she's just had her final jabs. Do you have something to tell me?' he asked, looking at the contents of Clara's basket.

'Yes,' Clara replied, still smiling. She was surprised how pleased she was to see him. 'I'm getting a dog, on Friday. His name is Gus. And I've left my job, and moved here permanently, as from this week.' Clara felt slightly giddy as she blurted out her news, trying hard not to stare into those blue eyes. She made more fuss of Lottie, grateful for the distraction.

Clara waited for William to be served and asked if Freya could meet Lottie, and him of course. Freya jumped in with both feet, asking questions Clara would never have dared to.

'Oooo, a play mate for Gus, how exciting. Do you live far William?' Clara was mortified, Freya was so forward but Clara waited eagerly for his answer.

'Not too far.' She was disappointed William didn't offer any more information. 'Well, I must get Lottie home, it was lovely to see you again Clara. Bye.'

Getting back into the car Freya scolded Clara, 'You kept that quiet.'

'What do you mean?' Clara replied, purposely not meeting Freya's gaze.

'A dishy auctioneer who's clearly into you, *and* he has a gorgeous puppy. Why didn't you invite him 'round for a play date?' Clara started the car engine.

'Because he's probably married and I didn't want to embarrass myself when he turns up with Mrs Auctioneer looking at me suspiciously. Besides, I'm not here to find a man, I'm fine on my own, with Gus.'

Tomorrow was a big day, she needed sleep but her mind span in circles thinking about Gus and William. She placed Gus' bed in the corner of her bedroom, unable to bring herself to have him next to her bed, that would always remain Minty's place. She eventually fell asleep remembering Lottie, and William, and wondering where 'not too far' was.

They spent the following morning preparing for Gus's arrival and carried out a risk assessment of the house and garden. His previous owner had lived in a bungalow so he'd have to learn to climb up and down the stairs. They found several more shards of glass where the greenhouse had stood, cleared a designated toileting area and moved the fallen apples to a far part of the garden. Clara found a local carpenter in the monthly parish magazine who would call by at the weekend to measure and quote for a gate. They were ready.

Tina greeted them with a wide smile as they approached the kennels. She had given Gus a bath that morning and a clean blanket for him to lay on.

'He's just been to the loo, so I think he's good to go. Can you take him to the office? They all want to say goodbye to him. There's a bag of food there too.' Clara could see the tears welling up in Tina's eyes.

'I'm assuming they're happy tears?' Clara gave her a hug.

'I always get emotional when one of our babies goes to a new home, I'm such a wuss.'

'I promise to bring him for a visit, he can help me walk the other dogs.'

Everyone in the staff room gave Gus a hug while Clara paid for his food and the adoption fee. Clara secured him into his travel harness and plugged it into the seat belt fastener. Freya volunteered to sit next to him ready to distract, give hugs and reassurance if needed on the journey home. To their amazement he lay down and went to sleep.

The sound of the gravel under the wheels woke him and he rose to look around. Standing, he shook his whole body, stretched and yawned. Clara connected the long lead to his harness, lifted him out of the car and put him down on the driveway.

'Welcome to your new home Gus.' The three of them marched around the garden as Gus pulled them along, exploring areas where Clara hadn't even been before, under trees, through overgrown shrubs and closely investigating several mole hills. Once indoors Clara took off his harness to let him run around. He dashed from room to room, sniffing the history of the house, learning about the people and animals who had lived there before. In half an hour he knew more about the previous occupants than Clara did. He spent his first evening curled up on the sofa, his head resting on Clara's knee.

'I think you've made the right decision.' Freya rose to pour them both another glass of wine. 'It's amazing here, so relaxing, and now you have Gus to share it with. What else will you do? Do you think you'll get bored?' She tickled Gus behind the ear before she sat down again, and he wagged his tail in appreciation.

Clara realised she hadn't thought that far ahead. Even if she wasn't made redundant the proceeds from selling her apartment would enable her to live comfortably for several years.

'I might find a part time job in a few months. First, I want to make this place feel like home, at least give it a lick of paint. I'll start on my bedroom, you never know, I might even make my own curtains!'

'I didn't know you could sew, that's amazing.' Freya looked surprised.

'No, it's not, I've never sewn a thing in my life!' Clara laughed,

'But this is a new life and I'm going to try new things.'

Freya raised her glass. 'I'll drink to that.'

Clara and Gus slept well that night and were sad to see Freya leave the next day. She promised to let Clara know about her new job and to be back soon. Clara turned to Gus.

'Well, I guess it's just the two of us.' With Gus still on the lead they walked around the garden and spent a while investigating his favourite spot near the barn housing the old red tractor. Clara walked him slowly towards the cliff edge, stopping every few feet, telling him to wait. Close to the edge, she stood and let him walk forward to see the drop for himself. He stood as if looking out to sea, sniffing the air, the wind blowing his ears, then he turned and walked back to her. They continued along the clifftop, the strong breeze blowing and swirling Clara's hair around. The wind became stronger and dark clouds appeared on the horizon.

'Looks like we're in for a storm Gus. Come on, let's baton down the hatches, I'll race you!' They ran back to the cottage, Gus galloping and bouncing alongside her, excited by this new game. Indoors, Clara closed all the windows, made herself a coffee and they both settled down on the sofa. Clara with a book, and Gus, well Gus was happy just to be with Clara.

The storm arrived later that evening and the wind buffeted the windows and doors as they snuggled up in the living room. Clara became slightly worried that the roof might blow off, or a tree would fall on her car, or the house would blow away like in The Wizard of Oz and they would become Dorothy and Toto! Thank goodness Gus wasn't afraid of thunder and lightning. Neither was she, but she wasn't used to the noises the house made, it was usually so quiet. The power went off around 11.30pm.

'Gus, remind me to buy some candles tomorrow.' He looked at her sleepily through the dark, half lifting his chin from her knee, wondering why she'd woken him. The house was pitch black, Clara used the torch on her phone to try and read a book to take her mind off the crashes and bangs, but it wasn't long before she ran out of charge. With nothing else to do but go to bed, Clara felt her way up the stairs, but Gus was already at the top, he could see just fine! She eventually fell asleep an hour or so later when the storm began to retreat back out to sea.

Clara almost leapt off the mattress as Gus barked angrily. He sprang out of his bed, growling all the way down the stairs. Clara looked around in a daze, it was daylight but she had no idea of the time as her phone was still out of charge. Gus was barking at the front door. Someone was knocking. Scrambling out of bed, she pulled her dressing gown on over her pyjamas and made her way to where Gus was jumping up and down at whoever was standing outside. Wondering who on earth would be knocking on a Sunday morning she opened the door to find William standing there. Gus stopped barking.

'William! Hi. Erm, are you OK?' It was still raining and by the sight of his wet clothes it seemed he'd been out in it for a while.

'I, erm, I came to see if *you're* OK actually. I've had a look around the garden, you've got a tree down and the shed at the far end has lost its door. Apart from that you've got off lightly.' Clara stared at him, rain was dripping from his hair, streaming down his face, he wiped a droplet off the end of his nose.

'I tried to call you a few times, but it went straight to voicemail, so I thought I'd erm, come over. I'm sorry, I probably shouldn't have. It's just that I thought seeing as you don't know anyone, there might have been a problem and you wouldn't know what to do, and, I .... I'm rambling, I'm sorry. Anyway, I'll be off, sorry to disturb you and your friend, and you Gus.' He turned to go before his reddened cheeks revealed his embarrassment. What must she think of him? Why had he thought to check on someone he sold a house to two months ago?

'My friend's gone home. It's just me and Gus.' William turned back to face her. Clara opened the door wider, 'Come in, you're soaking wet. I'll put the kettle on.' William stepped into the hallway, his black jeans stuck to his legs, and how he wished he'd not worn his old brown shoes with the holes in the sole that he'd been meaning to replace for almost a year. He took them off and walked into the kitchen, his wet socks leaving footprints on the floor behind him. Clara almost skipped into the kitchen, feeling light-headed and just a bit giddy she switched on the kettle.

'Damn, the electricity's still out.' She had no idea what else to offer someone to drink on a Sunday morning. Milk? Water?

'Let me have a look at your fuse box,' William offered, and disappeared into the cupboard under the stairs. Moments later the kettle started to boil. 'The switch had tripped; it should all work now.' He emerged looking relieved to have served a purpose.

'I hope you didn't mind me popping over, it's just that when I saw you the other day and you said you were living here it struck me that you wouldn't know who to call if you had a problem. Anyway, no major damage. Call it our 'After Sales Service!' William half laughed, hopefully his explanation seemed genuine, hopefully she didn't think he was stalking her.

He'd not been able to get her out of his head since bumping into her at the pet store. *So, she's staying in Norfolk permanently. That's great, because now she lives much closer. But on the other hand that's difficult, because now she lives much closer!* At least during the week he knew she was in London so it was pointless hoping he might ~~see~~ bump into her in some random way. Clara Richmond had frequently occupied his mind since their very first meeting. At first he found it annoying, it distracted him at work, and he was too busy for distractions. At weekends he would wonder if she was at the cottage. Why couldn't he just forget about her?

Clara pulled her dressing gown around her in a fruitless attempt to disguise the fact that she was still wearing her pyjamas. It wasn't exactly how she wanted to look if she'd received notice that William was calling. *Goodness knows what my hair looks like,'* she wondered. *I must try and make a good impression, even if I look like Worzel Gummidge!*

'It was so kind of you, I really do appreciate it. I'd been up half the night because of all the noise. I used the torch on my phone to read but then it ran out of charge. Tea or coffee?'

'Tea please, white no sugar.' William stood looking out the window towards the sea. Clara glanced at him while she was pouring the water from the kettle. She wasn't sure what it was about him but there was definitely something that drew her to like him. *Yes, it's definitely the blue eyes, but there's something else... something extra. Why had he dashed over in the pouring rain?*

'Here,' Clara handed him his drink.

'So... how are you settling in?' William looked around at the sparsely furnished living room then sat in the armchair. Gus had jumped onto the sofa, he guessed that was where Clara would sit.

'So far so good.' Clara snuggled up to Gus, curling her legs underneath her, he put his chin on her lap. 'As you can see, Gus has made himself at home. He loves the garden, especially around the old barn where the red tractor is. I don't know why.'

William laughed. 'That's where the old pig pen used to be.'

'How's Lottie?' Clara asked, breaking the slightly awkward silence that followed.

'She's adorable,' William smiled as he thought about her. 'She slept through last night, she sleeps in a crate. It's her den.' Clara could imagine Gus's reaction to a crate. One of disdain and disbelief she imagined, then he'd ignore it completely!

'Well, perhaps she might like to meet Gus some time.' She couldn't believe how forward she was being. Freya would be proud of her, but what was she trying to achieve?

'That would be great,' William responded standing up. 'Oh well, I must get back, she'll be wondering where I am.' Clara wanted to ask if anyone else would be wondering where he was, but it didn't seem an appropriate question to ask. What if the '*she*' who was waiting for him wasn't Lottie?

Closing the front door Clara's first response was to look in a mirror to see exactly what she looked like. Realising for the first time there wasn't a single mirror in the cottage, she wasn't sure if that was good or bad, she made a mental note to buy a full-length mirror that week, just in case he came back.

12

Clara was thankful she'd had a good night's sleep as she began the three-hour plus drive to Kent with Gus. They broke their journey halfway with a drive-through meal and a quick comfort stop for them both, then Gus settled back down to sleep the rest of the way.

Linda was waiting at the front door for them when they arrived, she'd been looking through the window for the past half an hour. Even though he'd never met her Gus wagged his tail and allowed himself to be fussed, excited by her high pitched 'Oh you are a lovely doggy' voice. Clara stood waiting her for turn to be made a fuss of.

'I see, I come second now for your attention!' she joked. Linda gave her a big hug.

'Come and tell me all your news, it's lovely to see you both.' Clara let Gus into the back garden and left the door open so he could wander in and out. Linda poured the tea and cut two pieces of freshly baked cake, waiting to hear how her daughter owned a dog when she worked in London all day and lived in an apartment!

'... and so we can visit you any time now and we're not limited to weekends, which is fantastic.' Clara finished relaying part of her news and cut herself a second piece of cake.

'Well, I think it's high time you slowed down, so I'm happy for you. What are your plans for the cottage? I don't remember the inside that well, I've blocked out that part of my life for so long.' Linda still found it painful to think about her parents and her childhood in Norfolk. She trusted Clara's judgement so didn't question her decision to give up work as she knew it wouldn't have been taken lightly.

The next day they took Gus to Haysden Country Park, a local Nature Reserve on the outskirts of Tonbridge. Clara and Linda walked arm and arm around the lake while Gus weaved backwards and forwards on his long lead, sniffing and snuffling his way through the grass and investigating as much of the undergrowth as he could. They spent an hour sitting on a bench overlooking the lake, Gus lay beside them basking in the autumn sunshine, while Clara and Linda drank tea from their flask and ate the tuna mayonnaise sandwiches they'd brought with them.

Clara explained about the changes at work and how it seemed the right time for a lifestyle makeover. She spoke about Elsa and finally Minty. They leant with their heads together as they shed tears over their lovely Minty, sharing happy memories. Gus looked up at Clara then lay his head on her foot, as if to say *'I'm here for you.'*

The next day Clara received an email from the HR department of Coopers & Leigh acknowledging her conversation with Dan Sayer about her back injury and confirming the company sick pay arrangements. She would need to visit her GP for a sick note and send it to the office. It wasn't the clean break Clara had hoped for, but it was an interim solution. She called her doctor's surgery, but they didn't have an appointment until 3 weeks' time as it wasn't urgent. HR made an appointment with the company Doctor for the coming week. Linda was more than happy to look after Gus while Clara took a train to London to 'see a friend'. She felt guilty lying to her mum, but the truth would have meant revealing to her the horrors of her relationship with Dan.

Waiting in the doctor's surgery Clara rehearsed her story of how she had injured her back moving a sofa. She hoped she could feign an acceptable amount of pain to warrant a lengthy sick note. Dr Yvon Walker smiled as Clara walked slowly into her office and gingerly sat down opposite her, ready to fake it as much as she needed, but the Doctor's opening gambit took her completely by surprise.

'You've been with Coopers & Leigh for a number of years I see. If you could change one thing at work, what would it be? Clara sat dumbfounded; she had prepared for what she assumed the questions would be; *How did you injure your back? How does the injury affect you? What measures have you taken to improve your symptoms? Can you touch your toes.....?* But she was completely flummoxed and she couldn't think of anything except the picture of Dan that appeared at the front of her mind. Not the Dan that he was now, but from back then, his face inches from hers, menacing, threatening. The image was so intense she didn't notice the steady flow of tears trickling down her face.

After a few moments she realised the doctor was sitting quietly, waiting patiently, watching her reaction, not interrupting, just giving her time, time to speak when she was ready. Clara wiped her tears away with both hands. Dr Walker held out a box of tissues. Clara took one and blew her nose.

'I, erm, I wasn't expecting that, I'm sorry. I'm not sure where that came from.' The doctor smiled kindly.

'Was your reaction just now related to work?' Clara's carefully sculpted list of responses dissolved into pieces as she found herself opening up and confiding to this gentle lady sat in front of her.

She wasn't sure how long it took to say everything that needed to come out, and was surprised how the words flowed as easily as her tears.

'... so there is no way I can work with him, I *can't* be there.' Dr Walker deliberated for a few moments. Clara wondered if she'd said too much. Had she been wrong to confess?

'Tell me Clara, do you feel depressed by your current situation?' Clara thought it was an odd question and looked at the doctor who raised her eyebrows. 'Because if you feel depressed then I can offer you some medication and / or time off work until you feel able to return. I would recommend that you seek counselling for your past experiences, as well as your current circumstances, which may take some time to work through. If that were the case, I would recommend that you do not go to work until we review your situation in, say, 3 months. From what you have told me, it would be perfectly plausible for the events to be the cause of emotional trauma and depression, a form of PTSD. So, tell me Clara, do you feel depressed by your current situation?' Clara looked at her open mouthed. Could it really be that easy?

'Yes,' she replied quietly.

Clara was still in a daze as she walked out of Tonbridge train station but the sight of Gus and Linda brought a smile to her face, filled with relief she hugged Linda.

'That's a lovely hug. Has something happened?'

'I'm fine mum, just relieved I've left London and changed my life.' Clara hated lying to her mum, but the truth would have been too awful for her to bear. Gus sat patiently next to Linda waiting for Clara to notice him.

'Hi Gus.' At the sound of his name, he stood and wagged his tail as Clara bent to stroke him. Life was going to be so much better with Gus around.

The following days flew by with more lovely walks with Gus,

and Linda shared the few happy childhood memories she had of Norfolk. They were mainly about Granny but also about her best friend from school, Christine, whom she had not heard from since moving to Tonbridge. Her parents had forbidden any contact and she had missed Christine for many years.

'I could try and find her,' Clara offered. 'If she's from a farming family they're probably all still there.'

Linda was horrified. 'I couldn't possibly tell her what really happened, what would she think of me?'

'Mum, she won't care, it was so long ago. Write down what you remember about her and I'll make some discreet enquiries.'

After breakfast Clara and Gus set off for Norfolk. She was sad to be leaving her mum but was ready to go 'home'. Linda packed a huge magic ginger cake that would probably last a fortnight, and yesterday's left-over chicken for Gus. Clara wished her mum would be able to visit them in Norfolk, but neither of them had suggested it. She realised it may be some considerable time before she felt able to, or maybe she never would.

Clara and Gus both jumped out of the car into the driveway when they got back to Norfolk.

'We're *home* Gus! Let's go and see the sea.' As they looked across the dark, still waters Clara took a deep breath in, and she was sure Gus did too. 'Come on Gus, time for tea and cake.'

13

The HR department at Coopers & Leigh emailed to confirm receipt of Dr Walker's sick note covering 3 months, after which she would review Clara's situation. Three months felt like a lifetime to Clara, who hadn't dared believe the doctor would be so sympathetic. She'd been prepared for a full-scale interrogation which may have given her a couple of weeks' grace at most.

Following her meeting with Clara, an incensed Dr Walker sent her report to HR. As Dan was Clara's boss she was obliged to send him a copy. In addition, she included a separate note in his envelope.

Dear Mr Sayer,
Today I met with your employee, Clara Richmond. I understand you are aware of the circumstances forcing Ms Richmond into the untenable position she now finds herself, following your appointment as her manager. Perhaps you may find it is within your power to find a suitable solution to her situation and undertake to resolve the circumstances in which she finds herself unable to return to work.

Yours sincerely.......

A rush of blood to his head generated beads of sweat that trickled down his forehead and the back of his neck. His breathing became rapid and shallow. *What had that stupid bitch said?*

Clara's outburst had left him sitting open mouthed. It was exactly the opposite of what he'd expected.

Having discovered his ex-girlfriend would be working for him he'd fantasised about them hooking up again while his wife was in the States. Clara had always been so eager to please him, so compliant. He was sure he had time to rekindle her feelings for him, with a little gentle persuasion, and reawaken her accommodating disposition. Having received her email suggesting they meet he was confident a reunion was imminent, perhaps even that night. He couldn't believe his luck. He'd opened his briefcase and taken out three condoms. A spare in case the first broke, and one for luck. He was always careful to ensure his briefcase was locked, his wife didn't need to know about his extra-curricular activities. Besides, he'd never actually told her he wasn't going to sleep with anyone else, he felt their marriage vows had been a bit vague on the subject.

He stared at Dr Walker's letter as it lay open on his desk. What exactly did she know? It reminded him of the one he'd received a week before he left for England, from a New York solicitor acting on behalf of a young intern he'd had a one-night stand with two weeks earlier. He hadn't seen her at work after that, not that he was looking for her, he'd assumed she'd gone on holiday. Anyway, what right did she have to change her mind just at the wrong time? What was he supposed to do when she'd taken him past the point of no return? Having previously rejected the offer of returning to England, he reconsidered and magnanimously volunteered his services as a great favour to the company, and at great personal expense since his wife would remain living in the States. He packed his bags and left within a week; a month earlier than his contract stated. *Let them try and subpoena me from across the pond*, he thought. Even though it was her word against his he couldn't afford another costly divorce. He was looking forward to seeing Clara again and working his charm on her.

14

The parish magazine proved to be a rich source of information for Clara, with local news and small businesses filling its pages.

'This is better than Google,' Clara informed Gus.

'Fenced In' erected a small picket fence to create an enclosure around the patio so Gus could meander in and out of the cottage, and a gate gave them access to the rest of the garden when he was on the lead. Clara bought a garden swing chair so they could spend time outside together, she would read her book or close her eyes and listen to the birds singing. After sniffing the boundary of his enclosure Gus would eventually settle at her feet, his chin resting comfortably on her slippers.

Clara helped Malcolm, the local handy man, lay a path from the drive to the front door and decided it was a far more rewarding form of exercise than going to the gym had ever been. He fitted a wooden five bar gate spanning the entrance to the driveway and fixed a new 'A Stone's Throw' sign on it. Clara kept the old original sign as a keepsake.

Clara began to fill the garden with an eclectic mix of plants as she potted up planters she'd found hidden around the garden, enjoying arranging them on the patio. She resurrected the old clothes-line that stretched between two tall metal poles and the wind rolling in from the sea dried her laundry in record time. Malcolm also secured a bench to the ground at the end of the garden looking out to sea. She and Gus loved spending their evenings looking at the clouds reflected in the water. On rainy days Clara wrapped Gus up inside her oversized kagool with his nose under her chin poking out the hole. It was his favourite time of the day; laying against her beating heart and held in her arms, their bodies keeping each other warm.

Clara and Gus settled into an easy routine. He would wake early, Clara would take him downstairs, opening the door to the patio and leaving him to eat his breakfast. She would take a cup of tea back to bed and fall asleep again until about 8.30am, having drunk only half her tea. Gus waited patiently in his bed for her to wake up again. During the day they would walk to the next village and often beyond. She was amazed by the number of people who sold home grown produce at the end of their driveway, placing an honesty box for customers to leave their money. There was an endless source of fresh eggs and seasonal vegetables within a few short miles, she always took a carrier bag with her whenever they went for a walk, returning with fresh produce she would make into healthy, wholesome meals. She at last understood what 'cooking from scratch' truly meant. Ready meals were a distant memory from another life.

They visited Linda, who bought Gus his own bed for when he came to stay, and the three of them spent many hours exploring the open spaces in and around Tonbridge. Clara still hadn't invited her to Norfolk and Linda didn't ask.

Freya and Daisy visited together at the end of October. Daisy brought news of Coopers & Leigh, hot from the marketing department grapevine.

'Talk is that you had a breakdown because you were overlooked for promotion, *yet again*, as you've not been to work since Grant's leaving / Dan Sayer's '*appearing*' do. Some people suspect you've run off with Grant!' Apparently, Dan's been having loads of meetings with HR, everyone's worried there's a big shake up coming. If you don't come back soon Clara you might find yourself out of a job.' Daisy looked at Clara. 'What are you going to do with Gus when you're back in London? Will you get a dog walker?'

Clara wasn't sure why she hadn't seen that question coming. How could she keep up the pretence, wasn't Daisy her friend?

Clara took a second to answer, glancing first at Freya.

'I, er. I'm not coming back.'

Daisy looked confused. 'What? What do you mean? You've got to come back. You can't have just left!'

'I can't say anything just yet, you must promise not to tell anyone. I'll tell you when I can.'

Freya quickly changed the subject.

'I still haven't found anywhere else to live, I keep being pipped to the post, there are so many people looking to rent.' Clara wondered why she hadn't thought of it before.

'Move into the spare room at my flat,' Clara suggested. 'That'll give you more time to look. Freya held her arms open and ran to hug Clara.

'Really? That would be a-ma-zing, thank you so much. Oh my God, can I move in next weekend? I'll pay a decent rent, and I promise to keep it tidy.' It made perfect sense for them both.

When Freya and Daisy returned to London Clara was relieved not to be going with them. It did feel strange being alone again though. A quietness returned to the cottage, and Clara and Gus settled back into their country life.

Clara had thought, and quietly hoped, that William would have been in touch again, but she'd not heard from him since his surprise visit after the storm. She began to think he'd been telling the truth, that it was the company's 'after sales service' and perhaps she hadn't received preferential treatment at all. Had she and Freya read him all wrong? Perhaps he wasn't into her. She tried to push him from her mind but pictures of him would float into her head; the first time she saw him, waiting at the cottage door after she ran across the driveway, standing at the edge of the garden looking out to sea, holding Lottie in his arms and appearing at her front door with rain dripping down his face. Clara turned to Gus laying in his bed, gazing back with so much love in his eyes.

'What am I thinking of Gus, I don't need a man in my life, I've got you. Besides, they only complicate matters. Whereas you, my boy, are an absolute joy.' Gus wagged his tail, he loved it when she spoke to him in that voice. It was the kind of tail that curled elegantly over his back, the hair left long so it waved like a flag. He was asleep long before Clara, who tried to push pictures of Dan Sayer out of her mind. So many nights, as she was about to drift into sleep his face would appear. Why did he have to come back and haunt her?

15

The inevitable email Clara had been dreading arrived, a date for her follow-up appointment with Dr Walker. Another trip to London would have evoked concerned questions from Linda. Clara and Gus stayed at her London apartment the night before her appointment so Gus could get used to the new environment. He settled quickly as he could already smell Clara there.

Her meeting with the doctor was brief. 'I'm sorry but I can't give you any more time off, just the two weeks remaining on the certificate I gave you. You need to find a way forward. Either resign, find a way to go back or tell HR why you can't work with him. I wish you well, and good luck.'

She'd known the doctor couldn't protect her indefinitely. She would contact the estate agents and set things in motion.

Clara stood at the entrance to her apartment block hoping Gus had been okay. Searching in her coat pocket for the fob to activate the door she felt a strong hand firmly grip her shoulder. Her entire body flinched then stiffened with fear as she caught her breath. It took just a minutia of a split second for a hundred scenarios to flash through her head as her body and mind prepared itself to stave off an attack. Her stomach churned; she dropped her bag. What did they want? With fists clenched she began to tremble, her voice caught in her throat, would she even be able to scream? Clara prepared herself to fight, to run, to do anything to stay alive.

'Clara, hey Clara,' she heard her name from behind, but panic had already unleashed itself from deep inside her. She turned to lash out with her right fist. Dan caught it mid-air before it brushed his face.

'Clara! It's me.' Her hand was still in his grip, her eyes wide open like a wild banshee, but seeing his face certainly didn't make her feel any safer. The built-up adrenalin inside her exploded.

'You fucking idiot, what do you think you're doing? I thought I was being attacked.' She hated that he made her swear, she'd always prided herself on being able to find other ways to express herself. 'What the hell do you want? And let go of me,' she demanded, trying to pull her fist from his tight grip, but he held onto it. She hated that he'd touched her.

'I just needed to talk to you. You've obviously been saying some stuff to that doctor woman, you could get me into a lot of trouble.'

'I told you to leave me alone,' she shouted. 'You're so wrapped up in yourself you don't give a damn about who you hurt.' Suddenly, the door to the reception of her apartment building opened, Clara heard Bill, the concierge, ask if she was OK. Clara pulled her hand free from Dan's grip, picked up her bag and walked into the building. Bill closed the door behind them, giving Dan a *don't mess with me* look through the glass.

'Do you know him?' He asked.

'Unfortunately, yes. But he frightened the life out of me. He's an ex who I told to leave me alone.' Clara was still trying to get her breath back. Bill pointed to the cctv camera.

'If you ever need any evidence, it'll be on there. I'll make sure we keep a copy.'

Clara let herself into her apartment, shaken and angry, but Gus greeted her with such ebullience she couldn't help but smile at him.

'Did you miss me Gus? You've been such a good boy.' She swept him up in her arms and buried her face into his neck.

'Let's get out of here and go home.' Clara looked around her apartment. It looked the same, but it wasn't, it was different. Someone else lived here now and she wasn't sure she ever wanted to come back.

They arrived back home not a moment too soon for them both. Gus ran around the cottage relieved to be back to the peace and quiet, he ran upstairs and put himself to bed, exhausted from his ordeal of strange London noises.

Clara made a mug of tea and buttered a large fruit scone. Spooning on her favourite peach jam she put her feet up on the sofa and sighed. Thank God she was here, safe. Here she was happy, here she would stay. Tea and scones, '*Home Sweet Home.* '

That night Clara saw the clock pass every hour whilst Gus slept soundly in his bed. *How do dogs sleep so much and so easily?* she pondered, wishing she knew their secret. Dr Walker's words ricocheted in her head like a pinball machine. She had two weeks sick leave to make a decision. She weighed up her options. Tell HR the truth, but it would be her word against a senior Director who had only just been relocated at great expense to the company. Besides, their lawyers and barristers would wipe the floor with any solicitor she could afford if she smeared his name and their reputation. She could simply resign, but that didn't seem fair. Going to the police wasn't an option, it was so long ago and she didn't have any evidence.

Clara eventually managed a fitful doze somewhere between 5.30am and 6.45am. Gus woke up full of beans after his marathon sleep, he scratched at the door and whimpered, alerting her to the fact that he really needed to go outside as quickly as possible.

Clara dragged herself out of bed, her head woozy with confusion, where was she? Hardly able to open her eyes she felt around with her feet for her slippers, which weren't in their usual place under her bed. She remembered they were in the washing as she'd spilt jam on them the morning they left for London. Barefooted, and still with her eyes barely open, she made her way down the stairs holding onto the rail.

'Wait Gus, I'm on my way,' she called out to him as he paced back and forth by the kitchen door. With her eyes barely open, and reaching what she thought was the last tread, she let go of the handrail to step onto the hallway floor but instead stepped into thin air. She caught her heel on the edge of the last step and fell onto the floor in a crumpled heap. She let out a piercing scream as she landed sideways on her right foot and a bolt of pain shot through her leg. Gus came running, licking her face and nudging her, clearly still needing to go out. Clara felt sick and light-headed, telling herself not to faint, and despite the excruciating pain, she dragged herself to the front door. Gus danced in circles around her, barking with more urgency now. Clara was able to just about lift herself high enough on her left leg, stretching her arm as far as she could, her fingertips somehow able to turn the latch and open the door.

'Don't go far Gus,' she warned him as she slumped back onto the floor and leant her back and head against the wall. She left the door slightly open, welcoming the cool air on her face as it eased her light-headedness. Clara took several deep breaths. After a few moments the cool air became a little too cool for her in her light cotton pyjamas.

'Gus,' she called out. 'Gus!' She listened for a sign of him but there was nothing. Clara pulled the door open wider. She was starting to shiver in the cold morning air.

'GUS!' she shouted. Looking out Clara saw that in her haste to get indoors last night she'd left the gate open. 'GUS!' He was no-where to be seen. Clara briefly forgot the throbbing pain in her right ankle as she realised her predicament. Her iPhone and Apple watch were upstairs charging on the bedside table, she lived in the middle of no-where, she guessed she had broken her ankle and her dog had gone missing. Wishing she'd had a landline phone connected when she had the chance, Clara realised she had to somehow get back upstairs. She couldn't go looking for looking for Gus, she could only hope that he would find his way home after whatever adventure he was on. First, she needed to get help for herself. Leaving the door closed to, just enough so Gus could push it open, Clara dragged herself towards the stairs. Very slowly, using her left foot to push herself up, she made her way up the stairs backwards, sitting on each step on her way up. Her right ankle was beginning to swell but she gritted her teeth. Her ascent took a few minutes as she stopped and breathed through the pain, but there was still no sign of Gus. Eventually, she reached the top where she bottom-shuffled into her bedroom and leant against the side of her bed. With her phone now in her hand, and help within reach, she hesitated. Who would she call? Why did she want to call William? He'd think it was very odd. Instead, she dialled 999 and was told an ambulance would be with her once one was available. She managed to get herself onto the bed and under the duvet. Although the pain was agonising she was so tired she dozed off. She was woken by the sound of a voice calling out from downstairs. Were the paramedics here already?

'Hello. Hello, is anyone at home?' It was a man's voice, noticeably an older man with a strong Norfolk accent. 'Hello, ha' you lost a dawg?'

'I'm upstairs,' Clara called out. 'I've hurt my ankle. Is it a small fluffy black and white dog?'

'It is,' the voice answered. Gus rushed up the stairs to find her, jumping on the bed and licking her face.

'Gus where have you been? I was so worried about you.' She was relieved to see him and particularly thankful to hear the sound of a human voice.

'You OK?' the voice called.

'Erm, not really, I'm waiting for an ambulance, I can't walk.' Clara heard slow, heavy footsteps climbing the stairs before stopping at the top.

'I'm in the room directly in front of you.' Clara stared at the door in anticipation, wondering momentarily if she'd just invited a serial killer into her bedroom. A small head appeared wearing a flat cap, peaking from behind the door. It belonged to an elderly gentleman.

'What ha' you gone and done?' he asked. Clara explained about the stairs and how she hadn't lived here long and didn't know anyone.

'Well, I'm Fred and I live across the field there, been 'ere all me life. Just like my father, and his father afore 'im and his father afore 'im. Just me, now the missus has passed. I saw your dog a runnin' in my field. I shouted "*slow you down*" but he dint take no notice a me.' Clara was mesmerised by Fred's accent; he seemed such a lovely old gentleman and she warmed to him instantly.

'You dint wanna let that dawg run out, he could get run down like what that dog and young lad did on that there road all those years ago. That were a roight shame, he were only a little lad.' Clara was confused. There was very little traffic that passed by the cottage but what did he mean a dog and little boy got run over?

'What happened to the dog and the little boy?' She wasn't sure she actually wanted to know, it sounded horrific.

'That lad's father, David what lived 'ere back then, well 'e left 'is new tractor out the front and went in for a cup o tea, like always. The young lad, he climbed on the tractor. He'd been crazin' his father to drive it so I spuz he took his chance. David, he dint harf gev him such a holler when he came out, the lad jumped down and ran ahind the tractor. Well, he musta released the handbrake cuz that tractor rolled backards as the road's on the huh. The lad saw his dawg was in the way and tried to save her. Well, nuff to say they dint make it in time.' Fred looked down at his feet, then turned and looked out the window. Clara was horrified by the story, but the bit about the boy didn't make sense, David's son was Michael. She didn't have time to ask Fred any questions as a woman's voice called out from downstairs.

'Hello, paramedics here.'

16

Six weeks in plaster! How on earth was she going to manage? Fred had kindly said he'd check in on Gus while she was at the hospital. Clara gave him the key to the kitchen door so he could let himself in. For some reason she trusted him completely, even though she'd just met him.

Clara arrived home late in the evening. The main accident and emergency department was in Norwich and Fred hadn't been joking when he said she'd be there for hours. The taxi driver kindly helped her across the shingle driveway on her new crutches. Gus leapt up and down when she opened the door, she had to wait for him to calm down before she could get indoors.

Clara guessed that going up and downstairs on her bottom was probably the safest thing to do. She was certain she'd be awake all night trying to get comfortable, but was so exhausted that in the two seconds it took for her to pull the duvet over her, she was asleep.

By lunchtime the next day she had to concede that she needed help. She ordered a food delivery online for the next day and then called her mum.

No sooner had Clara told Linda that she'd broken her ankle she announced, 'I'm on my way.' After she'd put the phone down, Linda packed a case and set off for Norfolk. It wasn't until she reached the M25 heading north she realised the enormity of what she was doing. She'd not returned home in all these years. She'd only learnt about her parents' deaths after the event, just like David's. There had never been a reason to return. Until now. But her daughter needed her, and even if she lived in Timbuctoo, she was going. She'd deal with her feelings later. Linda turned on the CD player and twisted the volume dial up in anticipation. She only had one CD in the car. Michael Bublé kept her company the whole way as she followed the satnav app on her phone and didn't stop until she pulled slowly into the driveway of A Stone's Throw.

It was much as she remembered it, but as Linda stepped out of the car she felt as though she was fourteen years old all over again. Was she ready to be back in Norfolk, to face so many ghosts? The memory of the last day she was at A Stone's Throw engulfed her.

* * *

Linda was sure even the birds were too sad to sing their songs on that August day as she walked alone, yet surrounded by so many. Just ahead, her parents and David and Janine held onto each other, arms linked, fused together, coexisting in their grief. But who did Linda belong with? Granny had passed away barely a year earlier, for no particular reason other than she decided she was ready. Linda wondered now if somehow Granny had known, had a premonition about what was going to happen. Known that she'd be needed to help little Stephen cross over to the other side, so that he wasn't alone when he got there.

The hearse carrying the small white coffin adorned with sunflowers, slowly led the way while most of Norfolk's farming community walked behind, heads bowed, united in their sorrow. Together they walked the mile to the church, never changing pace, adorned in black, holding each other's hands, mourning the loss of 'Tinker', as he'd been affectionately known. As Linda walked behind the rest of her family, she felt disconnected. Since the accident they hadn't shared their grief with her, nor acknowledged hers. She was an addendum, an incidental member of the family.

They seemed to notice her even less after Stephen died. Their grief was insurmountable. David and his wife moved into the big house with her parents. When she wasn't at school Linda fed the family, did their laundry and kept the house clean and tidy. The men carried on farming while the women sat with their sorrow in the parlour, knitting and sewing, but rarely talking. Linda felt invisible.

* * *

The sound of Gus' paws scampering across the gravel drew Linda's attention back to the present as he jumped around her, so excited that he was beside himself. Linda looked over to the cottage where her daughter leant against the open doorway, balancing on one foot. It was a surreal sight. With Gus still jumping up and down to get her attention, Linda walked towards her daughter with a mixture of emotions; relief at finally arriving after such a long drive, and memories of her family she'. She embraced Clara and gave her a worried look.

'I'm fine mum, honestly. Just a bit physically challenged at the moment. Thanks for coming.'

Linda stepped over the dip in the middle of the old wooden threshold, worn thin by the footsteps of her ancestors, and into the cottage. Apart from the furniture it seemed that nothing much had changed, as far as she could remember. Linda hadn't been back there since the day of the funeral.

Clara hobbled behind her on crutches as Linda walked through the downstairs living room through to the kitchen. Looking around she spotted the kettle and set about making cups of tea. She produced a magic ginger cake from her bag, which made Clara laugh and Gus get excited, as he loved ginger cake. They all slept well that night. Even Linda.

Later the next afternoon as they contemplated what to eat, Gus jumped up and barked as he heard footsteps on the gravel, then a face appeared at the kitchen door.

'Only me,' Fred called out.

'Hi Fred, come on in,' Clara replied, 'we're in the living room.' Fred stood in the doorway of the kitchen.

'Fred, this is my mum...'

'Cor blast me if it ain't Little Linda!' Fred announced. 'Well why dint you tell me yar mother's Little Linda? Blimey, it's a foo yars since you was in these hare parts.'

'Hello Mr Wells.' Linda smiled awkwardly at the familiar face looking at her in astonishment. *He looks the same age now as he did 43 years ago,* she recalled. Sensing her mum's discomfort Clara intersected.

'Thank you so much for looking after Gus. As you can see, the cavalry is here now. Mum was just about to drive me to the pub, weren't you mum?' Clara glanced at Linda, whose look of relief spread into a smile.

'Yes, no cooking for us tonight!'

Fred took the hint and turned to leave.

'Well, I thought I'd see how you're doin'. Keep yew a troshin.' Clara followed him to the kitchen door, beginning to master the crutches quite skilfully.

'Thanks Fred, I owe you a drink.' Fred touched the brim of his flat cap and left.

Clara returned to Linda. 'You OK mum? You probably didn't expect to see someone you knew quite so soon.'

'I'm fine, it was a bit of a shock seeing him, but I've survived it. So! Where are we going?'

Clara said she knew of a dog friendly pub a few miles away set in a deer park, so off they went. Returning home three hours later they were still talking about the food, friendly atmosphere and the herd of elegant deer that roamed freely outside as they'd watched mesmerised through the pub window. The chef had appeared during their dessert and offered Gus a roast potato, which he demolished in an instant.

'I'm so pleased you're here mum,' Clara gave Linda a big hug. 'I'm sorry you're sleeping on Freya's blow-up bed though.'

'I'll be fine,' Linda laughed, 'I'm so tired I could fall asleep on a washing line!'

The next morning, as Linda was making scrambled eggs on toast, Clara asked about the accident Fred had told her about.

'Mum. Who was the little boy who got run over by the tractor outside?' Linda stopped stirring the eggs for a few moments, then continued to beat them quickly. Clara thought perhaps she shouldn't have asked. Linda carried the pan over to the table and spooned the eggs onto the plates. Neither of them liked the eggs directly on their toast because it made it soggy, and neither of them liked soggy bread. Gus didn't give a hoot and golloped the small bowl of egg and toast crusts he'd been given. Linda sat down, picked up her knife and fork and started to cut her toast.

'He was David and Janine's first boy.' Linda stopped, staring at the food on her plate, deep in thought. 'It was a terrible time.' Clara sensed her mum was having difficulty speaking about it, perhaps she shouldn't have said anything. There was so much she didn't know about her life in Norfolk.

'It's just that when Gus got out Fred found him and mentioned it when he brought him home.' Thankfully Gus eased the moment by bringing Linda his favourite toy and putting it on her foot so she could throw it for him. They both laughed and Clara changed the subject.

The next afternoon Clara went back to bed for a sleep. She found it exhausting getting around on crutches, especially the stairs. Linda took Gus for a walk. It was a cold, dry but windy day.

'It's exactly the right weather to blow the cobwebs away,' Linda told Clara. In truth, she needed some space to process her feelings about being back in Norfolk, seeing old Mr Wells and telling Clara about Stephen.

17

Forty-five years had passed since Linda had travelled down to Kent by coach. Her parents took her to the bus station in Norwich, handed her an envelope with £100 in it, turned around and walked away. She never saw them again.

In London she'd been met by Gavin, looking sheepish, with his parents standing either side of him, looking disappointed. Linda stood holding her suitcase as they scrutinised her. She was petrified. The journey to their home seemed to take forever, and while she and Gavin both sat in the back of the car, they hardly exchanged words. Gavin's mum did ask her a little about her home life but mostly they all sat in silence. Eventually, they pulled up outside a small, detached bungalow, with a neat front lawn and just enough space for two cars on the driveway. It was much smaller than Linda had imagined. She was sure Gavin had told her his father was a solicitor. *Perhaps he wasn't a very good one,* she thought.

'Here we are,' Gavin's mother announced as she stepped out of the car and opened the rear door for Linda. Gavin and his father remained seated. Gavin's mother took Linda's suitcase from the boot and walked up the path, Linda followed. As they approached the door it opened. An elderly lady wearing an apron, her hands covered in flour, stood looking at them both. Linda thought she appeared rather stern.

'This is her, mum.' Gavin's mother announced. Linda was

confused.

'Well go on in girl,' she ushered Linda indoors. The small entrance lobby led to a large rectangular living room. Off to the right Linda could see a kitchen with a small table and chairs in the middle.

'Follow Grandma, she'll show you to your room.' Gavin's mother gestured for Linda to follow the elderly lady through into an inner hallway at the rear of the bungalow. She turned right, opening a door into a square room with a single bed and small wardrobe.

'This is your room dear,' Grandma told her. 'You can put your things in the wardrobe.' Linda turned to look for Gavin's mother but she was gone. She looked back at the elderly lady, confused.

'You're to stay here, with me. I know you're scared but you'll be fine. When the baby comes, I can show you what to do. I've had three of my own.'

That night Linda cried herself to sleep. She hugged her slightly swollen belly and vowed to never abandon her child. She wasn't even aware of where she was, only that she was somewhere in Kent, over a hundred miles from home. Except that wasn't home anymore, this place was. The next day she learnt she was in Tonbridge.

In the months that followed, Linda and Grandma settled into a quiet way of living. Grandma was a kind lady who shared her love of baking with Linda and taught her how to make her 'magic ginger cake'. Linda grew very fond of her, helping to keep the house clean, cook meals and do all the ironing, as Grandma didn't like ironing. Linda called her Grandma, and for the first time in her life felt as though she belonged. Linda and Grandma began to prepare for the birth. They decorated Linda's bedroom and bought second-hand furniture and equipment.

In many ways Linda was thankful she had come to live here; she imagined life with Gavin's parents would have been strict. She discovered soon after she arrived that his parents had taken him to Southampton for a new start. He was going to become a solicitor. There would be no contact. They had provided her and her child with a home, so had fulfilled their obligation.

Linda was seven months pregnant when Grandma collapsed one morning in the kitchen, holding her chest. Clara sat on the kitchen floor next to her, holding her hand, praying for the ambulance to arrive, telling her how she needed to finish knitting the blanket with the pom poms around the edge. The ambulance arrived within eight minutes of Linda's phone call. The paramedics asked Linda to stay at home.

'You look ready to give birth, it's probably best you stay here, we can't deal with you going into labour,' and they took Grandma off in the ambulance, their blue lights flashing as she watched them fade into the distance.

Shortly after five o'clock that evening the doorbell rang. Linda rushed to open it and saw Gavin's father standing there. Linda stared back at him, neither of them moved. It was then that she knew. She stepped aside, and he walked in. She was terrified of the news he brought.

Mr Richmond informed her that his mother-in-law had unfortunately passed away in the ambulance on the way to the hospital. *Unfortunately?* Linda screamed inside. *How bloody unfortunate for you! It's a tragedy, it's heart breaking, it's devastating.* Linda wrapped her arms around her stomach and wept. Mr Richmond produced a packet of tissues from his pocket, the small travel size wrapped in plastic. He'd obviously been primed by his wife that Linda may be upset. The tissues lasted two minutes. He lasted for seven, and then he left.

Grandma left home for the last time on a chilly morning in early May. Linda travelled with a neighbour behind the funeral car carrying Gavin and his parents. Her eyes never left the hearse they were following. Her wonderful Grandma. Not *her* Grandma; but '*her Grandma*'.

Linda vaguely remembered meeting Gavin's aunt and uncle, Grandma's two other children, and some cousins. It was only then she realised that in the five months they'd spent together, no-one had come to visit. They hadn't needed anyone else. Gavin quietly asked her if she was OK.

'OK in what way? OK about Grandma or OK about you getting me pregnant?'

'Ssssssh,' he said, quickly looking from side to side to see if anyone had heard.

'My parents have said you can stay at Grandma's until after... Well, until you've had... When you've given... you know,' and glanced fleetingly at Linda's bulging stomach. 'They own Grandma's bungalow, so there's no rush.' The service began.

'We are gathered here today to mourn the passing, and to celebrate the life, of Clara Elizabeth Thompson...'

The neighbour took Linda back home again where she sat alone in the living room until she realised it was dark. She thought about all the questions she wished she'd asked Gavin. *And what happens then? Where do we live? Are you going to visit us? Do you actually give a damn about us? Why don't you chop your dick off and stick it up your nose as you clearly can't cope with the consequences?*

Linda muddled through the next few weeks in a haze, growing larger by the day, growing more tired and feeling incredibly lonely and scared.

She attended ante-natal classes alone and met with her midwife who, because of her age and lack of support, contacted Social

Services to assist her claim for financial aid.

Linda joined the library. Now, at eight months pregnant, she realised how unprepared she was. She spent most days learning about breastfeeding, child development and nutrition. Grandma was supposed to teach her what to do. Now she was completely alone in the world. Until the day her waters broke.

18

As Linda and Gus strolled along the narrow country lanes they met very little traffic. Linda picked Gus up whenever a vehicle approached, welcoming the opportunity to cuddle him, until it was safe to walk again. There had been many times over the years when she'd needed a hug and none were available. She'd remained single all this time, never able to trust anyone. She hadn't minded. Clara was her world.

Hearing another vehicle approaching from behind Linda picked Gus up once again and turned to smile at the driver who had slowed to a crawl. It was an old pickup truck, scratched and dented, probably blue, but it was covered in too much mud to tell. The driver lowered the window. It was Fred.

'Cor blummy, you carryin' 'im all the way?'

Linda stroked Gus's head. 'Hello again Mr Wells.' She had hoped to avoid bumping into him so soon, and she definitely wasn't in the mood for small talk, or worse still, interrogation, especially as it was likely to rake up her family history and the reason she had disappeared so quickly all those years ago. Fred had already done the sums in his head. '*Thelma was right all along*,' he thought to himself, recalling his late wife's theory as to Little Linda's sudden disappearance.

Fred, sensing Linda's reluctance to chat, waved and drove on. She set Gus down on the ground and they strolled back to the cottage. As they reached sight of A Stone's Throw Linda remembered the day she heard the devastating news about Stephen.

* * *

She was collecting eggs before school from the chicken run next to the yard, the sound of her mother's scream pierced through her soul and she ran into the farmhouse to find her sobbing on the kitchen floor, the telephone beside her. Hearing a voice on the other end Linda picked it up,

'Hello' she said quietly.

'Linda. Get dad. Stephen's dead.' The sound of her brother weeping at the end of the phone haunted her for many years. She dropped the phone back on the floor, not wanting to end the call, and ran to find her father. As she hurried out of the farmhouse she saw him entering the big barn. Running towards him, she shouted.

'Dad! Dad! Dad!' He turned to see why this child, who he acknowledged only twice a day when she put his food in front of him, would be so eager to gain his attention.

David and Janine moved into the farmhouse. They were still living there the day Linda left for Tonbridge. Only Janine had hugged her that day. David hadn't spoken to her since she'd confided in Janine that she was pregnant. She'd hugged her that day too, but told her she couldn't keep her secret, the family needed to know.

* * *

As they approached the cottage Linda stopped to study the branches of the Christmas tree, running her fingers gently along the fir tree's spines, breathing in its scent.

'Hello Stephen,' she whispered.

Linda turned to look across the fields. It was time to reveal more of her past to Clara, before anyone else did. They walked around the back of the cottage, Linda let Gus off his lead as she opened the gate to the patio. Clara was lounging on the sofa reading when Linda and Gus returned. Gus quickly emptied his water bowl in the kitchen then curled up with his beloved owner.

'Time for tea?' Linda asked as she peered through the kitchen door.

'You read my mind. Yes please.' Clara stretched out, closing her book she stroked Gus' head lightly. He showed his appreciation of her affection with a slight wag of his tail. Hypnotised by her touch his eyes closed, his breathing slowed and he drifted off, dreaming of whatever dogs dream of.

Linda handed Clara a mug and sat in the armchair looking at her.

'What is it?' Clara sensed her mum had something to say.

'I saw Mr Wells again today.' Linda took a sip of her tea. 'There's so much I have tell you that I've spent so many years trying to forget. The trouble is, sitting here it's like it all happened only a short while ago, but when I look at you, I know that's not true.' Clara sat up.

'I'm sorry I brought you here mum, I should have known how difficult it would be for you. Perhaps I shouldn't have bought the cottage after all. Shall we go back to Tonbridge tomorrow?'

Linda knew her life would never be the same again the day the letter arrived, opening the preverbal can of worms. Seeing the Norfolk postmark as she signed for the large white padded envelope, she dreaded what was inside and the repercussions it would bring. She'd left it on the kitchen table unopened for two weeks. She could almost feel the contents stirring inside, anticipating their release, waiting to explode like an aerial firework, spitting out its insides, cascading, raining down, burning everything it touched.

Clara waited as Linda struggled to find the right words. There was no way to avoid it. If she didn't reveal it, others would, had already. Eventually, Linda looked back at her grown-up daughter. Where had all that time gone?

'The Christmas tree that's in the front garden, was planted shortly after Stephen died. He loved Christmas, even his dog was called Holly. Each year he crazed my brother for a real Christmas tree, but David said they were too messy and an artificial one lasted longer. So that's what they had, much to Stephen's disappointment. After the accident David dug a huge hole in the garden close to the cottage. He buried Stephen's dog there and planted the tree... for Stephen. Whenever he walked past he would touch the spines. He threw the artificial one away.'

Clara was horrified to think she'd considered taking the Christmas tree out. Although it was beautiful, it was enormous. Linda continued.

'The tractor David was driving that day was Stephen's favourite. It was bright red and had *Tinker* painted on the side. Stephen's nickname was *Tinker* because he was always into everything. '*You're a right little Tinker,*' we all used to say to him. In a way it wasn't surprising Stephen climbed onto the tractor that day. David never drove it again.'

Clara remembered the old red tractor she'd found in the collapsed barn.

'I've seen it mum, it's in one of the barns, it's still here.' Clara paused. 'Is there anything else I shouldn't touch? Anything else that has special significance?' Linda thought for a moment.

'You must make this place your own, don't dwell on the past.'

'As long as I don't find any skeletons in the cupboards,' Clara laughed. Linda smiled.

'More cake?'

Linda was thankful she didn't bump into Fred again for the rest of her stay. After ten days she had to go back home for an appointment but failed to convince Clara to return with her.

'I'll be fine mum. Besides, Freya and Daisy will be up at the weekend, Gus and I can survive until then. You've made enough ready meals to fill Marks & Spencer's food hall!'

It was a tearful farewell, and they hugged as though they weren't going to see each other for a long time. Gus pulled at Linda's laces on her shoes to try and stop her leaving. 'I'll be back for Christmas Gus, let go of my laces!'

Clara waved as Linda's car pulled out of the drive. Suddenly Norfolk felt a long way from everyone.

19

Freya tried once again to close her suitcase, but it refused to shut, as if objecting to being overloaded. *Why do jumpers take up so much space? Aren't they just wool and air?* she wondered, putting all her weight on the lid in an attempt to squeeze the teeth of the zips together so she could finally close it. She had taken the two weeks off from work running up to Christmas and was looking forward to spending it in Norfolk with Clara and Gus. She went over the rest of the contents of her case in her mind: *wellies, trainers, walking boots, slippers, jeans, waterproof trousers, dressing gown and pyjamas for sitting around the fire toasting marshmallows....* she had bought 2 huge bags of marshmallows just to make sure she wasn't disappointed.

The buzzer to the ground floor door sounded, Freya pressed the button to release the door and called at the intercom.

'Come up Daisy, I'll leave the door open.' Daisy was joining her for the weekend then getting the train back on Sunday afternoon. Finally able to pull the zip around the case, Freya dragged it off the bed and wheeled it into the living room. She was thankful Daisy would be there to help her lift it into the car.

'Damn. Toiletry bag!' Freya's toiletry bag resembled a small suitcase on its own, she'd left it in the bathroom. Stopping to look in the bathroom mirror at her newly tattooed eyebrows she heard a knock at the door.

'Come in Daisy,' she called out. 'Have you got room in your case for a few of my things? She walked back into the living room and froze as she saw Dan Sayer standing in the doorway.

'What are you doing here?' she stuttered.

'I'm looking for Clara,' he replied, confused at seeing Freya but walking further into the flat and looking around like he had every right to be there.

'She's not here, she's out.' Freya stepped back as he walked towards her, her heart pounding, she felt breathless and hot, yet cold at the same time. Dan turned away from her and sat on the sofa.

'I'll wait for her.'

'You can't,' Freya blurted out, 'She's not coming back tonight.' He thought for a moment, stood up and walked back towards the door.

'Tell her when you see her that I'll be back.' Suddenly he stopped. His eyes scanned the flat. Realising they were alone, he turned back to look at her.

'So, it's just me and you then,' he said, walking towards the door to close it. Fearing her only exit would be blocked Freya ran to the door, but he caught her arm.

'Don't you fancy a re-run of New York? I seem to remember you like playing hard to get.' Freya struggled to get free, but he was too strong. 'Just like your friend Clara,' he laughed. That lying bitch has been telling tales.'

Dan pulled her to him, her wrists tight in his grip. He drew her arms around his waist and held her to him, his lips trying to find hers, but she pulled her head away and spat in his face. Releasing her to wipe away her spit he pushed her backwards with brute force. Freya fell on the floor near the doorway. Sensing a chance to escape she quickly opened the door and crawled out into the hall. At that moment the lift door opened and Daisy stood there looking down at her.

'What are you doing on the floor? Are we crawling all the way to Clara's? It's a long way to Norfolk you know!' Seeing the fear in Freya's face Daisy looked up to see Dan Sayer standing in the doorway to Clara's flat.

'Dan!' Daisy could tell something had happened, but she was just as confused to see her boss standing there as she was to see Freya on the floor. Dan walked towards the lift.

'It seems Freya's had a bit too much to drink. Tell Clara I called.' The lift doors closed behind him leaving Freya and Daisy alone in the hallway. Freya burst into tears.

Daisy made them both a strong mug of coffee and sat on the sofa holding Freya's hand until she was calm.

'What did he want Clara for? Did he hurt you?' Freya wasn't ready to give any answers. She stood up and walked to the door, picking up her keys and handbag.

'Can we get out of here?'

Daisy walked over to her and held her hand out for the keys. 'I'll drive.' Freya didn't trust her own judgement behind the wheel at the moment so happily handed them over to Daisy. They loaded the car with their luggage in silence. As they pulled out of the underground car park neither of them noticed Dan Sayer's car following, carefully keeping at least one car between them and him.

On the way to Norfolk, Freya told Daisy about the incident in New York with Dan and what had just happened. Daisy was horrified. *That still didn't explain what he was doing in Clara's apartment*, she thought, but decided it was best to save that question for another time. Stopping halfway for petrol they remained unaware of the dark Audi that followed them off the slip road and parked next to the air pump, waiting for them to set off again. When they reached the narrower Norfolk lanes Dan made sure he was out of sight of their rear-view mirror. They were leading him straight to Clara. *Stupid cows!*

When they eventually reached the cottage Freya jumped out of the car to open the gate. The Audi stopped abruptly, and slowly reversed out of sight, almost colliding with an old pick-up truck that might have been blue if it wasn't covered in mud. Without anywhere to turn around Dan had no option but to drive straight ahead. Passing where Freya and Daisy had pulled in, he quickly took a sideways glance and saw them embracing Clara, who appeared to be on crutches.

'Gotcha,' he said out loud and continued along the road, looking for somewhere to stop and let the annoying truck behind him overtake. It was a hundred yards or so until he reached a widening in the road where he pulled into an entrance to a field. The truck slowly drove past him, its elderly driver watching him carefully. Dan waved him on impatiently.

Fred drove by slowly, looking at the driver of the Audi. Was he lost? The man waved him on so Fred continued, he was on his way to the church to lay flowers on Thelma's grave. Driving back half an hour later he saw the Audi, still where he'd passed it. The driver was walking around the car, looking puzzled. Fred pulled up beside him and opened the window.

'Aryorite?' he asked. The man looked confused.

'Pardon?'

'Aryorite?' Fred repeated. *Perhaps he be a mite deaf,* he considered. 'Ar y o rite boy?' he repeated a bit louder and slower. A look of understanding slowly spread across the man's face.

'I appear to be stuck in the mud.'

'Oh dare,' said Fred, turning off his engine and climbing out of his truck. He looked the driver up and down. His once shiny black shoes were covered in mud and the bottom of his suit trousers were caked halfway to his knees. Fred walked around the Audi, surveying the situation. His wellington boots hadn't been clean since the day he'd bought them, almost 15 years ago.

'We had a lot o' rain a'smornun. Thassa good for my crops but thassa no good fer such a fancy car in these here parts.'

Dan stared at the elderly man. Only understanding half of what he said he smiled, hoping that was the right response. The man spoke again.

'I afeared yew won't be goin' nowhere. That won't go forrards nor backards. Tha' do need towin'. Hold yew hard oil turn 'round and pull yew out.' With that, the man climbed back into his truck and drove off.

Dan had no idea what the man had said so sat back in his car, turned on the engine and put his foot down hard on the accelerator. Mud flew in all directions as the Audi sank further into the sludge. He turned off the engine and flicked through his phone to find the number of his breakdown insurance. Pressing the screen he waited to be connected but nothing happened. He looked at the phone again and saw the 'call failed' notice.

'No service! Jeez. This bloody place.' Dan hit the steering wheel in anger, sounding the horn and making himself jump.

At that moment Fred pulled up alongside the Audi. *Woss he a doon now?* he thought to himself. The driver stared back at him, clearly surprised to see he'd return. Fred parked in front of the Audi and attached a thick tow rope to it. Back in his truck he eased it forward slowly, gently tightening the rope between them, until he gradually dragged the Audi back onto the road. As Fred untied the rope the man thanked him.

'No problem. Dew yew keep a troshin,' Fred replied, climbed back into his truck, nodded at him, and drove off.

Dan followed the truck up to the church yard where he turned the car around and drove slowly back past the cottage. 'A Stone's Throw,' he read.

'So, this is where you've been hiding.'

Fred followed the mud-encrusted car back down the road, he was surprised when it slowed down outside Clara's cottage then sped off. *Thass strange,* he thought.

20

Gus danced around Freya and Daisy as he greeted them in the driveway. None of them noticed the dark Audi slowly driving past, closely followed by Fred's pickup truck.

Indoors, Clara had lit the open fire and made a huge pot of spaghetti bolognese for lunch. After washing it all down with a bottle of wine they sat in the living room, staring into the fire. Freya and Daisy looked at each other. They knew they had to tell Clara what had happened.

Clara was more concerned that Freya was OK than Dan was looking for her.

'Oh my God, he's unbelievable. You could report him for assault.' Freya just wanted to forget all about her ordeal.

'I'm not sure. I must admit I'm a bit worried about going back to the flat now he knows I'm there.' Clara was relieved she wasn't living there. *Thank goodness I'm safe and sound over a hundred miles away in Norfolk,* she felt sorry for Freya.

While Freya took Gus out for a walk Clara told Daisy about her history with Dan.

'So now you see why I've not been at work, apart from breaking my ankle, which was good timing in a way!'

'I don't think he should get away with it. Who knows if he'll do it again? I can be a witness for Freya, I saw the fear in her eyes.' Daisy wasn't sure how she was going to face him at work on Monday.

Freya and Gus returned an hour later. 'It's started to snow out there, Gus was trying to catch the snowflakes in his mouth and couldn't work out why they'd disappeared!'

Daisy put another log on the fire and announced she would be 'fire monitor.' They divided up the jobs for the weekend, with Clara being granted special dispensation. Freya and Daisy voted unanimously that she would be in charge of opening the wine bottles.

When they awoke Saturday morning the fields around them were covered in snow. Clara opened the kitchen door for Gus. He put one paw on the white fluffy blanket, stepped back into the kitchen, sniffed the air, then looked up at Clara.

'You've got to go out Gus. Come on, be brave!' Reluctantly he stepped into the snow, his little legs disappeared as he sank up to his belly. Clara closed the door behind him. *Poor Gus!* she thought.

Freya decided it would be wise to stock up on essentials. 'Just in case it snows again tonight,' and set off for the supermarket. Daisy brought in a supply of logs from the woodshed and stacked them by the fireplace. Clara was grateful for the freezer full of meals her mum had cooked for her. Freya returned with three loaves of bread, 3 bottles of milk, 8 bottles of wine, 3 huge bars of chocolate, a sack of potatoes, boxes of burgers, an assortment of sausages and bags of frozen vegetables.

'We can put some things outside if there's not space in the freezer.'

'Excellent!' Daisy said, unloading the burgers and sausages. 'Are we having a bar-b-que?'

'There wasn't much left and the shop was heaving so I grabbed them quickly before anyone else did. Oh! I left the loo roll in the car. Can you believe people were stocking up on loo roll?'

'Right! Who wants sausage sandwiches?' Clara asked. They all put their hands in the air.

That afternoon they lazed around while the snow began to fall again outside. They read books and played backgammon. It was a game Clara had loved to play as a child with her mum. Gus took it in turns to rest his head on each of them as they stroked his ears. Clara cancelled the booking she'd made at a restaurant in Cromer as she wasn't sure how clear the roads would be. That evening, after finishing the left-over spaghetti bolognese from yesterday, they binge-watched the latest series of Dynasty on Netflix, ate chocolate and drank wine. When Clara let Gus outside at bedtime the snow had thankfully stopped. Freya and Daisy declared they'd loved being snowed-in, even if it was only for a day, as they climbed the stairs slowly behind Clara.

The next morning they all slept in late, including Gus. They'd stayed up until the early hours and didn't wake until almost 10am. Her room was unusually bright when she awoke so there was no need to open the curtains. Gus was scratching at her door in desperation. Clara shuffled down the stairs as usual to let him out of the kitchen door. As she opened it a pile of snow fell inside onto the mat. A huge snow drift lay against the back of the cottage, there was no way they could get out. Clara hobbled through the hallway and opened the front door, thankfully it was shallower there and Gus could get out to relieve himself, but there was another tall drift against the gate and hedge. The branches of the Christmas tree hung low with the weight of the snow.

'Bloody hell!' Clara heard Daisy call out from upstairs. 'Have you seen the snow?' Clara heard the thump of Freya's feet as she leapt out of bed.

'Oh – My – God! I've never seen anything like it.' They ran downstairs like a couple of young girls on Christmas morning and met Clara in the kitchen. She opened the back door to show them.

'I don't think you're going home today, Daisy!' she pronounced.

As they suspected, the rail company's website reported that no trains were running today. Clara tuned into Radio Norfolk.

'Many parts of Norfolk are inaccessible this morning as the county woke up to a blanket of snow. The North Norfolk coastline has been particularly badly affected with snow drifts blocking roads and cutting off electricity to some homes.'

'I hope the animals are OK at Heathfields,' Daisy said to Clara. 'I know someone always stays there but I think I'll just check in.' She called Tina who reassured her that she and two other members of staff were there all weekend. Clara had a chat with Tina to update her on Gus.

'Actually,' Tina said thoughtfully. 'We're expecting a bit of an influx in the next few weeks. It's always the same at Christmas. People dump their old dogs on us to make way for new fluffy puppies. Would you be interested in fostering a couple of dogs for us in the New Year? You have all that lovely space around you and Gus loves being with other dogs.' Her request caught Clara completely by surprise, but she agreed to think about it and give her a decision before Christmas.

Sunday night brought even more snow and Daisy abandoned the idea of returning to London any time soon. The next morning she called the HR department to tell them of her plight, saying she was visiting family and couldn't get home. With most of the country covered in snow, Coopers & Leigh had advised their staff to work from home where possible and closed its office.

'Yippee!' Daisy danced around the living room, 'Can we go out in the snow?' Freya and Daisy found an old spade in the woodshed and dug a path in the snow drift big enough for them to get to the gate and climb over it.

'This is such an adventure,' Daisy declared, and off they set.

Clara and Gus stayed indoors as the snow was far too deep for him. Linda phoned to check they were all OK.

'We've got a fair bit of snow down here. I'm staying in. Don't you worry about me, I've got a freezer full of food.' Clara was sure she did. Linda believed in batch cooking, just in case.

Two hours passed and still there was no sign of Freya and Daisy. They'd both left their phones on charge in the kitchen in their haste to pull on their wellies and heavy coats to get out into the snow. Half an hour later Clara heard a car stop outside on the roadway with its engine running. It had been so quiet all day she would have heard a pin drop, so the sound of a car was like a firework going off. Clara hobbled to the front door with Gus. She could only just see the top of a black car over the snowdrift by the gate. She heard Freya and Daisy's voices in unison, 'Thank you so much,' and the sound of two car doors slamming before they appeared, climbing back over the gate. The car drove off.

'Are you OK? Who was that?' Clara quizzed them.

'That,' answered Freya, 'was that lovely man we met at the pet store who sold you this cottage.' Clara was dumbfounded.

'William?'

Freya walked into the hallway and took off her snow-covered boots. 'Yes, that's it. William.' Her answer didn't satisfy Clara who wanted to know more.

'What's he doing 'round here?' Daisy walked into the kitchen and hung her coat on the back of a chair.

'He lives near here. Didn't you know?'

'No, I didn't.' Clara was shocked. Why hadn't he told her. Freya joined them in the kitchen and filled the kettle to make hot drinks.

'We walked miles, then on the way back I slipped over and fell on my bum. William came along as I was sitting in the middle of the road laughing.'

Clara felt a pang of jealousy - *how can they say his name so easily, as if he was their friend? Why hadn't he been in touch?*

Freya poured them all drinks. 'Anyway, he offered to give us a lift back, so we said yes.'

It took Clara hours to get to sleep that night, so many thoughts swirled around in her head. *So that's why he came over after the storm, because he wasn't far away. Which means he definitely hadn't made a special journey to see me. I'm so stupid. Why did I imagine he'd been thinking about me? He was probably just being neighbourly.* Eventually, Clara wore herself out thinking and managed to find some respite in sleep. In the morning she made a promise to herself to not think about him anymore. She didn't want a relationship anyway.

Daisy was finally able to go home on Thursday. Although the major roads had cleared, Clara's narrow lane had remained covered in thick ice until the sun came out and the temperature rose above freezing. Freya drove them all to the station, Gus went too, where they all hugged Daisy and said their goodbyes.

They made the most of Freya's remaining few days in Norfolk, both dreading her leaving. She drove home two days before Christmas with tears in her eyes, sad to leave Clara and Gus, yet acknowledging she could no longer push Dan Sayer to the back of her mind. She had no other option but to go back to the apartment.

Freya parked in the underground car park, quickly got out of the car, grabbed her luggage and made for the lift, looking all around her, just in case. Once indoors she closed and locked the door behind her, turned on the TV to distract her thoughts and sat in the armchair. She couldn't bring herself to sit in her usual seat on the sofa, where he had sat, even though it was only for a moment. Flicking through social media diverted her mind, she'd been careful not to post any pictures of her stay with Clara. Norfolk was their hideaway, a well-kept secret, their safe place.

With Daisy and now Freya gone back to London, Clara had time to think about Freya's narrow escape with Dan. Although she'd put on a brave face Clara knew Freya was anxious about going back to the apartment. Now he knew where to find her, Freya wasn't safe. How glad Clara was to be hidden away in Norfolk. Fearing for her friend's safety, Clara decided it was time to expose him for the evil bastard that he was. She called HR and asked to speak with the Director.

21

Linda arrived on Christmas Eve. She hung some tinsel on Stephen's Christmas tree as high up as she could reach and decorated a smaller tree in the living room that she had brought with her.

'It has roots so we can plant it in the garden after Christmas, you have plenty of space.'

On Christmas Day they played backgammon and Linda cooked a roast turkey lunch, just like she always did. She took Gus for a walk around the garden, she didn't want to bump into Mr Wells again. As was their tradition, they watched The Queen's speech, followed by The Sound of Music, singing along while cracking nuts and drinking mulled wine. They always saved the Christmas pudding and cream for their tea. Linda opened a tin of chocolates and they settled down to watch the BBC Special, during which they both fell asleep. It was their perfect Christmas Day.

Christmas came and went far too quickly for both of them and all too soon it was time for Linda to return to Kent. Having prepared several more ready meals to stock up Clara's freezer, she drove home a day earlier than planned as further snowfall had been forecast. She had offered to stay longer but Clara insisted she'd be fine.

'You can't cancel your plans mum, they were arranged months ago. Besides, one of us has to party on New Year's Eve!'

The forecast for the last day of the year was just as predicted.

Clara awoke to find freshly fallen snow, but thankfully not as much as before. Just after lunch there was a knock at the front door, Gus barked and ran ahead as Clara hobbled behind him. A lady holding an enormous bouquet of flowers stood smiling at her.

'Clara Richmond?'

'Er, yes,' Clara replied, wondering who on earth would be sending her flowers.

'These beauties are for you. Happy New Year.'

She handed them to Clara who held them for a moment before placing them on the floor so she could open the small envelop that accompanied them. As she turned to close the door Gus spotted a black dog walk past, and ran out to say hello. The delivery driver had left the gate open.

'Gus, Gus!' Clara shouted, but he was far too excited to listen. Standing on one leg, with only a woolly sock for protection, she stepped out into the freezing snow. Scared he would run off again Clara called for him.

'Gus, come here boy. GUS!'

Gus blatantly ignored her as he and his new friend danced around each other by the gate. Clara stepped out into the snow, wearing only her woolly socks on her feet, she didn't have time to find her slippers. She gingerly made her way towards him on her crutches as quickly as she could, but her left sock had quickly absorbed the cold ice and her right foot dragged behind in the snow. She could feel both her feet beginning to freeze. *Surely that dog belongs to someone. Where the hell is its owner?* Her sodden sock became heavier and heavier, making it harder for her to walk, suddenly the crutches slid away from her, and she fell face first into the snow. She lay there, helpless, feeling the heat of her body melting the snow beneath her as her clothes soaked up the ice.

Struggling to get up she slipped again. She heard heavy footsteps getting closer, crunching the ice beneath them, then a pair of strong hands under her arms. Someone, a man, picked her up and placed her upright onto her good leg.

'Are you OK Clara?' She recognised his voice instantly.

'I'm fine. I'm fine, I'm just cold and wet and... actually I'm not fine. I need to get indoors.' Clara began to shiver. Still holding her upright he walked 'round to face her. She'd recognise those blue eyes anywhere. They exchanged smiles.

'Excuse me,' William said and before she knew it, he scooped her up in his arms and carried her back into the cottage, setting her down on the sofa in the living room. Gus and Lottie, who had grown so much since Clara had last seen her, followed them.

'I'm a dripping mess!' Clara declared, sitting on the edge of the sofa and peeling off her soggy socks. The dogs curled up together in front of the open fire while William stood looking at her.

'What can I do?' he asked. Clara thought for a second, she needed dry clothes, but she could hardly ask him to carry her up to her bedroom. Not like this anyway. She remembered the present from her mum was still next to the Christmas tree.

'Could you pass me that bag over there please?' William brought it to her, awaiting the next instruction. 'Perhaps you could wait in the kitchen while I get changed?' she suggested.

'You can come in now,' Clara called to William. He emerged from the kitchen with a mug of hot tea in each hand and burst into laughter at the sight of her, almost spilling the drinks. Clara stood in front of him, leaning on her crutches, wearing a bright pink fluffy onesy!

'You look like a huge candy floss,' he laughed. Clara couldn't help but laugh with him.

They sat with their tea, easily chatting as if they were old friends.

Clara told William how Gus had run away when she fell down the stairs and broke her ankle.

'So that's why I hopped out in the snow to get him. The delivery driver had left the gate open and I didn't want him running off again.' Clara suddenly remembered the bouquet of flowers she'd left in the hallway.

'I'll get them for you,' William offered, and returned to the living room with his face hidden by the huge bouquet.

'He must like you a lot,' he said, handing them to Clara.

'I have no idea who they're from,' she replied, opening the envelope and reading the card.

'Happy New Year, see you soon. DS'

Clara froze. She re-read the words, trying to make sense of them. *How did he know where she was? Had they been re-directed from her apartment? No, they couldn't have been.* Terrified and feeling vulnerable Clara threw the card to the floor as if she'd been burnt by it. *Where was he? Was he close by?* She stood up and made her way to the front window. *Was he outside?* William could sense Clara's fear.

'Who are they from?' He picked up the card. 'Who's DS? Clara is someone threatening you?'

Clara sat back on the sofa, William sat in the armchair, allowing Clara time to compose herself.

'He's an ex, from a very long time ago. It wasn't a good relationship, let's say, he always made sure he got what he wanted. Then he moved abroad for work, and I was free… until he reappeared this summer as my new boss. I haven't been to the office since.' William tried to read between the lines as Clara continued.

'The thing is, no-one knows I'm here, except my mum, Freya and Daisy. Even work think I'm still in London, I haven't told them about this place.' She sat back on the sofa and began chewing her nails. She hadn't done that since before Dan left for New York.

'I had to tell HR why I wasn't returning to work. They've obviously spoken to him. This was my safe space; he couldn't touch me here. But now I'm more vulnerable because there's no-one around and I'm stuck like this.' Clara held up her broken ankle. William could see her predicament.

'Look, just because they arrived today doesn't mean he's here. He could easily send them from London. If it's OK with you I can stay here tonight, I'll go back and grab a few things. Lottie can wait here; she'll make a big noise if she hears anyone.' Clara was taken aback by his gesture.

'But don't you have a family to be with, someone to be with?' She held her breath waiting for the answer.

'It'll be fine, I'll explain the situation.' Lottie stood up to go as he put his coat on, 'Lottie, stay,' he commanded, and she lay back down with Gus again. 'I'll be back in an hour.'

After he'd left, Clara checked she had a signal on her mobile phone, she had to use Wi-Fi calling as the cottage was so remote. Even though Clara assumed Dan would be celebrating New Year in London, rather than stalking her in Norfolk, she kept the doors locked.

Clara shuffled upstairs to change out of her onesy and into something more appropriate, then slowly climbed back downstairs again to take two of her mum's ready meals out of the freezer for them to eat that evening. She hadn't thought to ask him if he liked spaghetti bolognese, but seeing as most people she knew ate it, she hoped it was a safe bet. Looking in the freezer she hesitated for a moment. *What about garlic bread? That's only OK if you both eat it. Don't be stupid,* she reprimanded herself. *It's not like we'll be getting that close. He's just being kind.*

William walked back to his childhood home as quickly as he could. He'd recently been staying there as his house was being renovated, but he knew he'd probably be the only one awake by 11pm. The house was empty when he arrived, so he left a note to say he was staying with a friend. He packed an overnight bag, threw it in the car, paused, then took it out again and went back indoors. Opening the bag, he took out his toothbrush and cleaned his teeth. *Why am I doing this? It's not as if we're going to get close. I'm just keeping her company because she's scared.*

Gus and Lottie jumped up, barking as they ran to the front door hearing William's car pull into the driveway.

'Goodness you two make a noise,' Clara told them as she unlocked the door to let him in. The dogs greeted him enthusiastically and Clara was more pleased to see him than she allowed herself to show.

'Do you eat spag bol?' she asked, wishing she'd checked before he left.

'I love it,' he replied. 'And if you have any garlic bread then you'd have my favourite meal.' Clara felt as though she'd hit the jackpot. *Let's hope he likes wine!*

They spent the evening half-watching the television while Clara tried to teach William how to play backgammon.

'I don't think you're paying attention,' she teased him.

'I've had too many glasses of wine to concentrate. That's my excuse and I'm sticking with it,' he laughed.

At quarter to midnight Jules Holland began to whip the studio audience into an excited frenzy. Until then Clara and William had hardly noticed the Hootenanny, but with the anticipation of the approaching celebrations they turned their attention to the screen. William threw a log on the fire and poured them both another glass of wine, glancing at his watch as he sat back in the armchair. Clara sat on the sofa resting her leg. Her cheeks were flushed in the glow of the fire, and quite probably because of the two bottles of wine they'd shared so far. It occurred to her that she was unsure of the etiquette for the evening. *Would they kiss on the stroke of midnight? Perhaps just a polite hug maybe?*

William fidgeted in the chair. *A kiss on the cheek ought to be acceptable,* he hoped. He'd really wanted to tell her of his childhood memories spent in this house with his best friend Michael, but he couldn't risk spoiling the moment. He also really wanted to kiss her. Like he'd wanted to kiss her since the first time they'd met, since he saw her open to the door to the outside toilet and almost throw up in the hedge.

With just a few minutes to midnight William topped up their glasses. 'Just so we're ready to celebrate Old Year's Night.'

'Old Year's Night?' Clara looked at him puzzled. 'Don't you mean New Year's Eve?'

'No! It's Old Year's Night,' he insisted.

'I think you'll find it's New Year's Eve,' Clara continued. William stood up with his glass aloft.

'Absolutely not. Here in Norfolk, it's Old Year's Night, and you're in Norfolk now. So, you'd better make sure you speak properly.' Clara stood up to face him, balancing on one crutch.

'Me? Speak properly? You're the only person I can understand around here. Do you know Fred? He's absolutely lovely, but I don't know half of what he's said until ten minutes after he's said it.' William laughed.

'So you've met my father then?' Clara began to splutter as she choked on the mouthful of wine she'd just taken. William halfheartly patted her on the back. Turning to apologise for speaking about Fred in that way Clara lost her balance. William caught her in his arms and she fell against him. Their eyes met for the briefest of moments as Clara stared in those now familiar blue eyes. She could feel the warmth of his body against hers, their faces centimetres apart. Somewhere in the distance Jules Holland was counting down from ten to one. Clara heard Big Ben begin to strike… their lips met on the stroke of midnight.

22

Clara daren't open her eyes. She knew it was morning. She knew she was naked, apart from the cast on her ankle. She knew William was lying next to her as she could hear him breathing. What she didn't know was whether to pretend to still be asleep until he woke up, or whether to quickly get dressed and go downstairs so she wasn't there when he did.

Gus solved her dilemma by scratching at her bedroom door to signal he needed to go out. Clara panicked. *Oh no! Gus, don't wake him up. He can't see me naked.* She looked at William who was beginning to stir. Her dressing gown was on the back of the door but where were her crutches? Clara stood up on her good leg and hopped across to the door, she hastily pulled her dressing gown around her and tied the belt. *Phew! Made it.* Thank goodness he hadn't seen her.

'Morning!' Clara felt herself blush from top to toe. How could she face him now?

'I can't find my crutches,' she said, still facing the door and holding on to the handle. 'Gus needs to go out.' She heard William stand up and pull on his clothes.

'I'll let him out. And I'll get your crutches.' Gus raced down the stairs, Lottie followed behind them; she had been sleeping on the floor beside William. Unsure what to do Clara hopped back to the bed and got in, still wearing her dressing gown. She made a futile attempt at tidying her hair with her fingers.

Ten minutes later Gus and Lottie chased up the stairs to greet her as if they'd been gone for a week, followed by William who appeared carrying two mugs of tea in one hand and her crutches in the other. He placed Clara's mug on her bedside cabinet and sat at the end of the bed, holding his. Clara wasn't sure if this was going to be an embarrassing moment or not as his blue eyes seemed to see right into her thoughts. Will he act like nothing happened? William smiled at her.

'Hi!'

'Hi. Thank you for the tea.'

William laughed. 'Thank you for the cabaret this morning!' Clara was mortified, unsure of how to hide her embarrassment she threw a pillow at him and pulled the duvet over her head. She'd have to stay here until he left. William pulled the cover off her.

'Come on, I'm making sausage sandwiches for breakfast.'

Shuffling down the stairs on her bottom Clara stopped to pinch herself, she couldn't believe she'd spent the night with William.

She remembered the kiss. She'd *always* remember that kiss. His lips were soft, he'd put his arms around her waist, and she felt so… secure, and safe. They'd stood with their lips pressed together for several moments until William pulled away gently.

'Would you think it presumptuous if I carry you upstairs?' he asked, gazing into her eyes.

'Very,' she replied, kissing him again. 'My room is at the top of the stairs.'

When she reached the kitchen William had already laid the table and was cooking the sausages. He walked over and kissed her on the lips, then returned to the stove. Clara watched him, he didn't seem the slightest bit embarrassed, so why was *she*? At that moment she realised she had no idea if he was single. What if he belonged to someone else? What if she had no right to think of those blue eyes and his soft kisses? What if he was with someone and using her for sex and taking advantage of her?

'William, are you single?' He swung around to face her. Clara tried to read his expression. *He looks worried, I've caught him out. Oh no, what have I done? He's smiling, why is he smiling?*

'Of course I am! I wouldn't be here otherwise.' Clara took another mouthful of tea; she couldn't believe her luck. What a great start to the year.

After breakfast William said he ought to go and see his father for a while but would be back after lunch if that was OK. Clara called Linda to wish her Happy New Year. The phone woke her up as she had been at a neighbour's house until the early hours. Clara decided not to reveal her own New Year celebrations.

The bright sun began to melt the snow and the weather matched her mood. William, true to his word, returned with Lottie after lunch. He'd refreshed his overnight bag but left it in the car, not wanting to appear even more presumptuous.

'Shall we go for a drive?' he suggested. Clara had been housebound for so long she was excited at the prospect of a trip out. He suggested they go to Walcott. They could park on the road overlooking the sea.

'It will be like a first date,' he said, winking at her. Clara felt her cheeks colour, feeling about 15 years old!

Although what seemed like half of Norfolk had the same idea, they did manage to find a parking space. William put the leads on Gus and Lottie and took them for a walk. Clara felt a lump in her throat as she watched them wander up the road. This was how she imagined relationships should be, something she'd only experienced briefly at the start of her relationship with Joe so many years ago. *I mustn't get my hopes up, it could all be over by tomorrow.*

Just a fling. Just something lovely to remember. Clara reminded herself that she hadn't been looking for a relationship, so it didn't matter if it was a fleeting encounter. She hoped they could stay friends after though.

William walked on with Lottie and Gus, the sun was warm, but the wind was biting as it hit him in the face. *Ok, so how does this go after this afternoon? Shall I offer to stay? Perhaps I'll wait for her to ask me. Don't blow it. Maybe it would be best if I went home and contacted her in a couple of days. Maybe.. maybe... oh I don't know!* He looked down at his new little family trotting alongside him, they really did get on well together.

William returned to the car, put the dogs in the back and sat back next to Clara. Now he was back in the car he wasn't sure what to say, so he playfully put his freezing cold hands on her cheeks. Clara gave a little shriek.

'Blimey, they're like ice.'

'I thought I'd give you a taste of what it's like out there, I felt sorry for you sitting in the warm car!' The dogs fell asleep on the back seat while Clara and William looked out to sea.

'This reminds me of the day we first met, looking out across the sea when you viewed the cottage,' he recalled.

'You remember that?' Clara was amazed he remembered it too.

'Of course,' he replied. 'The sun was shining on the water just like now and we were standing next to each other. The wind blew your hair in all directions. I wanted to take you in my arms and kiss you right there.' Clara was speechless. William continued. 'I think I fell for you the moment you almost vomited after opening the door to the shed then came running towards me like a mad woman! Or it might have been when I saw the look of horror on your face when Kenneth announced he was happy to let A Stone's Throw fall into the sea!'

Clara at last found some words.

'So why didn't you contact me? Especially after the storm?'

'Ah!' said William. 'Therein lies a story.'

Clara dreaded what was coming next. *I knew it was too good to be true. Here's where he tells me about his complicated relationship, and they're on a break at the moment; but they've been together for twelve years and have three children.* His answer took her completely by surprise.

'I promised a friend I wouldn't see you.' Clara was confused.

'But no-one knows me up here.'

William took a deep breath and continued. 'That's not entirely true. My best friend is Michael, your cousin. We grew up together, we're the same age. There's exactly two months difference between us. I'm the eldest of course! We went to school together, and as we lived across the field from each other we were always in and out of each other's houses. At the time it seemed that Michael's mum was being overly protective, but she had lost Michael's older brother in a terrible accident when he was six. She wouldn't let Michael go far, so we played in his yard or mine. I didn't mind really. There used to be an old well in what's your garden now but Mrs Reid got her husband to fill it in when Michael was little.'

Clara wasn't sure what to say but William hadn't finished.

'A few weeks after his father died, Michael came to see me straight from the solicitor's office following the reading of his father's will. He was livid that his father had left part of his inheritance to a cousin he'd never even heard of. Apparently, there was a letter with the will explaining what had happened to the sister when she was sixteen. How she'd been sent away to Kent to have a baby. A bungalow had been left to the sister and Michael thought that should have been enough. I pointed out to him that he did have the main farmhouse, and all the land and business, but he wasn't in the mood for being swayed. Anyway, I couldn't tell him about you until after the auction because of client confidentiality, but once you bought it the paperwork had your name on it. He'd tried to buy it himself. He was the telephone bidder at the auction, but he couldn't keep up with you and Kenneth. I told him what a nice person you are, but he didn't care. 'You just fancy her,' he said. So, I admitted to him that I did. Anyway, he said we'd have a hard time being friends if I was seeing you, so I had to say that I wouldn't. He's been there for me over the years, especially when my wife passed away. Jenny was diagnosed with breast cancer when she was thirty-four but unfortunately it was too advanced by the time we spotted it. Fourteen months later she was gone.'

Clara couldn't believe what she was hearing but her mind was racing. *He's best friends with Michael, who doesn't want to know me. He's a widower, that's incredibly sad. So, he had cared about me! But what does all that mean?*

'Sorry if that was a bit much,' William said, turning to her. Clara was still looking out to sea.

'I'm sorry to hear about your wife.' She could only imagine what a terrible time William had been through. 'So, should we stop seeing each other, because of your friendship with Michael?'

'I decided yesterday when I went back to get my things that this was my decision and not his. Losing Jenny was the worst thing that ever happened to me. Losing Michael's friendship would be terrible, but bearable. I've got through tougher times.' William held out his hand towards her, Clara took it. It was slightly warmer than before but as he touched her she felt a tingle race up her arm and through her whole body.

'So, are we a 'thing' then?' she asked. William lifted her hand to his lips and kissed her fingers.

'I guess we are.'

They spent the next two days and nights together until it was time for William to return to work. They agreed that Lottie would stay with her for extra security; her loud, deep bark would make any potential intruders think twice. William would come back at the end of the day.

Clara called Daisy at work and told her about the bouquet from Dan. She held back telling her about William, that could wait for another time. Daisy said she'd let her know if Dan was out of the office for any length of time. If Daisy could see him then at least they knew he wasn't in Norfolk. She'd just spotted him in the library, complaining he'd been given the wrong information. Clara relaxed.

The following day Clara had a hospital appointment to have her cast removed. She was so excited she hardly slept that night. It was an early morning appointment and William had juggled a few work commitments so he could take her. She watched him sleeping, the moonlight glowing through the curtains as he lay beside her. She gently stroked the grey hair that grew at his temples.

'I can't believe I'm wearing a pair of shoes!' Clara declared to William excitedly wiggling her newly mended right ankle in the air. She'd bought a pair of Sketchers online just for the occasion, they were soft and padded. The sole of her right foot felt strangely uncomfortable as she put it to the ground for the first time in six weeks. Every millimetre of it tingled, a strange sensation she could only describe as spongey and tickly. They walked slowly out of the hospital with Clara holding William's arm, using one crutch to help support her ankle.

Over the next two weeks, with Clara becoming more mobile, they enjoyed trips out to country pubs, took the dogs to the woods and William showed off his culinary skills in the kitchen.

As soon as Clara was able to drive again she and Gus visited Linda. She told her about William, hoping she wasn't jinxing the relationship. William hadn't told Michael about her yet, but he was meeting with him while she was away. It was going so well she couldn't quite believe it. Surely Michael wouldn't end their friendship?

On the way back home Clara and Gus diverted to Heathfields. Tina had messaged Clara to ask about fostering again, they were getting desperate. Gus was excited to see a few of his old kennel companions who were still there, but there were also several new residents.

'Goodness,' Clara exclaimed, 'You're fit to bursting here.'

Tina looked around. 'Now you can see our problem.' Tina boiled the kettle while Clara sat holding on to Gus' lead.

'I'm not sure I can do anything as I'm seeing someone at the moment and he has a young black Lab, a bitch. But tell me what you're proposing and I'll have a think about it.'

Tina wanted to hear about William first, so it was half an hour before they got back on track.

'There are a couple of possibilities, the first is two Springer Spaniels who arrived yesterday. They are brother and sister, both neutered, aged five. The family have a new baby and their house is too small for all of them now. They could have coped with one dog but they need to remain as a pair. Billy and Brandy love to race around together and they need a lot of space to do that. You have all that land to wear them out on! They could potentially be a longer-term foster as we need someone to take both of them on.' Clara took a few seconds to consider it. She imagined two boisterous dogs charging around.

'What's option two?'

Tina disappeared for a couple of minutes and returned with a beautiful tan coloured Bulldog slowly ambling along behind her.

'This is Bessy, she's three and a half. She's struggling with being in the kennels, but we can't rehome her yet because she's not used to walking on a lead. She sits down and won't budge, and there's **no** moving her.' Clara looked at Bessy's cute, wrinkled nose and sad eyes. Tina stroked Bessy's ears. 'She's fit and healthy, gets on brilliantly with the other dogs, but can't cope with living outside and not being attached to a human. She doesn't need much exercise and the owner said she loved laying on her feet. It's a divorce situation and neither of them can give her a home. We could have a cuppa with them here together and see how they get on.' Clara called Bessy to her and to Tina's amazement she wandered on over to her. Bessy and Gus sniffed each other, then Gus laid at Clara's feet, Bessy lay down next to him. Tina handed Clara a mug.

'So far, so good!'

'So, you want me to get her used to the lead, that's all?'

'I thought if you walk Gus on the lead in the garden she'll follow, and then gradually introduce the idea to her. It's up to you and Bessy how long it takes, just tell us when you've cracked it and we'll come and collect her. We don't have the time to do it here, we're swamped as you can see.'

Tina helped Clara to load Bessy and her few belongings into the car. She couldn't jump in on her own as she was so heavy, they lifted her together.

'She's as solid as a rock, I hope she can get out when we get home!' With both dogs safely secured on the back seat Clara headed home. *I'm such a pushover,* she decided, glancing in the rear-view mirror. *But she is very cute.*

Bessy quickly made herself at home. Gus showed her around

the cottage and where to go to the toilet, then they both settled down in front of the open fire in the living room. When William knocked on the door that evening Clara discovered what a huge bark Bessy had. Even Gus was taken by surprise. Clara walked through the living room to open the door.

'Goodness Bessy, anyone would think a huge bear lived here!'

William and Lottie were standing ten feet back from the door when Clara opened it to greet them. Both looked wary and more than slightly afraid.

'What on earth is that noise?'

'This is Bessy, she's come to stay until she learns to walk on the lead. We're fostering her for a little while,' Clara shouted over the noise of Bessy's low, gruff bark. 'It's OK Bessy, you don't need to scare them off!'

William looked down at the rather stout Bessy and her squashed, wrinkled face, her tongue hanging out the side of her mouth.

'That is one ugly dog!' he declared.

'She's beautiful!' Clara retorted, 'Don't say that, you'll upset her.' Clara bent down to stroke Bessy who was sniffing hello to Lottie. Bessy snuffled William's shoes and trousers, sizing him up, snorted, then wandered off, leaving a trail of dribble on his trouser leg. She followed Gus and Lottie into the living room. William looked down at his trousers.

'That's charming! She kisses just like you!' Clara feigned being horrified and declared he'd be sleeping with the dogs tonight.

23

'Clara, it's Daisy. It sounds like you don't have a signal where you are. I'll try and call you again but just to let you know he's not in the office today, and he's booked the rest of the week off. I'll send you a text as well. Let me know you've got this message.'

Gus, Lottie and Bessy followed Clara up and down the garden, keeping her company while she carried each length of picket fence up to the cliff edge. Bessy had been with them for two weeks, but the almost constant rain had made it difficult to spend much time outside with her on the lead. It had also prevented the delivery lorry from going any further than the driveway, she'd have to carry them herself. William had gone away for a few days to a conference in Brighton so Lottie had come to stay. As much as Clara enjoyed standing like Kathy and Heathcliffe looking over the craggy rocks out to sea, she decided for safety's sake a fence was needed to create a barrier for the dogs should they get a bit overexcited running after each other and forget about the edge. She hadn't realised her mobile phone had fallen out of her pocket onto the grass, but Bessy had. She'd picked it up in her mouth and followed Clara to where she was piling the fence panels at the end of the garden. Every few trips Clara stood and looked out to sea, stretching her back, until she returned for the next panel. Bessy stood next to her now, feeling pleased with her treasure. The phone was still hidden in her mouth when Daisy's text arrived. Startled by the vibration tingling in her head Bessy ran forward towards the cliff edge. Clara screamed.

'Bessy!' She dived forward to catch her, just grabbing her back legs before she reached the edge. Bessy's mouth opened as Clara's firm grip jolted her backwards and the mobile phone flew out, smashing onto the boulders below.

Clara lay on the floor, gripping Bessy in her arms, too petrified to let go. She thought her heart would beat right through her chest as she felt the ground around them to check they were safe.

'Oh my God, oh my God! Bessy, what were you doing?' Bessy was licking her face. They were soon joined by Gus and Lottie licking her hands, not wanting to be left out of the fun. Clara rolled far away from the edge before she felt safe enough to stand up. She quickly led the dogs back to the cottage and took them into the kitchen where she poured herself a large glass of water. She drank half of it straight away and lay on the sofa in the living room, her heart still in her mouth. *The sooner the fence is up the better, but I think I'll leave it to 'Fenced In' from now on.*

Clara felt in her pockets for her mobile phone. She needed to tell someone about her near death experience and that she was OK, but she couldn't find it. Damn! She went upstairs for her Apple watch but it was out of charge. She plugged it in and went back in the kitchen to make herself a strong cup of coffee. She'd activate the search for her phone when it had a bit of juice in it. Gus scratched at the back door and whimpered.

'Gus, didn't you go while you were out? I'll have to keep that patio gate closed, you three aren't going back out there until that fence is up.'

Two hours later Clara woke up on the sofa feeling cold, she'd left the kitchen door wide open but the dogs were lying next to her on the floor. Lottie suddenly leapt to her feet, ears pricked, then began to bark, deep and agitated. Gus and Bessy joined her.

All three of them ran to the front door, their protests becoming louder and more urgent. Clara followed them. The tone of their barks alarmed her, she wondered whether or not she should open the door. If someone was outside they may have left the front gate open. Lottie was sniffing madly at the bottom of the door while Bessy stood still, growling. Gus jumped up at the door, his bark matching the intensity of the others but two octaves higher. Clara opened the door slightly; the gate was closed so she opened the door wide enough to allow the dogs to run outside into the driveway. Lottie was first, picking up a scent, she turned and followed it away from the gate, down the side of the cottage and into the back garden, barking as she ran. Gus and Bessy followed her but Clara stayed in the doorway, unsure of what to do. Something, or someone, was out there and they weren't happy about it. She closed the door and walked back through the living room to the kitchen. *That's funny,* she thought to herself. *I'm sure the kitchen door was open. Perhaps it blew closed when I opened the front door.* Clara could hear the dogs in the garden. The patio gate was open but she was sure she'd closed it. Clara turned the handle of the kitchen door to let the dogs back in but it was locked. She looked at where the key hung on the hook, but it wasn't there. *What the....?*

'Hello Clara!' She recognised his voice in an instant and spun around to see Dan Sayer standing behind her in the doorway to the living room. The dogs were barking frantically outside and scratching at the back door. She stood with her back against the kitchen cupboards, she was trapped.

'What the hell are you doing here?' She tried to sound calm as she slid her way across the kitchen to the sink, wondering if there was there something there she could defend herself with if needed.

'I thought it was time we had a chat. Nice place you've got here, hidden away in the middle of nowhere, with no-one around.' His voice sounded menacing, threatening. She didn't need telling that no-one would hear her protests. If only she could let the dogs in, surely they could offer her some protection.

'What do you want to talk about? I said everything I had to say in the pub.' Clara tried to control her breathing. *Slow, shallow, even. In through the nose, out through the mouth.*

'But you didn't leave it there, did you? I know you fed that Doctor and HR a load of crap. Did you seriously think I wouldn't find out? You and your friend Freya, you're just money grabbing bitches.' Dan walked towards her. Clara desperately looked around her. Why had she cleaned the kitchen earlier? Usually there was a sink full of crockery and knives and forks. All three dogs tore at the kitchen door, desperate to protect her. Clara had never heard them sound so ferocious as they tried to claw their way in, their breath and saliva leaving marks on the glass. Her fear of Dan momentarily disappeared as she worried about the injuries the dogs would suffer if the glass broke. His voice jolted her back to her current predicament.

'You should never leave keys in the door you know.' Dan held up the old key to the kitchen door as he walked towards her, stopping two paces away, then placed it in his trouser pocket.

Sweat began to drip down her back and her cleavage, her breathing was shallow, reminding her of earlier that day as she'd clasped Bessy to her chest. *Stay strong, stay calm.*

'Just say what you want to say and go.' The cold sweat was making her jumper damp and her stomach began to churn. She desperately needed to find a way out. Her eyes flicked momentarily towards the living room door, but he saw her look for an escape route and moved to block her way. He looked around the kitchen, out of the window towards the sea view.

'Well, I'm not sure I want to go. A romantic country hideaway for two, a log fire, no-one else around. The dogs will get fed up barking soon, we'll have peace and quiet. Just the two of us.'

'My boyfriend will be home soon; he's coming to collect his dog.' Lottie was still pawing at the door, but Clara could tell she was getting tired. She needed to find another escape route, and she needed to think fast.

'The dogs are so noisy; let's go into the other room so we can hear each other better.'

Dan walked into the living room and stood blocking the doorway to the hall.

'Sure.'

Clara sat in the chair so he couldn't sit next to her. Her fingers gripping the arms, she was ready to fight or fly, but for the moment she froze, until she got the chance to... but chance to what? What would she have to do to stay safe?

Dan remained standing, glaring at her. Clara had seen that look before; it had haunted her dreams for years. While he was talking she tried to work out an escape route.

The front door's unlocked. If he turns around I'll run for it. She cursed her newly mended ankle, it still wasn't very strong. *Could she make it in time? Then what? Run out to the road? The gate is closed, he'll have caught me by then. Anyway, the chances are no-one will be around.*

'What happened to you Clara? You were always so... what's the word? Good. Yes, you never complained, never had so much to say for yourself. Life was easy with you, we always had a good time.'

Words stuck in Clara's throat. Although she opened her mouth to speak, nothing came out. *If I try to pacify him, he'll see me as weak. Or do I stand up for myself and chance making him angry?* She looked at

Dan and shrugged. Maybe saying nothing was best right now.

'Your dumb friends drove all the way here without noticing me following them. Stupid bitches. Ha! I suppose that cow Freya told you about our 'liaison' in New York? Did she tell you how she played me? Led me on, had her hands all over me? She couldn't wait to get me upstairs. You can't take a guy that far and then change your mind. There should be a law against that.'

He was pacing now, backwards and forwards in front of the fire. A horrific thought crossed her mind. Could she push him into the fire? So far, he hadn't laid a finger on her. Was making a Guy Fawkes of him a bit extreme?

'What do you want Dan?' She managed to spit out.

'At last Clara! Thinking of someone other than yourself. Well since you asked, I want you to tell HR you told them a pack of lies. I want you to admit to everyone that you were jealous I got the job, so you made up a story. Then you can resign.'

Clara thought very carefully about asking her next question.

'What happens if I don't?'

'I can't let you walk around telling tales. You are on the verge of ruining my career and my marriage. I won't have anything else to lose. If there's nothing left for me, then I may as well serve time.'

In that moment Clara realised the seriousness of her situation. She needed to buy herself some time.

'I need to think about it. Consider what to tell HR. Give me a few days.'

'Oh no! You can tell them now.'

Clara remembered she still hadn't found her phone.

'I don't know where my mobile is, I lost it earlier today. Can I borrow yours?' If only she could make someone aware of her predicament, raise an alarm in some way. The dogs had stopped barking. No-one was coming to help her.

'You don't think I'm that thick, do you? Email them.'

Clara's laptop was upstairs. Could she make an escape? The old bedroom doors had metal keys, if she could get ahead of him she could lock herself in a room. Her bedroom was at the back of the cottage but no one would see her there. She could pretend her room was at the front. Freya's room had a wooden chair. She'd seen it lots of times in films where a chair was wedged against a door to stop it from opening, but would it really work? She remembered the key was in the lock but she'd never tried it. Then what? She couldn't chance it.

Dan was staring at her, she needed to make a decision fast.

She looked around and saw her crutches leaning against the cupboard under the stairs.

'I need to get my laptop from upstairs.' Dan followed her into the hallway.

'Well this is a nice surprise, going upstairs with you again after all these years!' Clara felt her skin prickle as she pushed away the memories of all those years ago.

'I still need a crutch to help me upstairs.' Clara took one of the crutches and leaned heavily on it as she slowly climbed the stairs. She could hear his footsteps on the wooden steps behind her. As she neared the top Clara quickly turned around, taking Dan by surprise. For the briefest of moments she met his gaze, before planting the base of the crutch into the centre of his chest and pushing with all her might. Catching him off-balance, she watched him fall backwards down the stairs. Clara ran up the remaining two steps into her bedroom, closed the door and felt the relief as the key turned. She quickly pulled the chest of drawers across the door and dragged her heavy king-size bed to build a barricade. She'd previously struggled to move it when she dropped her phone down the back last week so she was surprised she found the strength. She grabbed her laptop and sat on the bed. Her extra weight would add to the barricade. She strained her ears to listen for the sound of him climbing the stairs, but heard nothing. Opening her laptop and logging on as quickly as she could, her hands trembling, Clara hastily sent an email to William, Freya, Daisy and HR.

Subject: HELP ME, DAN SAYER IS AT MY HOUSE AND IS THREATENING ME

As she quickly added the postcode and hit the SEND button Clara prayed someone would open her email in the split second it took the universe to zap it through light and space. She listened intently. She was sure several minutes had passed but she couldn't hear a thing. Where was he? She tried to keep her breathing shallow and silent, despite the tightness of her lungs; she was sure they were about to explode.

The dogs had become quiet but were still on the patio, ears pricked, sniffing for a sign of what to do next. With all her senses on alert, Clara gently stepped off the bed, trying not to make a sound, and walked softly to the window overlooking the patio below. Gus and Bessy were laying together under the table. Lottie was still at the kitchen door. Now what? Stay where she was? Climb out of the window? But to where? She could make the dogs bark again but it was rare for anyone to walk past her cottage.

At that moment she saw something move out of the corner of her eye. Gus and Bessy rose to their feet, barking viciously and Lottie joined them as Dan appeared and quickly closed the patio gate, shutting them inside. He briefly held his hand to his head then inspected it. Was that blood? Was he injured? Was this her chance to escape? Now she knew he wasn't in the house she could quickly move to a front bedroom to try and get some attention, if anyone happened to be passing. But she needed to keep him at the back of the house to make sure he didn't come back inside. Did she have time to move the furniture and get downstairs to lock the front door? Remembering he still had the key to the kitchen door Clara abandoned what had fleetingly seemed like a great plan. Instead she opened the bedroom window. Gus and Bessy looked up at her in earnest, not understanding. She called out to them softly. 'It's OK guys, good dogs.'

'You bitch. I could report you for attempted murder,' Dan shouted at her, holding the back of his head. Clara quickly stood back from the window for a few seconds, pulled the bed slightly away from the door, then returned so he could see her. Gus and Bessy were scratching wildly at the fence, trying to get at him, and Lottie was attempting to jump over it. Dan looked around then walked towards the woodshed. Clara quickly pulled the bed and chest of drawers far enough away to make a quick exit, or pull them back into place if needed, then returned to the window. Dan had reappeared with a metal poker in his hand. *What does he want that for?* Her heart sank she saw him walk towards the patio, shouting at the dogs to shut up, wielding the weapon above his head. To Dan's surprise, Lottie opened the gate with her nose and was growling at him, still a young dog she showed great bravery. Dan shouted at her, sweeping the poker across her face, narrowly missing her. Frightened, she backed away and ran into the trees as he shouted at her.

Poor Lottie. She's still a baby, she must be petrified. Clara was glad she'd got away, but what about Gus and Bessy?

Dan turned and walked back towards the patio, towards them. 'Don't you dare!' Clara screamed as Dan swung the metal poker at them. Gus was quick to dodge out of the way, but Bessy was too slow and Clara heard the sickening thud as the poker struck her right shoulder then again across her back. Bessy yelped out in pain. The sound tore through Clara's heart. Bessy limped towards the kitchen door and lay down on her side, breathing heavily, whimpering. Gus sniffed her then ran towards Dan, snarling and growling. Clara watched helplessly as Dan took another swing at him, but brave Gus dodged the blow and ran behind him. In the next second Clara saw Dan's face contort, then he screamed out in pain as Gus sunk his teeth just below his left calf muscle and clung on tight. Dan fell to the ground with Gus still attached to his leg. Dan reached and grabbed Gus by the scruff of the neck, Gus let go of his leg but snapped at his hand. Dan writhed on the ground, alternating between clutching his leg and looking at his bleeding hand.

Clara took her chance. She ran down the stairs, grabbed her car keys from the hall table and ran out of the open front door calling for Gus. She had to get him somewhere safe, indoors wasn't an option. Besides, Bessy was still in danger. Gus heard her call and ran towards her from the back of the house, Clara opened her car door and put him inside. She ran to open the gate but as she turned to run back to the car, she saw the tyres were flat. Dan was limping towards her down the side of the cottage; the poker still in his hand. Clara pressed the button on the key fob and locked Gus inside the car, then ran out into the road. There wasn't a person or car in sight.

The sound of metal hitting glass made her turn on the spot. Dan was smashing the poker against the windscreen of her car. A petrified Gus was barking frantically inside. Clara ran back into the driveway screaming.

'Stop it! Stop! Stop! I'll do what you want, just leave him alone.'

Dan glared at her, pausing momentarily, then continued to attack the windscreen like he'd been possessed. Clara ran as best she could, screaming as she jumped on his back and clawed at his face. He swung around with her still attached to him, but her extra weight was too much for his injured leg and they fell onto the gravel. As Clara lay on the hard stones with Dan's heavy frame on top of her, she realised she was unable to move. Pinned to the ground, she froze with fear. She could feel and hear him breathing heavily. They both lay still for a moment before he quickly turned himself around to face her. His breath invading hers, his eyes piercing, inches from hers. It could have been twenty-five years ago in that very moment.

'Ha! Gotcha.' Clara felt drops of saliva from his mouth land on her face. 'This brings back memories.'

As Dan raised himself onto his hands, his body still heavy on hers, Clara brought her knee up as hard as she could and made solid contact with his groin. He gave out a deep groan and rolled off her, clutching his balls. Clara scrambled to her feet, unsure of what to do or where to go. Dan pulled himself up gingerly and stood between her and the gate. She'd gone too far. She had never seen him this angry, even more now than when he'd held a razor blade to her throat. From then on, she'd known he was capable of more than she'd realised and had taken care not to provoke him. Right now she feared for her life.

A vehicle drove by but disappeared before Clara could get their attention. Running out of options she needed to entice him away from Gus. Clara was desperate to know if Bessy was OK but she daren't draw him near her either. Instead, she ran towards the dilapidated barn where *Tinker* the old red tractor stood. She remembered there were some old tools among the debris under the collapsed roof, and pieces of metal frame from the old greenhouse. She was sure there was something there she could use to defend herself. She ran as fast as she could, her weak ankle causing her to limp heavily. Dan gave chase and Clara prayed she could get there first. What she was prepared to do when she got there, she had no idea. Had anyone opened her email? Was anyone coming?

Dan stumbled and Clara took her chance to get further ahead. She heard him curse and swear after her. Making the most of her head start Clara ran around the back of the barn, hoping he'd think she was hiding inside it. All she had time to pick up was an old wooden fence post, it would have to do. She remembered the small shed at the end of the garden where William had been the day of the open house. Surely that would buy her some more time. Clara made her way as quietly as she could, keeping low through the fruit trees, thankful for the tall grass providing cover. When she eventually reached the shed she remembered the door had been blown away in the storm.

'CLARA!' he was getting angry now, she needed to get out of sight. Perhaps if she got her breath back she could outrun him and get to the road. She crept into the shed and crouched in a corner trying hard not to breath in case he heard her. An old tarpaulin, covered in spider's webs, in the opposite corner of the shed moved slightly. Clara put her hand over her mouth to stifle a scream. It moved again. It was too big for a rat, she hated rats. Maybe it was a cat, or a fox, or a badger or... Whatever it was she'd have to be brave and not blow her cover. A thudding sound repeatedly reverberated on the floor. Clara held her breath, what on earth could it be? The sound of a quiet whimper emanated from underneath the tarpaulin. Clara looked closer as it moved again. She could see a black nose and dark eyes looking back at her. She pulled the tarpaulin away.

'Lottie! Here you are! Good girl,' she whispered. Lottie was shaking with fright and relief at seeing Clara. After running off she'd hidden in the trees and seen Dan attack Bessy whose cries had frightened her again. She'd run towards the cliff-edge then taken refuge in the shed. Clara shuffled over to Lottie, cuddling her close, pulling the tarpaulin over them both.

'Ssssh.' They sat as still as statues, each breathe silent. Clara felt as though her ears were on stalks, like antennae, listening for any sound, but it was fruitless as the noise of the waves below drowned everything else out. Several moments passed as they waited. His voice was closer now.

'Clara! Clara! I *will* find you.'

Clara pulled Lottie to her. Her chest pounding as though it would explode, her heart thumping against it. Without warning Bessy suddenly appeared at the doorway. Clara and Lottie almost jumped off the floor. She limped over to them, her breathing heavy, her tail making an attempt to wag. Clara noticed she had something in her mouth. It was a mobile phone! It had fallen out of Dan's pocket when he struggled with Gus. As Bessy looked at her Clara could see the pain in her eyes. Bessy turned and limped out of the shed, almost dragging herself along to the cliff edge where she sat, panting heavily.

'What are you doing here you stupid dog?' He was here! Clara could see he still had the poker in his hand. She felt as though her head would explode. If he touched Bessy she would have to break cover, she gripped the fence post tightly in her hand and hoped it would be enough to defend herself and the dogs. As Dan approached Bessy she dropped to the ground, she had used all her energy to find Clara and now her injuries were too much for her to put up a fight.

'Do you fancy a short walk off a tall cliff you squat nosed ugly bitch?'

Bessy slowly opened her mouth and dropped the mobile phone onto the grass.

'That's my phone you bloody thief,' Dan walked over to her, shouting. 'You've slobbered all over it you disgusting mutt.' He bent down to pick up the phone but Lottie must have thought he was going to attack Bessy again. In a split second she tore herself from Clara's arms, ran out of the shed and launched herself at Dan, hitting him with the full force of her weight on his backside, catching him off balance. Clara watched open mouthed as Dan Sayer disappeared over the edge of the cliff. She heard him scream, then she heard... the sound of the sea.

She wanted to scream; scream to let out the fear, the relief, the shock and disbelief. Instead, she scrambled to her feet and ran to Lottie and Bessy at the cliff edge. Sitting down on the grass she pulled them to her.

'Oh my God! What just happened? Bessy, are you OK?' Bessy was laying on her side, still panting heavily. The wounds Dan had inflicted on her clearly visible now. She gently stroked Bessy's head. *Please God, let her be OK.* They all sat huddled together on the ground, buffeted by the wind, unable to move. Clara couldn't bring herself to look over the cliff. Was it really all over?

Lottie's ears pricked up and Bessy let out a low growl, her only remaining defence as she lay helpless and injured on the ground. Clara heard sirens in the distance; getting closer, then men's voices shouting, dogs barking. Dare she believe they were safe? 'Over here!' she called, surprised at the rasp in her voice as it caught in her throat and the tears that flowed freely down her face.

24

Linda had tried to talk her out of it. 'Are you sure you're going to be OK?'

'Yes mum, I'll be fine. Anyway, we'll see you next week when you come up, won't we Gus?'

Going to Tonbridge had been the right thing to do, six weeks ago. She'd had given Linda a watered-down version of her history with Dan. There was no need to reveal all the details. Now it was time to return home. William had arranged for the cottage to be professionally cleaned after the police had completed their investigations and cleared the crime scene, plus he'd organised for new door locks to be fitted.

The police returned the old kitchen door key. It was still in Dan's pocket when his body was found washed up on a beach several miles up the coast. Clara felt sorry for the couple out walking their dog who found him. Sometimes she felt sorry for herself too, and more times than she cared to admit, she had terrible nightmares.

Linda often heard her daughter making tea in the early hours of the morning. She left her bedroom door open, and for the first week Clara was there Linda awoke each morning to find her sleeping beside her, Gus laying at her feet.

William, Freya and Daisy had been regular visitors to

Tonbridge, taking it in turns to keep Clara busy and listening to her recall what had happened, gradually talking it out of her system.

Daisy brought news from work that Dan's wife had been visited by the police shortly after he'd left for England. They were there to arrest him for rape. The rumour circulating at work was he'd jumped off a cliff to avoid being sent back to the States. HR had, so far, managed to keep Clara's desperate email a secret, but Clara knew it was only a matter of time before they all learned of her involvement. Chrissie, Director of Human Resources, visited Clara in Tonbridge.

'... and he'd rearranged the whole department which effectively made your position redundant. We believe he was trying to pay you off. The company is sympathetic towards your situation and regrets the trauma you've suffered at his hands. We have a couple of options for you, moving forward.' Chrissie shuffled in her chair; Clara could sense her discomfort. 'The first is a phased return. We can find you an alternative role, same pay grade of course...'

'What's the second option?' Clara interrupted her. Again, Chrissie looked uncomfortable, sometimes she hated her job.

'Erm, we can offer what we hope you feel is a generous redundancy package. The changes he made actually make sense and ...'

'I'll take it!' Clara interrupted again. 'I can't go back there, I'll take it. Did you bring the paperwork with you?' Chrissie reached into her oversized Michael Kors leather tote bag and took out an A4 envelope.

'I hope you find it acceptable. We at Coopers and Leigh, hope that we can all put this episode behind us and move forward.' *Episode?* Clara hoped Chrissie knew exactly how unsympathetic and utterly unfeeling the company's rhetoric sounded, *It's not bloody Eastenders!* She pulled out the paperwork and flicked through the pages to find the figures. Even Clara had to raise an eyebrow at the amount staring back at her. Chrissie continued.

'I suggest you show this to a solicitor before you sign it.'

Two weeks later Clara received a hefty lump sum deposited into her bank account. Having returned her company car, she ordered a second-hand Black Range Rover Evoque. *Just the ticket for those Norfolk roads,* she thought.

Even Clara had questioned whether she could return to the cottage, but only for a fleeting moment. She had enough money now to make the changes she'd planned. The fence had already been erected along the cliff edge; William had arranged that too. He was waiting for her when she pulled into the driveway.

Lottie ran to greet them both and she and Gus danced around, clearly pleased to see each other. William hugged Clara, lifting her off the ground and swinging her around. He kissed her, then looked questioningly into her eyes.

'Are you ready?'

'I will be when you put me down!' Clara was smiling into his eyes. She'd never tire of them she decided.

Gus and Lottie rushed past them into the cottage, William followed Clara inside. She walked directly into the living room where an open fire was roaring in the hearth. It all looked the same. What had she been expecting?

'Are you OK?' William asked.

'Yeah, I'm fine. I suppose I should take a look around just to make sure he's not here. I know he isn't, but my eyes need to tell my brain that.' Slowly they took their time to look around the cottage. As she climbed the stairs Clara tried hard to push away the memory of the last time she was there. Her bedroom furniture had been returned to its original position but a vase full of a dozen red roses stood on the dressing table. Clara turned to smile at William.

'You're such an old romantic.'

'Hey! Not so much of the 'old' thank you very much.' They walked over to the window to where Clara could see the new fence. William put his arm around her waist and she leant her head on his shoulder.

He'd had taken the week off work having liaised with Linda. Neither of them admitted to Clara they had planned not to leave her alone, but she guessed as much. They took long walks, saw a show at the end of Cromer Pier, ate out, slept in, and went to sleep in each other's arms every night. Clara's nightmares had started to subside but Bessy was always in them.

Bessy had spent a few days at the vet following an operation to repair her wounds. Tina had taken her home with her to recover but yesterday messaged Clara to say she was ready to be rehomed.

William was fast asleep, but Clara had been woken by another bad dream. She snuggled up to him causing him to stir.

'Do you think Bessy will find it too traumatic being here?' she whispered to him. She lay her head on his chest and wrapped her arm around his waist. The hairs on his chest tickled her nose.

'I think only Bessy will know the answer to that,' he replied sleepily, yawning and turning to face her. 'Are we awake now then?' He was becoming used to Clara's disturbed sleep, which often resulted in tea, biscuits, and meaningful chats in the early hours. Gus and Lottie would eagerly hoover up the crumbs in the morning. Instinctively William knew they would be visiting Tina and Bessy later that day. Clara fell asleep in his arms, comforted by the thought of seeing Bessy in a few hours, she'd tell William in the morning!

They left Gus and Lottie at home and drove to Heathfields. Tina thought it best Clara and William see Bessy without them. As they walked towards the kennels Clara's hand gripped William's. Tina had seen them arrive and was waiting for them with Bessy at her side, Clara called out to her. Bessy had been sniffing Tina's boots, but her head whipped around at the sound of Clara's voice. Her whole body weaved from side to side as she wagged her short tail and strained on her lead as Clara approached, dragging Tina towards her.

'She doesn't get that excited when she sees me!' Tina laughed, letting go of the lead. Bessy rushed to Clara who knelt with her arms open wide, Bessy ran into them for an emotional reunion.

William stayed with Tina while Clara took Bessy for a walk.

'How's she doing?' Tina asked. William thought for a moment.

'She's coping, but we're taking it a day at a time. Seeing Bessy will be good for her. Do you think Bessy would be okay if she came back to live at the cottage?' Tina shrugged.

'Take her back for a visit, see how she reacts. She'll let you know.'

25

Gus and Lottie jumped up at the sound of the knock on the front door and ran barking into the hallway. Bessy lolled along behind them growling deeply. Clara looked at William, he saw the flicker of fear in her eyes.

'I'll go.'

It was Saturday morning, but her mum wasn't due for at least another hour. William opened the door and Clara listened intently. She could tell by the sound of his voice he seemed surprised. Then she heard another man's voice in the hallway, it was getting closer. Clara stood up, who could it be? William appeared, followed by a man of around the same age, slightly taller with dark hair and dark eyes. He looked around the room before settling his gaze on Clara.

'Clara, this is Michael, my friend, your cousin.' Michael stepped forward to shake her hand. As she took it their eyes met and Clara felt a tingle, like an electric current, flow up her arm and down her spine. *That's weird*, she thought, somewhat startled as the energy zapped through her. *It must be the family connection, perhaps an ancestral ghost has passed through me giving me the eeby jeebies!*

'I've come to see how you are. I'm so very sorry to hear what happened.' His voice was soft with a slight Norfolk twang. 'William said he was staying with you this week, I hope you don't mind me dropping in.'

William disappeared into the kitchen to make tea. Clara smiled at Michael.

'Sit down, I'm so pleased to finally meet you, thank you for coming.' Michael took off his coat, the fire was roaring.

'That fireplace always did have a good draw to it. It heats up the place in no time.'

Clara turned in her chair to face Michael.

'I'm so sorry I offended you when I bought the cottage, I just fell in love with it.'

Michael held up both hands. 'I'll admit I was fuming when I realised what father had done, I still don't understand it, but it's done now, and you seem like a really nice person. According to William that is!'

Clara smiled, Michael smiled back.

'It's so strange,' Clara wasn't sure where she was going with this comment, 'but I'm looking at you for a family resemblance, but I didn't even know I had a family so I'm not sure what I'm looking for!'

'Well, I was always told I looked like my grandfather, but with my grandmother's eyes.'

Clara looked at him closer.

'Then my mum must have her eyes too because they're the same. See, I've found the family resemblance!' William returned with a tray of teas and homemade ginger biscuits he'd impressed Clara with yesterday.

'It's a miracle there are any left after Clara devoured most of them.'

William and Michael laughed as they recounted stories of their childhood for Clara's amusement; getting into trouble at school for taking Michael's pet toad, arguing over who was going to ask Susie Croucher to dance at the end of year disco and whose mum made the best jam roly poly. As Clara enjoyed listening to their banter she realised there was so much about William she didn't know.

Michael complained that as his birthday was always in the middle of summer he never had a birthday party as all their friends were too busy helping on their family farms.

'Unlike William, whose 16th birthday party is still talked about at school reunions, for reasons I am not at liberty to disclose!'

The dogs jumped up as they heard another knock at the door. This time Clara went. 'It'll be mum.'

William noticed how she seemed more relaxed, calmer. Linda followed Clara into the living room.

'Goodness it's hot in here!' she declared. Clara took her coat.

'Mum, you'll never guess who this is. It's my cousin Michael.' Linda stood open mouthed, staring at the stranger, her mother's eyes staring back at her. William greeted Linda with a kiss on the cheek then turned to Clara.

'Actually Clara, I've just realised, you and Michael have the same birthday. You could be twins!' he laughed. Clara looked at Michael.

'Bagsy being the eldest!' Clara turned to Linda, but she wasn't there. 'Mum? Mum, where are you?' Clara walked into the hallway to find Linda sitting on the stairs. 'Mum, you look awful, are you OK?'

'It's too hot in there, or maybe it's the long drive, I don't feel very well, I'll go upstairs for a while.' Clara returned to the living room; Michael was putting on his coat.

'I popped in to see how you are, and I suppose I was just a bit interested to meet my long-lost cousin. Now I've met you, it will be nice to come back and visit the old place, if you don't mind.'

William saw Michael to the door and Clara went upstairs to check on her mum. She tapped quietly on the bedroom door, but

Linda didn't answer. She opened the door and peeped inside. Linda was in bed; Clara watched the rise and fall of her breathing for a few moments then closed the door. It was a long drive from Tonbridge. *Perhaps she'll be OK after a sleep*, she thought. Clara joined William downstairs, he opened a bottle of wine and they lay on the sofa together watching the fire. William kissed Clara's head.

'Is your mum OK?'

'She was asleep when I went up,' she replied, 'I'll check on her again in an hour or so.'

Clara was woken by a wet nose on her face, she wiped it away with her hand and opened her eyes to see Lottie looking at her.

'What's up Lottie? Do you want to go out?' Clara untangled herself from William, who was snoring gently, and stood up from the sofa.

'Come on girl, let's go,' but instead of following Clara to the kitchen Lottie walked towards the hall, stopped in the doorway, and looked over her shoulder at Clara.

'What do you want Lottie?'

Clara followed Lottie as she slowly climbed the stairs and made her way to Linda's room where she lifted her paw to scratch the door. Slightly alarmed, Clara put her ear to the door. On hearing an unusual sound she knocked and opened it.

'Mum, are you OK?' Linda was sitting on the edge of the bed looking out of the window, her back to the door. As Clara walked around the other side of the bed, she could see Linda was crying.

'Mum! What's the matter? Shall I call a doctor?' Linda looked at Clara and let out the most painful cry Clara had ever heard. She sat on the bed beside her and hugged her as Linda wept in her arms. Clara sat in silence while Linda sobbed, letting out waves of tears, catching her breath, wiping her tears on her sodden sleeve. *Why didn't I put a box of tissues in here?* Clara thought, remaining quiet, holding her mother. She waited for her cries to subside, wondering what on earth could be wrong.

After what seemed the longest of times, Linda sat up straight, took a deep breath and held Clara's hand. Clara squeezed it slightly, letting her mum know she was there, supporting her, but wanting to understand what was wrong. Linda knew it was time. 'Please don't hate me,' Linda implored her. Clara was taken aback.

'I can't think of one reason why I ever would,' she replied hugging her mum. Linda searched in her bag, took out a small packet of tissues and opened them.

'I don't know where to start. I never dreamt I'd be having this conversation with you, although you would have found out eventually...' Linda paused, 'when I passed away.' Clara opened her mouth to say something, but she had no idea what, so she closed it again and Linda continued. 'There is a letter attached to my will, it's with my solicitor.' Clara's head was spinning.

'What's going on? What's so bad that you couldn't tell me?' She wasn't sure what she needed to prepare herself for, but she knew she was about to hear it.

'When Gavin's grandmother passed away before you were born, I had no-one left in my life to support me. She had become my best friend, my only friend. I relied on her completely, and she relied on me. We had it all planned out, how we'd cope, the things we'd all do together, we were all going to be so happy.' Clara watched her mother as tears yet again flowed down her face. She knew how close Linda had been to her paternal great-grandmother, she'd even named Clara after her.

Linda wiped away her tears and continued.

'You see... there's no easy way to say this to you. I was heavily pregnant when she passed away. *Very* heavily pregnant.' Linda sobbed and let out a stifled cry. Clara held her to her, but Linda pulled away, much to Clara's surprise. 'Clara... Michael isn't your cousin... he's your twin brother.'

Clara couldn't remember what happened next as her world turned dark. She stopped hearing, stopped breathing, stopped functioning. Her head felt solid and cold, like a block of ice, preventing her from speaking, from blinking, from thinking.

'Clara, Clara! Say something. Clara, Clara!' Linda was holding her daughter's hand, longing for her to look at her. Not even sure if she was being heard, she at last told Clara the last piece of the puzzle in her life, not sure if her beloved daughter would ever speak to her again. Could she even hear her?

26

~ FORTY FOUR YEARS AGO ~

Linda woke in the middle of the night to soaking wet sheets. After initially being horrified that she'd wet herself she realised in her sleepy state that her waters had broken. She called the hospital, cleaned herself up, got dressed, and waited for the ambulance, sitting on a chair in the hallway with her bag at her feet. She sat in silence, yet she could hear Gavin's grandma's voice; 'Now you be a brave girl, go and have those babies, and when you all come home, I'll be here waiting for you.'

Linda often heard grandma's voice talking to her, some days she wasn't sure how she got through without it. She never told anyone in case they thought she was mad, but then she didn't really have anyone to tell.

At the sight of the blue flashing lights approaching, Linda opened the door, turned around and whispered, 'See you later grandma,' then walked out to meet the ambulance crew who carefully transported her to the hospital.

'Who's your next of kin Miss Richmond? Is it still Mrs Thompson?' Clara hadn't been prepared for that question and stared at the nurse, tears welling up in her eyes. She shook her head slowly. The nurse, oblivious to Clara's reaction, continued. 'Well I need a next of kin, just in case we have to, erm, contact someone, especially as you're so young.'

There was no other choice but to give her parents' details, not that they'd care, or turn up to see if she and the babies were OK. But as it stopped the nurse from staring at her, Linda was satisfied she'd done the right thing. She was bustled into a room by a midwife who was soon joined by a second midwife and a doctor. The next twenty-six hours of her life were a blur of faces, machines, multiple examinations, voices telling her she was doing well, how many centimetres dilated, push, pant, breath, stop pushing, go again... Linda fleetingly wondered what Gavin was doing, living his student life, going out, sleeping in, getting drunk, sleeping around?

'Aaaaaargh, Grandma!' Linda heard herself call out at the start of yet another huge contraction as she sobbed unashamedly, feeling isolated and deserted. Exhausted, soaked in sweat, hungry and scared, Linda eventually gave birth to her two beautiful babies.

'We called your parents when you arrived and again when you delivered the babies. They're on their way.' Linda stared at the midwife in disbelief.

'Are you sure? Did they actually say they were coming?' Having just woken from four hours sleep, Linda wasn't sure she'd heard them correctly. Had they decided to forgive her, to help her raise her family now she was on her own? 'Where are my babies?' she looked around panicking, they were no-where to be seen.

'They're in the nursery, we thought you'd need the rest after all your hard work.'

Two more midwives wheeled the cots into Linda's side room. The decision had been made not to put her in a main ward because of her age. They didn't want the other mums talking about her, but also to allow her to get as much rest as possible.

'They've just been fed and changed.' The midwives wheeled the cots to the side of Linda's bed then they all left the room.

Linda stared at the two perfect little faces peeping out from the blankets. Everyone had been surprised by their weights, the little boy was born first weighing in at 5lb 12oz, followed by his sister, at 5lb 4oz. She loved them already and as she looked back and forth and back and forth between them, from one to the other, her eyes closed, and she fell back into a deep sleep.

She was woken by the sound of crying.

'What do I do?' Linda pushed the alarm and waited for a midwife to arrive. Little Clara had woken, and Michael was beginning to stir too. Overwhelmed by the enormity of her new responsibility Linda burst into tears.

'Oh, bless you my darling, it'll be alright.' A midwife Linda hadn't seen before walked into the room as Michael woke, demanding to be heard above Clara. Seeing Linda's tears, the midwife put her arms around her and gave her a hug.

'Look, I'll see to Mr, and you see to Mrs. We'll do it together.' Marion, the new midwife, showed Clara how to feed the babies and change their nappies. 'You'll have to decide which one has to wait when you get home, but you'll get the hang of it. Always have enough bottles ready in the fridge, and make sure you eat properly too. I always had the baby's bag packed in the hallway with everything I needed to go out, except milk. Then, if I wanted, or needed to go out, I was almost ready.'

The door opened and Barbara, one of the midwives that had helped deliver the twins, entered and smiled at Clara.

'Did you have a good sleep?'

Linda nodded. 'Yes thank you.'

Barbara handed Linda an envelope. 'Your parents were here earlier, they didn't want to wake you, but they saw the babies. They left you this envelope. I suppose they'll be back later.' Barbara handed the envelope to Linda and asked Marion to help her in room 2. Linda was on her own, again.

She stared at the envelope in her hands, it was strange to see her mother's handwriting after all these years. They'd been here, in this hospital, looking at her babies. Would they be back soon? She opened the envelope.

Linda,

We were surprised to hear your news, two babies. We realise it will be a huge struggle for you now that Mrs Thompson is dead. How will you cope with two babies when it would have been bad enough with one? You don't have any money, you don't have a permanent home, you don't have anyone to help you. Your children will grow up in poverty and may be taken into care if you can't cope.

We have a proposal for you which we feel is sensible all 'round. David and Janine will adopt the boy. Janine had a miscarriage just after you left, the doctors have told her she cannot have any more children. They have already lost our lovely Stephen, we have all suffered so much.

In return, we will buy the bungalow from the Richmonds for you and the girl to live in, on these conditions. You will NEVER tell anyone about us or our arrangement, even the girl. We don't want her to come looking for the boy and we don't have a daughter anymore; we hope you have better luck with yours. The boy will work on the farm, he will have a good life, with family, a good education and one day he will inherit the business. What better life could you give him? Furthermore, you will not return to Norfolk while any of the family members remain alive.

With only one child to care for, and a roof over your heads, you will have a better chance of keeping your daughter. David and Janine will collect the boy this Saturday, the day you are due to go home, they will collect you from the hospital and take you to the bungalow. They will have papers from our solicitor for you to sign.

Mr and Mrs D Reid

P.S. If you are in agreement, ask a nurse to call us and say thank you for our letter.'

The letter fell into Linda's lap as she clasped her hands to her mouth. It took all her strength to stifle a scream, a scream that started in the depths of her soul and shuddered through her body fighting its way out, sure to pierce anyone's heart who would have heard it. Linda rocked back and forth as she fought to keep it inside.

Her parents, to whom she'd only ever been a disappointment, wanted to take her baby boy away. They had it all planned. He'd replace Stephen, he'd be the apple of their eye, they'd give him the attention they never gave her. David and Janine would raise him as their own son. He'd never know his real mother, or his twin sister.

No! How dare they take anything else away from her. They'd taken away her home, her friends, and sent her away. She would never give up a child. But what if they're right? What if I can't cope? What if social services take them both away from me? What life can I give them? Where will we live? Can I keep them safe?

Linda barely slept that night, fretting about her parents' proposal, although it felt more like an ultimatum. The twins took it in turns to demand feeding, changing and cuddling. By the break of dawn Linda could hardly speak. Barbara came on duty at 7am, saw how exhausted she was and took the twins to the nursery so Linda could get some rest. Linda tried to object, petrified that her parents or David were close by, waiting for Michael to be separated from her so they could snatch him. She slept fitfully and woke to find Barbara looking through the window at her, she entered when she saw Linda was awake.

'Hello lovely. There's a lady here to see you, she's from Social Services, she just needs a chat about when you go home. I'll let her in then get you a nice cup of tea and a biscuit. The twins are fine, they're asleep at the moment.' Linda felt relieved that the twins were sleeping, but frightened by the prospect of a visit from Social Services so soon.

'... so you don't own where you live, or have a rental agreement? I see. The owners, Mr and Mrs Richmond, contacted us to say they are happy for you to stay there until you are 18, which is...' the lady from Social Services looked at her paperwork. '... in four months' time. So, we may as well look at getting you rehoused now. You will go to the top of the list for emergency housing, which may initially be a shared house with other young mums. But seeing as you have two babies we'll need a large room to become available. Sometimes, if we don't have space in our area, we have agreements with other authorities, someone will take you all. I assume you don't object to moving to another area as you don't have anyone close around here anyway.'

Barbara entered with a cup of tea for Linda, she looked at the lady as if to say, 'I'm not getting you one, I know why you're here.' Barbara smiled a kindly smile at Linda as she left the room.

'There are other options open to you,' she resumed. 'Have you considered adoption? There are lots of lovely kind people waiting for a baby. We may have to split them up though, not many people feel they can cope with two.'

Linda was horrified. They were all trying to take her babies away from her. She wished she could scoop them up and escape from there. But where would she go?

Clara and Michael seemed to sense something was wrong, they kept Linda very busy for the rest of the day but she refused to let anyone take them to the nursery. Barbara popped in to help as much as she could, but her shift finished at 7pm.

'You need some sleep lovely. Your babies need you to sleep too, you can't just keep going.' Linda didn't have enough energy to object anymore so Barbara took the twins off to let her rest. 'They'll be back in the morning before you know it,' she smiled as she wheeled them out. Linda was asleep before the door closed.

She dreamt about someone trying to steal her babies, she dreamt about them all living in one room with rats and soaking wet mouldy wallpaper, she dreamt about living back in Norfolk with Clara and Michael aged about six, running around the fields laughing together, she dreamt about Gavin's grandmother smiling at her. Linda awoke, scared for all their futures.

Barbara returned with the twins as soon as she was on shift. It was Friday. Linda asked to be left to cope on her own for the rest of the day. Tomorrow they were due to go home, with no-one to help, and soon they would have to move, again with no-one to help. By midday she was exhausted again.

'What would grandma do?' Linda quietly asked the twins. Looking at Michael, Linda knew with David and Janine he would have a good life, he would be well cared for and never be hungry. Should she let Clara be adopted too, allow her to live with a family and be safe and warm? 'What would grandma say?' Linda wasn't sure grandma would have the answer either.

The door opened. The lady from Social Services was back, questioning Linda about going home tomorrow.

'Who's collecting you? Do you have car seats for both the babies?' Backed into a corner, Linda lied, sort of.

'My brother and his wife are collecting me; they have suitable transport for all of us. He's twelve years older than me, so he's... grown up.' Never had Linda felt more helpless than at that moment. She couldn't even arrange her own transport back home for herself and two babies. She needed help. She'd need a lot of help, for a long time to come. What would their future be?

That night, Linda dreamt that Michael was riding with her brother David on a tractor, he was waving at her and smiling, but she wasn't there with him, she was looking through a crystal ball. Turning around she could see Clara playing in the garden of the bungalow with her friends from school, they were laughing. Clara had long dark hair, tied in a bow and she was wearing her new birthday clothes and shoes. In her dream, Linda had collected Clara and her friends from school after work and taken them out for tea, before a play date at home with games and a big birthday cake Linda had secretly made. But as the colour and the children's smiles began to fade, Linda felt cold and scared. Michael and Clara were lost in the woods, she couldn't find them. Eventually she stumbled across a ripped tent and found them cowering inside. To her surprise she crept into the tent, tucked them into damp sleeping bags and cuddled up beside them. This was their home.

Linda sat bolt upright in bed, grateful to still be in the safety of the hospital. She needed a wee. Sitting on the toilet in the bathroom attached to the room, Linda heard the babies wake and start to cry. She cried too, silently, but just as desperately. It was Saturday.

They were both still crying when she returned to the room. As she picked up Clara she heard the door open behind her. Turning to ask Barbara for help with Michael she saw David and Janine standing in the doorway.

'You're early!' Linda snapped. Janine walked towards her.

'I... we... just wanted to see if you are all OK.' Janine looked at Clara, then at Michael, but didn't move towards him. 'Shall I hold the little girl while you pick him up?' she asked. Linda was taken aback; she wasn't used to such kindness from her family. She hesitated.

'No, it's OK, you can pick him up.' Janine didn't need telling twice, but aware of Linda's fragile emotions she slowly picked Michael up and held him in her arms. He immediately stopped crying. The silence brought Linda a mixture of emotions: relief, helplessness and inadequacy. Both women stood looking at each other, each with a baby in their arms, each with a longing in their hearts. Their eyes met and Linda felt her heart would break as she nodded to Janine.

'Yes. OK,' Linda whispered. Janine couldn't suppress a sharp intake of breath, it was more than she had dared to hope for, it was more than she believed was possible. David stepped forward,

'We'll love him and care for him. He'll have everything he needs, and more.'

'Except he won't have his mum,' Clara corrected him. Janine looked at David then back at Linda.

'No, he won't have his mum. But his mum would have given him the best gift possible, a happy life, and we will be eternally grateful to you for that and be the best parents we can be. We will look after him for you.'

'I want a photo of them together, before you leave,' Linda insisted. She wanted to make sure she never forgot his face.

Janine produced a polaroid from her bag. 'We thought you might.'

They drove to Linda's bungalow in silence, the twins lay awake, calmed by the sound and motion of the car. David parked in the driveway and opened the rear door to take Michael out of the car but Linda stopped him.

'No, he's comfortable. If he comes inside then I won't be able to let him go. David carried Clara into the bungalow and Janine stayed in the car with Michael. Once inside, David produced an envelope from his pocket.

'The solicitor drew this up in case you decided... I don't know what to say Linda. Thank you, and, I'm sorry. I wasn't really aware of what was happening until after you left. We never did have much to do with each other. I'll be forever grateful to you.'

Linda quickly read the agreement and scrawled her signature; suppressing the urge to scream and run out to get Michael.

'Don't change his name. Promise me.' David took back the paperwork and handed Linda another envelope.

'I promise.' Then he turned and left. Linda couldn't look out the window, she carried baby Clara into her bedroom, lay her on the bed and snuggled up next to her. Later, when she opened the envelope, she discovered it contained £1,000 in cash.

27

All these years later Linda still remembered thinking a hundred million pounds wouldn't have been enough to take the pain away. Over the years the heartache and pain had softened, but it was always there, a permanent dull ache she carried with her every day. Clara was now a grown woman, she'd worked hard, and Linda had given her enough love and support for two. Each day when she woke, she said a quiet 'hello' to Michael and 'goodnight' before she fell sleep. She even left a soft light on in her bedroom at night to remind her of him. Not that she would ever forget. She prayed the twins would find it in their hearts to forgive her once she had gone, for it was a pain too great for her to bear while she lived.

Clara remained sitting beside Linda. She heard all she'd said, but it was as if her mum was telling her a story, a story about someone else, someone in the next street or a friend of a friend. Her mother had read her bedtime stories hundreds of times but none of them had been so incredibly sad.

Linda waited for Clara to speak but instead she stood up and left the room. Linda heard her go downstairs and out the front door. William called after her.

'Clara, where are you going?'

Linda watched out of bedroom window as Clara pulled on her coat and walked up the lane, Gus and Bessy following her. Then the front door banged, William and Lottie ran to catch them up.

He put his arm through Clara's and they walked along together

Linda waited more than three hours for Clara and William to return. She put her case back in her car, tidied the bed, finished a pile of ironing she found in the spare room and made a chicken casserole. She wasn't going to leave without saying goodbye, or trying to, if Clara would let her.

The sound of a vehicle pulling up outside drew her to the living room window. It was Fred's old truck. Clara, William and the dogs got out. Linda sat on the edge of the sofa, her hands on her knees, waiting. Clara walked in and stopped when she saw her. William took the dogs upstairs.

'You'll have to tell Michael. He has to know the truth,' Clara announced, then walked into the kitchen. She took a bottle wine out of the fridge, left it on the side then walked back into the living room. 'I will need some time to come to terms with this. I can't be angry with a frightened young girl who had everything to lose. I'm not angry with you. I get it. You *are* the frightened young girl, it's just that you're my mum too.' Clara was about to say '... and we don't keep secrets from each other,' when she remembered how she'd kept the truth from Linda about Dan Sayer to avoid upsetting her. She returned to the kitchen. Deciding she needed a clear head, she filled the kettle to make tea.

How could she be angry with her mum? Hadn't she given her a loving, stable childhood and made sacrifices for her? Linda had worked part-time once Clara started school, yet she'd always taken her, picked her up, been there for sports days, swimming galas, nativities and been home for the school holidays. She'd put wholesome food on her plate, kept her clean and well-clothed, tucked her in at bedtime and read to her, nursed her through sickness, coughs, colds and chickenpox. What more could she have asked of her?

William had remained silent while Clara poured out her mother's secret to him, allowing her to exorcise her emotions and feelings. She cursed her cold-hearted grandparents. She cursed her own father and his parents. How could they let this happen? How could they abandon a young girl to fend for herself? William held her in his arms as she cried. Gus, Bessy and Lottie stood next to them in the bitter cold. He took her to his parents' home, where Fred made them tea and listened to Clara's story. When it appeared that Clara had nothing more to say, Fred spoke.

'He were always a happy child, was Michael.' She looked at him surprised. Fred continued. 'They were a might overprotective you could say, but he wanted fer nothin'. Can't say the two of you would o' had such a gret life if yer mother had kept you together. Seems she dint ha' much of a choice. Hint no good you puttin' on yer parts now.' That was all Fred had to say on the matter.

For once, Clara understood every word Fred said. And he was right. She was feeling sorry for herself when she had no right to. It was Linda who had suffered all these years. It was time to stop thinking of herself and get back to her mum.

'Will you go and see Janine? She still lives at the farm with Michael and his two boys. Mum, you have grandchildren to get to know.' Clara handed Linda a mug of tea and sat down in the armchair. Even though Linda had wondered over the years if Michael had his own family she had never expected to meet them. How would they react to her? How would she tell him? Linda and Clara agreed it was best coming from Janine. William sent Michael a message the following day, saying Linda would like to visit his mother.

Michael took off his boots, he could smell dinner cooking, he was ready for a hot and wholesome meal, it was just what he needed to get him through the rest of the day. He hung his well-worn jacket on the old stand that had held the Reid family's coats for over a hundred years, and walked into the farmhouse utility room to wash-up. He'd been out since 4am. It was an almost daily regime he'd followed since he was sixteen years old. Janine was loading the washing machine. He bent down to kiss her on the cheek. Her small frame and features were so delicate now, almost like porcelain. He remembered how he towered over her even at age twelve; and had been looking down on her ever since, yet he looked up to her with every beat of his heart. He couldn't remember her ever having a cross word with anyone. She was the kindest, sweetest woman he knew, she had borne such grief and yet given him so much love. He understood why his parents had been so protective of him, having lost their first son. At times he'd tried to rebel, but they always explained things to him with kindness and understanding. His father David had been a quiet man, overshadowed by his own overbearing parents. They'd worked him hard, their only child, who was to inherit the farm and uphold the Reid family name in the farming community. David had not been a particularly tall man, and Michael sometimes wondered how he himself had crept over six feet by the time he was sixteen. His grandparents told him it was the fresh air, good food and hard work. Besides, his father hadn't eaten his brussel sprouts when he was young, which is why he stopped short at 5 feet 8 inches! If ever something would entice a young lad to eat brussel sprouts it was the promise of one day growing taller than his father.

Michael learnt of the existence of Linda and Clara at the reading of his father's will. He'd always been told his father was an only child, no one had ever mentioned a sister. Why would they all lie to him? The solicitor waited for him to calm down as he refused to believe what his father had requested. Janine sat quietly, praying her husband's will wouldn't reveal that Michael wasn't their real son. Along with the will, Michael also received a letter, written several years ago by David before his death. In it, he explained that he had a sister, Linda, who had been sent away for bringing disgrace upon the family at age sixteen. She had a daughter, who David believed was entitled to a small recompense from the family. After all, she wasn't guilty of anything. Michael had been furious, how could his father split up the family estate for some outcast who hadn't lifted a finger to help?

After William told him about her ordeal with Dan, he had visited Clara out of good manners. He'd expected to find a jumped up, spoilt, snooty London socialite. Instead, he was surprised at how he immediately warmed to her, feeling at ease in her company, he even thought he'd visit her again. The arrival of his disgraced Aunt Linda and her quick disappearing act led him to believe she was still ashamed of her behaviour, even after all these years. He was undecided how he felt about her. Perhaps he'd get to meet her another time.

Michael had kept his meeting with Clara secret from his mother as she'd seemed very upset when she'd bought the cottage. Janine had been even more quiet than usual ever since. He tentatively approached the subject.

'Mum. I met my cousin Clara yesterday.' Michael looked sideways at his mother while he dried his hands, to gauge her reaction. Janine stopped momentarily as she switched on the washing machine. Michael thought he heard her take a sharp intake of breath, but he couldn't be sure as the water gushed into the machine. He waited a few moments and then continued. 'I thought it was only right seeing she'd had that spot of trouble, so I went over to see if she was OK.'

News of the break-in at the cottage and subsequent death of the attacker had spread through the community faster than a plague of locusts. Janine managed a half-smile as she walked past him and into the kitchen.

'Dinner will be on the table. Christine has made lamb hotpot.' Michael followed her, kicking off his shoes.

'I was surprised by how much I liked her. She's dating William. What a coincidence ay? Anyway, her mum turned up while I was there, I suppose she's my aunt. Linda, that's her name. William said she'd like to come and see you.'

Janine felt her knees give way under her. She stumbled and grabbed onto a kitchen chair just in time to break her fall.

'Mum! Are you OK?' Michael reached out to her, holding her steady, pulling out another chair for her to sit on.

'Christine, get mum some water please.'

Christine was much like Janine in her build. She too came from a farming family, over near Kings Lynn. The youngest of three girls and two boys, she'd been brought up working in the house, supporting the men who went out into the fields in the early hours of the morning, reappearing at midday to be fed, then out again until long after it was dark. She'd rather be in a warm kitchen baking bread and weighing eggs than out in the freezing cold. In the warmer weather she got to help feed the lambs whose mothers had died while giving birth or didn't have enough milk to feed them. Michael had visited her family farm with David when he was ten years old. They were the same age, yet he was already tall and strong as he helped his father load several lambs onto the truck. He was invited into the kitchen for milk and homemade biscuits while their fathers chatted. Christine was sure she fell in love with him as they sat at the table together, his dark hair and eyes a sharp contrast to her blonde hair and blue eyes.

Michael offered her the last biscuit, when she declined he snapped it in half to share with her. She wrote to him after that, to enquire about the lambs. They married when they were twenty-one and two years later she gave birth to twin boys. Michael laughed when they discovered she was expecting two babies. 'It's just like breaking a biscuit in two, so we have one each!' he declared.

Michael helped Janine to sit down. 'I'm okay, probably a bit hungrier than I realised,' she lied. They ate in silence. Michael was worried. He'd recently lost his beloved father; he couldn't lose his mother so soon after. He decided not to push the subject of Linda visiting. It could wait a couple of days.

28

'Hello Janine.' Linda had taken it upon herself to call into the farm the next day. She couldn't wait any longer. It was time he knew the truth. She *needed* him to know the truth. Janine stared at Linda as she stood in the doorway to the kitchen. As their eyes locked a silent conversation passed between them, then Janine nodded.

'I'll tell him tonight.'

There was nothing more to be said.

As Linda pulled out of the yard she clung tightly onto the steering wheel. Returning to her family home, to the ghost of her past, had taken so much of the strength and resolve she'd acquired over the years. Hardship had strengthened but not hardened her. She was here to reclaim her son, to stand up for the young girl who was sent away, forgotten and abandoned.

Linda returned to the cottage and made far too many apple pies. She had to keep busy.

William called Clara late that evening. 'I've had a long conversation with Michael. He's on his way over.'

Clara sat in the living room as Linda paced up and down, periodically poking the fire in between looking at her watch and out of the front window.

'The dogs will tell us when he arrives mum.' Clara watched her walk back and forth, wringing her hands, breathing deeply and tidying her hair.

The dogs jumped up from their usual place in front of the fire at the sound of the gate opening followed by wheels on the gravel drive. They ran barking to the front door. Linda swung around and looked at Clara, fear, hope and tears in her eyes, she held her hands to her chest. Clara went to the door while Linda stood frozen to the spot in the living room. Several seconds later Michael appeared. His tall frame almost filled the doorway as he stood looking at Linda. She daren't breathe. Was he here to denounce or accept her? Clara waited behind Michael in the hallway. They had hugged briefly when he arrived, words hadn't been necessary, but he needed to see Linda.

At the sight of his birth mother looking at him, Michael let out a loud sob as he broke down in tears and hung onto the doorframe weeping unashamedly. Linda went to him, holding his face in her hands, wiping his tears away with her fingers. He sobbed as he bent to embrace her, and Linda held her son in her arms once again.

'I'm so sorry Michael, so very very sorry. I didn't know what to do, I was scared, it broke my heart to let you go.' Linda wept as she held him. Michael pulled gently away, holding Linda's hands, looking at the mother he never knew he had.

'They should have looked after you.'

The three of them talked until late into the night. Michael told them how Janine had confessed the true circumstances of his birth, how her own loss of Stephen had clouded her judgement in her need to have another chance at motherhood. She and David had indeed loved him like their own son, and he couldn't criticise them for anything except for being too weak to stand up to his grandparents. Yet they had been supportive of him and loving too. He couldn't deny he'd had a good life; and he and Christine were very happy. He laughed at the irony of having twins of his own, Connor and Jack, two strapping boys who were currently away at university.

Michael returned the following evening accompanied by a nervous Janine, she wept with relief as Linda embraced her.

'Thank you for looking after him and keeping him safe for me.'

29

Tina called Clara a few days later. 'Clara, I'm sorry to bother you but there's a problem with Bessy's paperwork from when you adopted her. It wasn't signed in the right place; you've got to come and do it again.'

'Really?' Clara asked. *What a faff*, she would have to take a detour on her way to Norwich with Linda to choose a new carpet for her bedroom. 'We'll come later this afternoon; will you still be there?' She'd be there all day.

'Sorry mum,' Clara sighed, remembering Linda was wearing her new boots. 'I know we're not dressed for it, you can wait in the car if you want.'

Clara parked on the grass, Linda decided as it wasn't too muddy and she would go in with her. Tina greeted them both.

'Sorry about this Clara. How is the lovely Bessy?' Tina opened a draw and took out a new adoption contract. 'I've filled in most of the details, if you can just check and sign it in the box on the left at the bottom.' Clara was sure that's where she'd signed it previously but took the paperwork Tina held out to her and she began to briefly read the contract. She stopped when she got to the name of the dog. It read, 'Elsa'. Clara looked up at Tina, her mouth open yet unable to say anything. Tina spoke for her.

'You don't have to, but I know how the two of you connected when she was here before. Her owner is moving to an apartment in New York for work.' Clara looked around at the kennels.

'Where is she?' Tina led her and Linda to a corner kennel where

Elsa was laying in her bed with her eyes closed. Clara gently called to her.

'Elsa, hello girl. Hello Elsa.' Elsa pricked her ears, then slowly looked up from her bed. When she saw Clara her long tail began to move from side to side. Slowly she stood up and walked over to the mesh fencing. Clara held out her hand, Elsa sniffed then licked it. It was decided.

Clara and Linda arrived back at the cottage with the latest member of the family and were greeted enthusiastically by Gus, Bessy and Lottie. When William arrived home from work later that day he looked at Clara, confused as four dogs danced around him.

'Have we just acquired another dog?'

'This is Elsa. That's it, I promise!' Her smile was contagious, and he laughed as he made a fuss of the newest member of the pack.

As Linda prepared to leave for Tonbridge the next day Clara brought a cup of tea up to her room as she packed.

'Mum, I've been thinking. How would you feel about leaving Tonbridge and living here? You could stay with me until we convert one of the barns.' Linda held her hands to her chest.

'I've been dreading leaving; leaving you, leaving Michael. Are you sure? I'd love to. I'll go back and put the bungalow on the market, my family is here now.'

And so it was decided, Linda would return to Norfolk and be with both her children, and her grandchildren. She would finally have the family she had been so cruelly denied.

Clara, William and all four dogs spent the next evening at their favourite spot looking out across the North Sea. Almost a year had passed since Clara had first viewed A Stone's Throw, just to be nosey. They sat huddled together under a blanket with the dogs curled at their feet, watching the waves dance in the moonlight. Clara briefly thought of her lonely London existence and pristine flat with views over the Thames. She'd thought it was the perfect lifestyle, how wrong could she have been? She'd not swap this for the world!

The dogs took their time to settle down that night, each trying out all of the beds until they eventually negotiated who was sleeping where. The sound of Bessy's quiet hypnotic snoring soothed Clara into a deep sleep and her familiar dream.

Once again, she found herself on that same familiar path, barefoot at the water's edge, feeling a gentle tickle as the water lapped around her ankles and toes. Her heels slowly sank a little into the soft warm sand, her jeans were rolled up to just below her knees and the water splashed at her calves as she walked a little further into its waves... but this time she felt a gentle tug at her hand, she turned to see a familiar face smiling at her. Together they held on as they moved forwards into the deeper waters, he went ahead first but Clara was right behind him, the current becoming stronger, drawing them on, they felt the flow of the ebb and tide, contracting, carrying them along what seemed like a tunnel...

This time when Clara awoke, she smiled. It all made perfect sense now, he'd been there all along, it was Michael.

Acknowledgements

Whilst I sat for four years writing this book on my own, I never felt as though I was 'on my own.' Here's who helped me along the way and to whom I sincerely thank for their time and input.

To Bryan Baxter of Auction House East Anglia for the riveting insights into the auction and bidding process.

To Zeb, my little black and white Havanese dog who, during the day regularly alerted me to the deer and dog-walkers who had the cheek to pass by our house, but also popped downstairs at 4 o'clock in the morning to see why I was still awake.

To my husband, you know who you are. You are 'lovely'. Thank you for always believing in me.

About the Author

'A Stone's Throw' is Louise Maclennan's debut novel. Originally born in London, she lives in Norfolk with her husband and their Havanese dog, Zeb. Louise has one son, of whom she is extremely proud.

Printed in Dunstable, United Kingdom

74670927R00150